A GREATER GOOD

A GREATER GOOD

A
Novel
by

Stacey A. H. Taylor

TATE PUBLISHING
AND ENTERPRISES, LLC

Published by Tate Publishing & Enterprises, LLC
127 E. Trade Center Terrace | Mustang, Oklahoma 73064 USA
1.888.361.9473 | www.tatepublishing.com

Tate Publishing is committed to excellence in the publishing industry. The company reflects the philosophy established by the founders, based on Psalm 68:11,
"The Lord gave the word and great was the company of those who published it."

Published in the United States of America

ISBN: 978-1-62854-942-3
Fiction / General
13.12.09

DEDICATION

This story is dedicated
To whoever truly loved another,
To whoever felt the concern for another's
welfare more sharply than their own,
To whoever understood, for at least a moment,
what it means to be fully human,
And, mostly, to the man who taught me
with his heart to believe in myself.

PROLOGUE

Sometimes, a beginning can seem more like an ending and an ending more like a beginning. One is required to be prepared at all times to recognize the moment of a life-altering event when it happens and, moreover, know what to do with that moment when it arrives. Life is like a moth-eaten overcoat, chewed up with mistakes and regrets, and sewn haphazardly back together with fortitude and hope. It is within this patchwork where we find purpose.

CHAPTER 1

APRIL 2007

She carefully navigates her way through the dimly lit, smoky bar and slinks down, like a python evading notice by its prey, into a chair in the darkest corner of the room. All five of her senses are heightened to the maximum, and her heart is beating fiercely. She hopes the murmuring, faceless shadows around her can't hear it. She's ached for this moment for three endless, miserable years. An abused captive of circumstance, she never believed she'd live to see this day. Her hands are trembling like a halyard struggling to stay attached to its mast in a violent storm. Her throat is a vine choking the trunk of its host. This is the second most difficult task of her life. She starts to doubt that she's ready for this, but decides she has to be, even if she isn't. What choice does she have, really? She calculatingly lowers her head so that her hair falls forward and is shielding her eyes, making her feel unidentifiable, and takes a stealthy inventory of her surroundings. No one has noticed her. Nothing has changed in the room since she walked in. People are still talking obliviously all around her, the bartender is still wiping down his bar, and weary cocktail waitresses are darting here and there with trays full of empty glasses and faces full of empty smiles. She makes a sympathetic mental nod in recognition of the empty smile. She's intimately familiar with it.

Then from the superficial safety of her dark hiding place in the corner, she hears the music begin. The music. The soft, gentle, embracing sounds coming from the stage. The reason for her being there. The reason for her being at all. The melody is the caressing fingers of a lover, barely touching, yet gently pulling her away from everything else. She dares not look, but as soon as she hears him start to play, she is drawn back into his world. The frigid shell covering her starts to melt away. She is suddenly an innocent child who has been lured by the hypnotizing sounds of the Pied Piper as he seeks his revenge against the world for past wrongdoings. She can feel her body relaxing into the chair, letting down its guard. A momentary false calm washes over her, as his guitar tenderly clutches her soul, lifts it, gives it wings. The familiar rhythm of his strumming starts to transport her to a different time and place. Her world is blurring, and her pulse starts to slow. His music is her opium.

As her body relaxes and her head falls wearily to rest against the wall behind her, the waitress approaches, laying down a coaster and asking sweetly, but economically, what she'd like. At this interruption, she snaps out of her trance, sits up straight, and composes herself again. What would she like? She'd like to stop the world, put it in reverse, and right all the wrongs, take back all the hurtful words, alter fate, and change the course of her life. That's what she'd like more than anything.

"Rocks or neat?" the waitress continues.

At the waitress's response, she realizes she only asked for a martini instead and mutters, "Neat, please." It's time for neatness in her messy life. The waitress retreats to fetch her drink, and she is left to soberly stare at the vacant plain white coaster lying motionless on the table. It awaits a glass to be placed upon it. That's its only purpose. It is only one-half of an equation; without the glass, its existence is undefined.

Her eyes have settled on every fixture in the room, scrutinized every detail as if she were going to paint a picture as soon as she walked out the door. But she has tactically avoided one thing. Not convinced that she won't come completely undone at the sight of him, she braces herself, clears the emotion from her throat, straightens her posture, smoothes back her hair to clear her line of sight, and haltingly looks in the direction of the stage. She doesn't chance looking directly at the stage, but lets her eyes get closer and closer by increments like the hunter she's had to become, trying not to scare off the unsuspecting game in her sights.

With the mellow, hypnotic tunes of the guitar as her reference point, she lowers her head and first rests her eyes at the table next to her, then a few tables over, then, daringly, the table right next to the stage where she pauses and inhales to fill her lungs as a diver would before his plunge into the abyss of the dark unknown. Her ravenous eyes slide cautiously five degrees to the left. Bull's eye. She sees him. As her pupils focus on his silhouette, she can almost feel them dilate and narrow to gain the perfect focal setting. The man playing the guitar is the center of her existence now, and every nerve ending in her body seems electrified. The blood rushes to her head in preparation for the sensory overload. She can't force herself to look away, even if she wants to. Her eyes are a compass needle, and he is magnetic north.

After three years that stretched out like three lifetimes. Peter is within arm's reach, and her arms seem to know it. They ache to hold him as if they have a mind of their own. It's been three lonely years filled with agony since she's seen him. It doesn't seem real, but it must be. The movements match the sounds; she could never have imagined the way she is feeling. It definitely isn't a dream this time. He's sitting and strumming in the very same room as her. He's so treacherously near that the air seems to be filled with his scent, his breath, his essence. Fantasy has blended with reality now, and it's making her a little dizzy. She finally exhales, just before she might have lost consciousness. She enjoys the luxury of drinking him in without anyone's knowledge for a brief moment. A sad smile filled with regret makes its way unconsciously to her mouth, and her head tilts, trancelike, to the side as she gets lost in the memories that are stirred.

He looks so small and fake—like a figure from a worn out novel. She's imagined him so many times over the years, only having a few photos, grabbed in a hurry, to draw on here and there. His familiar face, even downturned, fills her with a warm sense of belonging. It's as if her life hit the Pause button the last time she saw him and now somebody has hit Play. His eyes are closed in concentration, or maybe something else. Heartache, like her? His guitar, as it always was, is an extension of his body. They are one. She is consciously jealous of the instrument cradled in his tender hands. Each note is perfection under his lithe fingers. He is a master. He is her master. She can try to fool herself, but her soul is his, and she knows it.

This can't be real—it's too good to be real. It's been so, so long. Can she really be sitting in the same room with him? But she is, and she's loving it. As she falls deeper and deeper into the trance, something breaks the spell abruptly, and panic reclaims her. The waitress has set the drink down hurriedly, half on the coaster, half off, and it spills a few drops of cold, sobering liquid on her hand as she reaches to steady the glass. She imagines the silent sizzle as the alcohol meets her fevered flesh.

"Here you go, ma'am. Enjoy." the waitress mutters mechanically as if nothing else is happening here, as if she didn't just make a monumental mistake by coming here without warning and shouldn't be running for the nearest escape right now. Can the waitress detect her anxiety as they exchange niceties? All at once, she becomes painfully aware of the gravity of what she's done by coming here. Her panic escalates. What was she thinking? She can't do this. The longing and desire must be evident on her face.

She feels so naked. It's all going to end very, very badly for sure, and she should never have returned. She feels her face redden just as the waitress asks if there will be anything else.

She pauses a moment and attempts to compose herself. "No, thank you," she replies and smiles with a practiced calm, almost as a test or challenge to see if the waitress notices her agony.

She waits to gauge the waitress's reaction. Nothing. The waitress simply smiles, turns and continues her work. That is slightly comforting. Now after a few steady breaths, she calms a little. She can attempt to look at him again with renewed confidence in her anonymity.

Again, the same ritual. Drop the head, look toward the stage with the eyes only, pausing at no less than three tables along the way. Slowly, cautiously, almost there—and *boom!* Their eyes collide almost audibly. She freezes like a rabbit facing a wolf in the open field—nowhere to run, nowhere to hide. The hunter has become the hunted. She's not breathing, not blinking; her pulse may have actually stopped for a moment.

His eyes look almost empty at first as they meet hers. He squints—to see clearer or to shield the enormity of what he is beholding? Disbelief becomes evident, then shock. His bottom jaw drops slightly, his eyes widen, and he locks his stare on her as if he could physically hold her with it. His music continues so smoothly that not a head turns in the whole place. Everything is moving along seemingly undisturbed, except for the screaming, wild roller coaster of emotions that races up, down, and loops around their minds.

He lets his gaze fall away first. She is too stunned to even blink. After his eyes unlock their capture, she feels dropped and lands hard. She gulps air as if she has just broken the surface from a thirty-foot skin dive. Her lungs sting a little from the deprivation, her pulse is quick, and her face is flushed. He keeps his head down toward his guitar and plays on as if his hands know nothing of what the rest of his body is going through. What does she do now? She planned everything out so painstakingly but made no preparations, neither emotional nor physical, for this moment. She couldn't possibly have, even if she tried. Did she think she would be able to sit and listen to him play without being noticed? Or deep down did she want to be noticed?

Her palms are sweating, but she rubs them together as if they're cold. She realizes that she doesn't even know if she's hot or cold. She looks around at all the other faces in the room—but carefully not at his. No one seems to know what trauma has just occurred. Don't they hear the warning bells? Can't they smell the smoke? This is a five-alarm fire! She has never felt so alone, yet so alive. She decides the best thing to do is to take a big throat-burning swig of her martini and try to melt away. She doesn't dare draw attention to herself by getting up to leave. She'd probably collapse if she stood up right now anyway. He keeps playing and never lifts his head.

Finally, his song ends. The sudden silence draws her head to center stage reflexively. Damn it, she took a big chance—he could have been looking her away. She quickly turns her head away but keeps him in her periphery. He bows his head in thanks for all the muffled applause of people who are half-listening and stands with a quick motion to turn toward backstage. He's gone. He's disappeared behind the curtain. She is staring now at the curtain swinging back into place and becoming still as if he was never there. Did this really all happen? She makes a sweep of the room as if he might magically appear in another corner like Houdini, with a puff of smoke and a whoosh of cape. Seconds turn into minutes, which turn into an eternity. His set isn't due to end for at least another hour. This is her chance. He's obviously taking a break to collect himself. She could escape now, and he would be left wondering if she was only a figment of his imagination. She could leave him a note—something witty and contrite like in a

Bogart and Bacall film. She could leave her cell-phone number and put the ball in his court. But something tells her from the look on his face that he's not interested in playing ball, at least not with her.

There's movement in the room that makes the nape of her neck prickle. She can sense it. She hasn't seen him come out, but she knows he's there, getting nearer. Her head slowly rises as if from telepathy, and her eyes land directly on his. He's approaching—with purpose in his step. As he nears, she summons a strength in herself that she didn't know existed and never releases the stare. She knows instinctively that if she's the first to look away, she loses. She didn't live through the hell of the last three years only to come back here and lose.

The closer he gets the more determined she gets. He's standing less than a foot away, preparing for a confrontation. She's sitting down but still somehow manages to give the appearance of looking down on him as he stands before her. One eyebrow is lifted slightly, and her chin is set, giving a false air of confidence and superiority. Her face remains emotionless. They are poised as if in a duel. Words hover in the air as a swordsman's hand hovers over his trusty blade at his side, ready. An old familiar phrase fills her mind: "A still tongue makes for a wise head." She refuses to say the first word. He is forced to.

"Emily."

He says the name cautiously as if it might bite him. No inflection of a question or greeting, more of a summing up. His voice is too controlled, and his nostrils flare slightly from the stress of withheld emotion and restrained anger. His eyes are guarded, and she can't read the emotion in them.

She is on the defense now. She must say something or flee in shame. A dramatic pause for effect to keep him hanging on and then—

"Peter."

There. Done. That was tough. Her voice came out steadily, slightly weak but not noticeably, and a little quieter than it should have been in order to put him on the defense. They've traded rook for rook. No upper hand yet on either side. He finally makes his move. He leans from the waist to lower his head so that his mouth is distractingly close to her right ear.

She can feel his hair touching hers, feel the heat from his body, and his familiar scent floods her nostrils. All five senses are inundated with him at once. She takes advantage of the fact that he can't see her face, and she closes her eyes in an effort to absorb as much of him as she can before he notices. She struggles to hold on to whatever reserve of emotion she has left. It's a very fine line between fight and flight, and she's walking the tight wire on that line right now—without a safety net. He draws his breath to speak, and simultaneously she feels the breath being taken from her.

"Please leave here immediately," he says in monotone.

That's it. That's all he says. He pulls away and regains his visual connection with her eyes. This is definitely not the Peter she knew three years ago. She can see he's not the same shy, even-tempered, compassionate man he once was. He's grown very cold and callous. She feels slapped. This shakes her up a bit, but she is working with adrenaline now, and she steadies herself like a gymnast on a balance beam who has just wavered. She doesn't even recognize the cool exterior she is portraying. She simply looks him in the eye without emotion and mutters, "Okay, if that's what you want."

She has just moved her knight to the right and forward for a flank attack. He didn't see it coming. They both expected a different response. She didn't try to explain everything she'd been through to get there. She didn't ask why. She didn't beg him to reconsider. There would be no second chance for him to reconsider his tactic. She very simply complies as if it makes no consequence to her either way. Stay, go, what does she care? It's only her life that depends upon it.

His eyebrows knit together ever so briefly at her quick withdrawal. Then he remembers himself, takes a physical and emotional step back, seemingly replacing his saber in its sheath, checks his person, nods, and is gone. She is left watching his back and feeling the blood rushing through her veins like mounted soldiers racing thunderously across the battlefield. Stop him! Her caged heart is pleading with her to let him rescue it. It can't be ending like this! We've waited so long and journeyed so far! Stop him! But her exterior remains cool, even as her vision blurs with unshed tears. She sniffs her emotion back in, locks it up tightly in the little steel box she calls her heart, and takes a long familiar swallow of her martini. It smacks of a loser's rubdown after a boxing match in which she lost without ever taking a swing. She'll leave all right, but not until she finishes her drink—call it a consolation prize.

That went *so* differently in her head. It was supposed to open with him walking silently over to her with longing in each step. Then he would take her hand and very gently pull her up to stand an inch in front of him. He would look purposefully into her eyes, his own eyes darting back and forth between hers as a thirsty dog laps feverishly at a cold bowl of water drinking her image in. His hands would rise timidly, adoringly to each side of her face and gently embrace it. Then without a word, and so slowly it was barely noticeable, he would tilt his head and lean toward her. His lips would meet hers as softly as a bee lands on a flower to draw out the nectar without damaging the petals. As he released her from his embrace, a smile would slowly unfold on their faces and somewhere in the distance violins would start to sing. She stares at nothing for a whole ten seconds as she privately mourns the moment that could have been. That's what was supposed to take place. What the hell was this crap? Leave here immediately? Okay? *Now what*, she thought to herself.

She shivers slightly from the chill of defeat that descended upon her, and her hands begin to tremble a little again. Her breathing is shallow. Her temples become damp. She steals nervous glances around the room as if she has just committed a crime. Had she? She prepares to take another sip to calm herself and then waves the waitress over to ask for her check when she hears the music start again. The guitar sounds different this time. Distant and lonely and it makes her pause and look. The spotlight gives the appearance of closing him in as if caged. He is keeping his eyes very carefully on his instrument and playing with such deep emotion that it appears as if his heart were itself caged inside that guitar. She is so torn between wanting to lovingly brush the hair off his face and say something to bring a smile to his lips or tossing the contents of her glass in his face. She doesn't blame him for his reaction, though—she completely understands. She has only herself to blame.

As her thoughts turn inward to the past, she doesn't notice the inebriated man stumbling over to her. He leans down so she can smell the stale odor of cheap alcohol on his breath. He asks her in slurred speech if he could buy her a drink. It takes a moment to register in her mind that he is flirting with her. She absently thanks him but says she has to get going.

"A pretty girl like you should never be drinking alone," and so on and so on. This guy won't take no for an answer.

Now she feels his fingertips sliding up and down her bare arm, and she imagines indelible lines where his skin touched hers and made it crawl with disgust. This idiot picked the wrong time and place. She is visibly irritated now and doesn't know what to do or say to make it clear that she isn't interested in him without making a scene.

She looks him directly in the eye, tightens her lips, and mouths a very firm and undeniable no.

He backs up menacingly and skulks back over to his ruddy-faced laughing friends. She stands, fishes in her purse for a ten, slaps it down on the table, drinks the last swig while she is standing, as if she were a fearless pirate, self-assuredly places her purse strap on her shoulder, and saunters toward the door, head high in an attempt at confidence. She has nothing to be ashamed of. She went with her heart. Sometimes it works out, and sometimes it doesn't. This time was a doesn't.

As the cold air slaps her damp cheeks it makes her tears more noticeable. Standing on the curb, waiting for a taxi, she feels so small that she could fall into the crack of the sidewalk and never be seen again. The scene in the bar was replaying and replaying in her head. Peter seemed like such a stranger to her. It shook her up. She could still faintly hear the lonely music coming from the trapped-looking man in the spotlight on the stage. The wind gusts up and reminds her that her cheeks need wiping. She involuntarily rubs the back of her hand across her face, and the motion makes her feel even more vulnerable. *Where the hell are all the taxis in this town?* she wonders angrily with misplaced aggravation.

—◡—

The loneliness of a broken heart is an uncrossable chasm.

—◡—

CHAPTER 2

It's his first solo performance. He's feeling very vulnerable up on the stage. He hasn't performed in public in a very long time, and the last time was with his band. They are his clothes; without them, he feels naked. Why did he think he wanted to become a solo artist? Now he remembers. That's who he's become—the solo.

Everything seems to be going well. The audience has no idea that he feels lost without his band. As usual, his playing is so smooth that he can actually let his mind drift and let his fingers take over and do their own thing. He is a born musician. His guitar is as integral a part of his body as his eyes or his legs. He's starting to feel comfortable now. He's in a groove, and as he looks around, he sees everyone enjoying his playing.

Some people are conversing softly with the music. It's providing a comfortable backdrop for their whispering of sweet nothings. Some people are watching him and swaying absentmindedly in time with the music wearing vague unforced smiles on their faces. Others are on the small dance floor stepping lightly in time to his rhythm and holding on to their partner as if separation would require surgery. That brings contentment to his troubled soul. If he can get just a few minutes of peace from the mental anguish he's been suffering since he's been back in town, facing ghosts from the past, then his old six-stringed friend will have done its job.

He closes his eyes to get lost in his own musical world. A calm he hasn't felt in a long time washes over him, and he opens his eyes again to let them fall unsuspectingly from person to person. He grows more and more at ease—until. There is a speed bump in the room. His mind stumbles over a dark figure in a shadow in the corner of the room. Something looks vaguely familiar about this person. He squints to focus more clearly, and when it registers, it does so with a colossal shock.

No, it can't be. But it is. Emily? It is definitely her. And she's looking right at him. What the hell is she doing here? How did she find him? It must be a coincidence. His mind starts moving in fast rewind as memories flood through the gates. On top of everything else that's going on in his life right now, he can't possibly deal with this. His pulse is quickening, and it's getting hard to concentrate on his playing. He forces his head down to the safety of his beloved guitar and submerges himself in his music without daring to lift his head and show his hand. His vision is blurring with lack of brain power from the event that has stolen his ability to think. He decides to end the song a little short. He intuitively picks a good ending phrase, and as he finishes, he nods in thanks to the crowd and slowly walks backstage, letting the curtain fall behind him like a bank-vault door keeping the "bad guys" out.

Once he's backstage, he gently sets down his rosewood companion and pauses dramatically while his mind catches up with the recent discovery. His hands involuntarily rake his hair on either side of his head as if he could rake the image from his mind. She was just sitting there as if she had every right to stroll back into his life unannounced and uninvited. The world is upside down right now, and he has to hang on to his head to keep from losing it.

He stares at his flushed face in the mirror, silently beseeching his reflection for a suggestion on what to do. He knows that he can't just ignore the fact that she's in the same room as him. The emotions are too big—the ceiling would burst. He already knows what he wants to do; it's just a matter of getting his body to actually go through with it. He has rehearsed this scenario in his mind many times over the past three years just on the off chance that she might show up somewhere, sometime. He had almost completely given up that possibility, but here she is. He takes a few deep breaths, rakes his hair one more time for good measure, pivots determinedly on his heel, and marches militantly into the lounge. As he pauses at the bar to take a swig of cold water, he almost imagines himself in fatigues heading out to fight the age-old battle between good and evil.

Luck is on his side. As he approaches her, her head is down. This affords him two advantages. One is the benefit of surprise; the other is the benefit of soaking in the soft lines of her silhouette without being noticed. However, just as he approaches her, her head rises slowly and seemingly confidently. She looks him squarely in the eye. Jesus, she's beautiful. It almost makes him cave. Almost. She's more fragile than he remembered. And her cheekbones are more prominent. She's lost weight and could now be considered skinny rather than just thin. Her hair is cut short and businesslike; the girlish tresses are gone. She seems somehow to be the outer shell of the girl she was. So much so, it sends a chill down his spine. Maybe he's just prejudiced by their history. In any case, it's clear that she has changed—a lot. And it's obvious that she won't speak until he does. Women. Head games. He knows exactly what he has to do. He throws the first punch.

"Emily."

He thinks he managed that without too noticeable an effort.

She gives him that look that makes him feel measured and found wanting, then she replies, "Peter."

Did she say his name or sneeze it out as if it were irritating her sinuses? No matter. He has even more resolve as a result. He bends to her side so she can't watch the emotional struggle on his face as he delivers the message that must be delivered.

"Please leave here immediately."

He did it. He only had one chamber loaded, and he was able to pull the trigger and effectively hit his target. As he withdrew and saw the hurt look on her face, he thought fleetingly that he wished it was a misfire. But the thing is done now, and it can't be undone.

She pauses, blinks, almost regally, and mutters a very unexpectedly simple, "Okay, if that's what you want."

Did he hear her correctly? Yes, he did. Poised for advancement, he now realizes he has to holster and retreat. Nothing more is needed to say. He pauses for a fraction of a second before he remembers himself, turns, and, taking great effort, walks effortlessly backstage. He can feel his back burning under her stare, and he imagines he hears the whimpering of a wounded innocent animal as it lay struck in the field. *Nope, definitely no innocent animals in this room*, he reminds himself. *Just coldhearted snakes.*

Her face remains in his sight, even with his back turned to her. Her image is burned into his retina. He finally executed the retaliation plan he had formulated and practiced over and over for the last few years. Living out his fantasy of retribution feels so liberating—for the first thirty seconds.

Then something in her face keeps turning over in his mind. There's a disconnect, a mental roadblock, a warning signal of some sort. He can't put his finger on it, but it's taking the vengeful wind out of his sails. By the time he reaches backstage, he is almost completely full of the deepest regret he has ever felt. Sixty seconds and one hundred eighty degrees later, he has to work in order to steady his hands and recover a normal respiratory rate. It takes him a few moments, but once this is accomplished, he bestows upon himself an imaginary purple heart and invisible red badge, lovingly picks up his only true friend in the world, and reenters the spotlight of his lonely, confused world. Feeling like a complete schmuck, he then sets about playing the saddest song he knows. There is no sadder sound in this world than the music of a tormented soul.

As his guitar moans, he can think of only one thing. *What did I just do? Why did I just send her away? Why? I've thought of her so many times over the last few years that it's almost as if I beckoned her here through mental telepathy. And when she amazingly appears, what do I do? I ask her, no, tell her to leave?*

As he plays, he notices a local drunk talking to her. He feels even worse as he watches her having to put up with the guy alone. He has no reason to feel protective over her now, but old habits die hard. He knows the guy is harmless, so he doesn't get overly concerned. It serves her right for messing with his life after so long. What business does she have for being here in his world? Why did she come here? For that matter, why did she ever leave in the first place? He's starting to feel completely schizophrenic as the war rages silently in his mind.

He sees her stand up, take a swig, and walk with her head held high, purposefully, without looking back, straight out the door. *Good show*, he thinks. His mind is battling and finding itself at the losing end of the rope in an emotional tug of war with his heart. He realizes that he only has a few minutes before she walks down the street and out of his sight forever. He's sweating now, and his mind is racing. *Think, think!* He could probably still catch her if he runs.

As he plays on robotically, he sees the drunk walking toward the door after Emily. This is his golden opportunity. He can rush out there as if to protect her from the unwanted advances of this intoxicated fool.

He finishes the song a few phrases early and sets down his guitar. "Be right back," he promises his inanimate wooden comrade, and then he leaps off the small stage and takes long strides to hasten out the door. He is delayed slightly by the crowded bar and cocktail waitresses with big trays. This heightens his excitable state. He has got to get to that door before it's too late. He is now hopelessly desperate to jump simultaneously into his past and his future.

She is still waiting for a taxi to appear when she hears Peter's music get louder as the door to the bar opens behind her. She turns to see a man emerge, stumbling, from the bar. As the door closes behind him, the music is softer again, and she feels cut off. It's her new suitor. He grins drunkenly at her and begins to walk/stumble toward her. He is accusing her of being the cause of blatant ridicule from his companions in the bar. He is set on bringing them back a bit of victory, perhaps a cell-phone number? As he tries to speak through his alcohol-laden brain, it begins to rain. The first few drops are fat and land with a decisive splat. No question. It's going to pour.

Within moments, the sky opens up, and the man is harassing her, and she is struggling just to deal with the events from inside the bar, let alone this new situation. It all boils over, and she is overwhelmed. As the man drones on and on about what he'd like to do with her, she reacts without thinking. She draws back her hand and slaps him square across the cheek. It stings her palm and leaves a bright-red mark on his face. She realizes she has just made him the victim of her misplaced anger and frustration but can't do anything about it now.

The rain is coming down in buckets, and they just stand there without speaking. The slap and the rain have sobered him enough to make him offer a wide-eyed apology. A cab pulls up to the curb, and the sobering drunk opens the door for her in an attempt at a peace offering. She knows she overreacted and feels a little remorseful, so she smiles forgiveness and thanks him as she gets in and closes the cab door.

Embarrassed, the drunk turns back toward the bar. His mind is cluttered with his thoughts and recent events so he doesn't see the crazed guitarist bounding toward him as he reenters the bar. They collide in the doorway. He falls to the ground, but the lunatic musician just stumbles, rights himself, murmurs an impatient "Look out," and reaches for the door. It takes Peter less than a few seconds to rebound, but those few evil seconds make all the difference.

As Peter thrusts the door open with a little too much force, rain lashes him in the face, and all he sees through blurry eyes are the taillights of a yellow cab and the silhouette of his soul in the rear window. Probably one of the saddest sights he's ever laid his eyes upon. He stands in the rain, staring at the ground in distress and disbelief for a longer-than-necessary time. For a split second, he ridiculously considers running after the cab. The mental image awakens him from his quiet hysteria, and he turns dejectedly back into the bar.

As he re-enters the crowded room, he mutters an expletive under his breath. So close. After such a long, miserable time. What the hell is he going to do now? He knows people are looking at him, but he doesn't care. Just inside the door, he pauses for a somber moment of renewed loss, walks with his head down across the bar, climbs back up on stage, and gently retrieves his faithful guitar. He holds it a little too tightly and begins to finish his set. He knows he'll have to deal with this catastrophe eventually or risk losing his sanity, but for now, he just gets lost in his music—again.

———

Love is the lack of all reason in the face of desperation.

———

CHAPTER 3

Ten minutes later, the cab pulls up to the lobby of Emily's hotel. She hugs her purse to her chest for comfort and slides slowly, almost unwillingly, out of the back seat. As she hands the cabbie his fare, she feels slightly reluctant to say good-bye. It feels as though she is saying good-bye to any chance of reuniting with Peter. Once she passes through the front doors of her hotel, she will have entered some new unknown phase of her life, uncharted unplanned virgin territory. For the past three years, she has known exactly what she wanted to do in each situation. Though none of it was easy or necessarily what she would have chosen—if she'd had a choice. At least, she was able to react to the circumstances around her with full knowledge of what her goals were. Not anymore. She is, for the first time in her life, completely at a loss for what to do next.

She nods a silent, blank greeting in reply to the desk clerk's "Good evening, ma'am" as her heels make a companionless sound, tapping out her loneliness in Morse code across the cold marble floor. Her hand reaches for the elevator call button mechanically. She sees her own trembling fingers and feels detached from them. Each movement she makes, each step she takes, each second that passes takes her further away from Peter, while her mind clamps steadfastly to his image.

It had been an exhaustingly long day. She had left San Francisco early this morning, flown six hours to Virginia, and had just enough time to check into the hotel, change her clothes, and race to the bar to find Peter. For the past few months, ever since making her decision to find him, every single moment had moved her forward toward him. She had, for the first time in a long time, foolishly allowed herself to become optimistic and hopeful. Now, in contrast, everything seems to be moving her away from Peter at about 100 miles per hour.

Somehow she is standing in front of her hotel room door inserting and reinserting the damn card key until she finally sees the green light indicating that she may now enter. *Enter what?* she thinks. Every door she opens seems to close with a sad finality behind it. She enters her lonely, dark hotel room. The "Sanitized for Your Protection" scent of solitariness immediately mocks her. She leans back against the interior of the door for support. Eyes closed, shoulders slumped, for a full minute before exhaling exaggeratedly and tossing her purse dismissively on the desk. She mindlessly undresses and prepares a hot bath, too hot, a little punishing. It feels good.

How could she have been so stupid? The whole scene was so humiliating. Did she seriously expect him to throw his arms wide open and welcome her back into his life? After what she did to him? Or more accurately, what he believed she did to him? She lies in the tub for one full hour before her gooseflesh skin is shivering so badly she has to get out. She wraps the towel around her bony, frail body and looks at her withered face in the mirror. Her eyes are sunken and bruised. Her skin is slightly sallow. Her hair is lifeless. It had been a long day. But it had been an infinite three years. As tears threaten, she can't help but think how differently he would have treated her if only he knew how agonizingly far she's traveled to find him; it was much more than the merely 2,400 miles listed on her voucher as points.

As she lies alone in the dark room, trying to convince her mind to let go and fall asleep, images from the evening haunt her, like a video playback of the missed field goal that cost the team the championship. *Please leave, please leave, please leave.* She hears it over and over.

In her growing wariness, she thinks she sees a siren going off in her room, a red flashing light trying to alert her to something important. On closer inspection she realizes it's the little red light on the phone. A message? Her heart quickens reflexively. The first thought that pops into her mind is that it might be Peter! She never heard the phone ring. She snaps on the light, examines the phone, finds the ringer in the off position, and curses loudly. Some idiot turned off my lifeline! Her mind goes further down imaginary hallways in a chase after Peter, obstinately ignoring the obvious fact that she never even had the chance to tell him what hotel she was staying in.

She calls the message center. "One new message." Another turn down another promising hallway. "Press 2 to play messages." Maybe he called all the hotels in the area trying to find her, she reasons much too optimistically. Further down the hallway. "At 12:45 a.m. today," it begins. She can almost hear Peter's voice apologizing and desperately begging her to meet him somewhere, anywhere. Her heart is thudding wildly. It has to be him. It has to be.

Then, of course, the message lady's voice morphs into her mother's voice, asking if she arrived in Charlottesville safely and going on to ask why she hadn't answered her cell phone. Emily is dropped abruptly from a five-story window at the end of the imaginary hallway that was supposed to be leading to Peter. All the air goes out of her at once. She set herself up for that one, she thinks. Ridiculous. Convincing herself that he scoured the town looking for her as if she were Cinderella or something. She mentally blames that one on the cruel social convention of reading preposterous fairy tales to little girls throughout their childhood, convincing them that everything always ends with a charming prince and a happily ever after.

She knows she should have called her mother when she got back to the hotel, but she didn't trust her voice, and she didn't want any more sympathy. She'd had enough sympathy in the last few years to last her a lifetime. Sympathy is now the enemy. After fretful hours of tossing and turning, Emily finally falls into a fitful and restless sleep.

She awakes, several hours later, to the new day, but the same pain. She is a little fresher at least and feels a glimmer of something akin to pluck. Having been accused all her life of being the eternal optimist, Emily starts to feel that if she fans the embers of that pluck, she might just work it up into enough energy from which to form a new plan. The survivor in her slowly returns, and she looks around her hotel room admonishing herself for the disarray in which she left it last night. She starts to put things in the drawers, hang things up, and get herself together. With each movement she feels more and more confident.

As she works to organize the room, she is organizing her thoughts as well. So this was going to be a little tougher than she originally thought. She can certainly handle adversity. Could it be any harder than the past few years? Hell no. She's starting to feel encouraged. She came all this way, and she's not leaving without a fight. There's certainly nothing left to lose if she is unsuccessful, she tells herself. She subconsciously feels her spine straighten and her pace quicken. The embers have ignited, and she's ready to begin anew. It is exactly that undefeatable can't-keep-her-down attitude that Peter loved about her once upon a time, and she feels closer to him just by recognizing this. It took a few hours, but she's back. First things first, though. Breakfast. She's all too painfully familiar with what happens if she doesn't eat in the morning.

Peter finishes his set around midnight. He has no idea what he played. But the crowd appears pleased. The drive home seems superfluous. Home? What's that? He trudges up the stairs, falls into bed with an empty thud, and tries to block out the events from the night. It would be easier to block out the sun in a glass house. With his ears ringing and his conscience shouting at him, he attempts to fall asleep.

It's very early the next morning when he finally waves the white flag. He has been tossing fitfully for a couple hours, and he is in the same clothes that he had on last night. He can still see the red taillights of the cab as they got smaller and smaller. They seemed to be mocking him like two red eyes of a demon carrying away his last chance at happiness. He is so full of regret that he can feel it in the back of his throat. He's choking on it. He had hoped that somehow she would have come back to the bar last night. But that was ridiculous. Why would she return after the way he treated her? Now he may never know why she came back, where she'd been all this time, why she left, or what she wanted. How did the old proverb go? Pride goeth before destruction? Yep.

The silence around him is deafening. Still dark outside. No one in the house is awake yet. Peter lay there thinking, thinking, thinking. She looked so different, but three years can change a person. He knows that from personal experience. The sound of his name on her lips was unnerving, and it reverberated around in his head like a pinball in a pinball machine. He feels guilty for dwelling on her. He promised himself when he returned to Charlottesville that he would make a fresh start and not waste his life on memories and hopeless expectations.

After he has grown numb to the regret and remorse he's feeling, he decides that last night probably worked out for the best, after all. If he had caught her before the cab pulled away, he would have undone all the work of the last few years. Who needed to reopen that can of worms, right? He was finally over her, right? He had finally already made peace with the fact that she didn't care for him any longer, right? Whatever or whomever she left him for was obviously more important to her than the life they had built together, right?

As he pushes himself along this train of thought, like the little engine that desperately wants to, he starts to feel the anger and animosity that was stirred in him last night finally ebbing with the morning tide. He just wishes there weren't so many damn unanswered questions. Had she achieved the raging success in her career that she had obviously been so hungry for? Had she fulfilled all the things she apparently couldn't have done with him at her side? Had she found someone else to share all this with? He feels that he may go mad. Peter isn't a praying man, but when the pot boils dry of everything tangible, you have to turn somewhere. He just wants peace of mind. He thought he had found it, until last night.

He found himself imagining alternative ways that their little tete-a-tete could have played out, everything from him yelling and shouting at her, to him grabbing her close and kissing her hard, to him just completely ignoring her. Yeah, he finally decides with absolute certainty that last night ended as it should have. The last thing he needed was Emily back in his life, anyway. He wishes he could just fall asleep and escape his thoughts for a while.

Just as he thinks sleep might be near, he hears the baby start to cry. An involuntary smile curves his lips at the sound, and he gets up and walks courageously into the dark of the early morning to answer those cries.

They are only a few miles apart at this moment but feel worlds away from each other. Emily is in her hotel room pushing away a room-service tray full of food that, though hungry, her weak stomach still can't handle. Peter is sitting in the dim light of the new dawn holding the precious tiny life that has become the fulcrum to the lever on which he exists. Neither one knows of the other's deep pain and longing from the past three years. All they share now is the hollow space in their lives where each other used to be. That hollow space is ever-increasing and threatening to devour them both like a black hole. Simultaneously, and unbeknown to the other, they allow themselves to fall into a deep reverie, reliving their idyllic early days together.

CHAPTER 4

It was back in 1999, during her sophomore year at University of Virginia, when she walked into the local campus hangout and saw him for the first time. He was a senior. His hair was longer. He had more spring in his step. And he smiled all the time, but shyly, with his head down slightly. He was in a band with three friends from school, and they had a permanent gig at a favorite local watering hole. His friends were very popular, and the girls always flirted with them. He was the quiet one, whom no one seemed to notice, except her. His seemingly low confidence never matched his copious talent. He rarely gave eye contact to anyone, but when he did, it was electric. His eyes held the universe. She could see her future so clearly when she looked into his eyes. She was immediately and powerfully attracted to him.

Her friends noticed her interest in him and dared her to approach him and request a song. She finally worked up the courage. She walked slowly and apprehensively toward him during a break. As she neared him from behind, he turned around in slow motion as if he sensed her presence. As soon as their eyes met, they could feel it. It's was so cliché, but all cliché's have a basis in something. She finally managed to stutter her request and he simply nodded in response—no words. She had asked him to play "You've Got a Friend." It was one of her favorites.

The band and her friends gave her strange looks because they didn't hear that request too often. Dave Matthews, Smash Mouth, Everclear. Those requests, they expected, but James Taylor?

Peter never even raised an eyebrow; he simply asked his band members to step aside as he took a stool into the spotlight, sat down with his guitar resting companionably on one knee, strummed the first few notes, and began to sing, looking shyly at her occasionally. Her flesh melted, her face grew hot, and her legs weakened. They were inseparable ever since. Until three years ago.

———

Peter Howard Daniels was born in 1977, in a small town in Florida. It was just outside of Gainesville, Florida, where his father was a math professor at the university. His mother mostly did volunteer work at the hospital, and as he got older, he was drawn more and more to the hospital to volunteer with her. At first, he visited patients just to cheer them up. Eventually, he was volunteering as much as his mother. He excelled at sciences and grew to love medicine. His pursuant medical-career choice was not unexpected. He was accepted to the University of Virginia on a very generous scholarship, and the medical school at UVA was a shoo-in.

His parents were the real-life version of Mister Rogers and Donna Reed. His older brother and sister, Michael and Jennifer, were born twelve and ten years before he was, respectively. His parents' priorities were family, health, education. Period. Finances were never discussed. Credit was only something you got at school for passing a course successfully.

Consequently, Peter grew up to be a very down-to-earth, caring, compassionate soul who wanted to become a physician solely in order to help out in the world, not to fatten his bank account. Some girls on campus sought medical students to date because they were looking for a certain lifestyle. Those girls were disappointed in Peter Daniels, who wanted to spend his free time volunteering and who didn't even own a car. He was not flashy, superficial, and wild. He was serious, committed, and humble. It wasn't until Emily came along that those qualities were appreciated. She was the proverbial person in the woods who validated whether a sound was made when a tree fell, so to speak. Without her around to appreciate Peter, he seemed to not exist.

Emily Renee Waters was born in 1979, in the bay area of San Francisco. Her parents, in partial contrast to Peter's, were in the business world. Her mother was an attorney with a law degree from Harvard, and her father was a member of the board of directors with an international insurance firm. They had only Emily, and she was raised attending very selective private schools, expensive summer camps, and white-gloved holiday cotillions. They could have easily been snobs, but they weren't. Emily could have easily been a spoiled brat, but she wasn't. Her mother always pushed pro bono cases where she felt children from underprivileged families needed representation, and her father was a champion to providing insurance at lower premiums to families in need. They had compassion for people from all walks of life and instilled a sense of civic duty in Emily that most of her prep-school friends didn't understand.

While they were all planning their country-club futures, she was planning her education and career as a journalist. She dreamed of bringing awareness to people in need around the world through journalism. She wanted out of life only what she could earn herself, and she had very high ideals. She'd had all the luxuries her parent's income could provide, such as cars, vacations, and a credit card of her own at sixteen. She was looking forward at eighteen to leaving that all behind and embarking on a journey with whatever she could fit in her backpack. She had been easily accepted to her first choice, UVA, and couldn't wait to get to Virginia and start chasing her dream. She felt like a runner at the starting line, waiting for the gun to go off.

Emily and Peter were born on opposite sides of the country two years apart and grew up in different worlds. They never met until she walked into a bar one unsuspecting evening and saw the shy, sincere, adorably boyish man playing his guitar straight from his heart. He was in the background, but to her, he was the only one on the stage.

———

Life in Charlottesville, Virginia, in 1999 was heaven on Earth. They spent most of their free time lying on the cool long grass of "the lawn" underneath the landmark omniscient oak tree that was more than 150 years old. Peter was usually sprawled on a blanket, studying, with Emily on one side and his faithful guitar by his other side, the ever-present text book in his hands, preparing for an exam. Emily often wondered why he even bothered studying; he could have taught most of his classes. He was an academic phenomenon as far as she was concerned. He had probably waltzed out of the womb, tied his own umbilical cord, and proceeded to give the OB a few pointers for the next delivery, and not in a superior way, simply in a "Let me help you out" way. Emily teased him occasionally by calling him a boy scout because he had that always-prepared, brainy, gentle-and-kind persona that boy scouts are supposed to have.

Theirs was an idyllic world viewed through eyes full of optimism, enthusiasm, and passion. The lawn was the social heartbeat of the campus and was usually peppered with students studying, relaxing, throwing Frisbees for their dogs, etc.

A typical day would find the sounds of the bird's songs mixed with the gentle dancing of leaves on the breeze and distant shouts between friends all formed a peaceful medley that soothed the soul. They were part of a world that offered a safe present and promised a bright future. Emily was probably giggling because

Peter was tickling her and teasing her about her lack of knowledge pertaining to the endocrine system of the human body.

"Well, I'm not the premed student here, you are. So I don't need to know about all that stuff, now do I?" she would taunt.

"But it's part of your body—you should want to know it anyway!" He would half joke as he slid his glasses back in place with one finger.

"I only need to know that if I'm seeking a PhD like you, Mr. Peter Howard Daniels," she teased one time in an exaggerated tone. "Hey! I just realized something! You're going to be Peter Howard Daniels, PhD. Do you know what that means? You'll be PHD, PhD!" She laughed uncontrollably.

He loved her wit. He loved her laugh. He loved everything about her. As he covered her mouth with his in a silencing slow, warm kiss, he wondered how he ever got this lucky. She pulled away after a few moments and stuck out her tongue to tease him. Usually, they would both end up laughing like five-year-olds in the middle of the stately campus.

It was the same scene day after day, and it was perfection. He listened to her thoughts, worries, and desires with complete devotion, and she believed in him limitlessly. She finished his sentences; he finished her ice-cream cones. She baked cookies for him when he needed to stay up late studying; he brought her flowers for no reason at all. She trusted him with her life and the lives of their unborn children; he trusted her with his heart and his soul. He was the timid, quiet, studious type, almost brooding. She was the outgoing, full-of-life, fun-loving, and clever type. They were born to be together and couldn't imagine life any other way. They had it all figured out—or so it seemed.

He would be graduating soon and entering the medical school right there at UVA in the fall. She would be entering her junior year at UVA, seeking her bachelor's in communications. They talked for hours about the plans they had for their future.

They planned to wait until he finished his residency before getting married because of the demanding nature of the work. She still wanted to be a journalist, and he was going to be a general physician. He wanted to practice at a large research hospital, and she was after a Pulitzer. They had big aspirations. They would live in a small farm community just outside of the city and have acres and acres for animals and children to run around.

Peter's grandparents, Hank and Louise, lived in a similar town in Kentucky, called Hazel Green. It was only a little over six hours from campus so Emily and Peter traveled there occasionally for visits. They loved the quiet, peaceful pace of Hazel Green and knew someday they would build a home together that would duplicate his grandparent's home. A slice of the American-dream pie.

⁓

Oh, but dreams are funny things built on the delicate wings of imaginary fickle creatures.

⁓

While visiting Peter's grandparents' home one weekend, during Emily's junior year, she and Louise sat down to have a girls' heart-to-heart. Emily would forever remember the images from that warm afternoon. The sun was filtering through the window to adorn the kitchen in a golden glow. The long graceful branches of the willow in the backyard were swaying tenderly in the breeze, the delicate fingers playfully tickling the grass beneath. A pie was cooling on the windowsill, filling the room with the aroma of fruit, sugar, and home. They were sitting at the table chatting and having tea. Louise smiled maternally at Emily, her face weathered and wrinkly, her eyes glistening, and she covered Emily's hand with her own soft, aged hand.

After a thoughtful moment, Louise said only this to Emily, "I can see that you and Peter love each other very much. Remember, Emily, people only love like that once in a lifetime."

Surely it was meant as a compliment, but it rang slightly as a warning, and Emily could only nod silently in reverent response. Though Louise passed away shortly before Emily graduated, and Hank followed her six months later, as was typical with older couples who had spent their lives together, these words engraved themselves on Emily's heart, and she thought of them often.

It was obvious that starting a family was the most important goal to Peter. They both loved kids tremendously and spent many hours during the week at the community center, volunteering as counselors for the underprivileged children who attended the daycare while their parents, many of them single moms, worked. They really enjoyed those days the best. Emily would sometimes catch a glimpse of Peter through the window, and she could actually feel her heart swell at the sight of him holding the small figure of a boy up to the basket so that he could slam-dunk the ball or teaching a little girl in pigtails how to properly hold a guitar. Like most young women in love, she ached to share the joy of having children with him.

Peter sailed through medical school and began his residency at the local hospital. Emily graduated and took insignificant jobs at local newspapers to begin her ascent into the news world. They shared a small apartment in town so they could be near their jobs, but they never let go of their dream for that heavenly country home filled with happy kids.

———

Into each life a little rain must fall… enter the monsoon.

———

CHAPTER 5

It was finally nearing the end of his first year of residency, and they were going to start planning the wedding and search for their country property. She had waited for this for so long and couldn't believe they were at last so near to their dream. She had been feeling a little disillusioned lately because her progress at the paper had stagnated a bit, and she was losing confidence, especially in contrast to his raging success at the hospital. Everyone was more than impressed by his natural abilities as a physician.

Though Emily had her mind keenly set on marriage, it was during that year that Peter was offered the chief-resident position. This was not surprising since he graduated summa cum laude from the medical school at UVA. His work as resident rivaled seasoned physicians at the hospital, and despite her own career slump, she truly could not be more proud of him, year after year. She hated to put their future together on the back burner yet again, but taking the chief-resident position was a no-brainer. Their dreams would have to wait a little longer.

In direct contrast to the progress of her own life, a co-worker of hers had gotten married last year and was already having her first baby. Emily suppressed the pangs of jealousy that stabbed her conscience and would just have to live vicariously through her friend for a while. She often went to the hospital to have lunch with Peter and the other doctors and nurses, but he was so busy now he told her he only had time to grab a quick sandwich so she shouldn't bother coming in. She pictured him surrounded by all his colleagues and couldn't help feeling left out and left behind. Life was moving in fast motion for everyone else, but not for her it seemed.

At least their love life wasn't showing any signs of stress—yet. From the very first time, way back in undergraduate school, it was always fresh and meaningful. She had had little experience when they met. At nineteen, she was a little older than the average American female who loses her virginity. She hadn't planned it that way; that's just how it worked out. She hadn't had a serious boyfriend until Peter. And she wasn't the casual-sex type. They dated for several weeks before the relationship became physical.

———

It was a cool summer night in Virginia, and they had been out all evening. Peter took her back to her apartment very late and walked her to her door. As they stood on her front porch, the man in the moon shone down on them with an approving smile. He held her close and looked at her with an expression that was something between caring affection and ravaging passion. He stepped closer to her so that she could feel the warmth of his body against hers and kissed her so delicately on the lips that it made her whimper with loss when he pulled away.

"I want to spend the rest of my life with you. I want…I want you. I want you—now." His breathing was getting heavy. Then he enfolded her tightly in his arms so that his powerful hands pressed on the small of her slight back and molded them into one. He gave her a long, deep, soul-searching kiss, as if he could consume her and they would truly be one. He was taking and giving at the same time, and she could hardly keep up. She got a little lightheaded with the motion of the kiss, back and forth, give and take. The kiss begged something from her, something she had never given to any man. She pulled back for air breathlessly and looked into his face to find a fire in his eyes that scared her a little and enticed her at the same time.

She silently and bravely took his strong, capable hand in her fragile, delicate hands and whispered, "Follow me." She led him inside her home, her body, and her heart. As they made their way up to her bedroom, they didn't say a word. Words could not do the moment justice. Emily walked over to the window and opened it slightly to let the crisp night air kiss their skin. She gazed out at the stars, the trees, and the dark endless sky as if she were looking at it for the last time through innocent eyes. She had thought about this moment often, as most young girls do, and wanted to make sure that her mind, heart, and soul were all on the same page.

Peter stood quietly in the shadows as she said her silent good-byes to her childhood. This was her decision and hers alone. He would not make one move nor utter one syllable to persuade or dissuade her. He could wait a lifetime for her if he had to.

Emily turned slowly to face him, and as his eyes adjusted to the dim light in the room, he could see the desire on her face, a child's mischievous eyes with a woman's come-hither smile. He crossed the room into the breeze from the open window and felt intoxicated by the fresh air and the mysterious darkness. They undressed each other slowly, never taking their eyes off each other's, bathed in the cerulean moonlight pouring in through the window. After a slight pause in recognition at the enormity of what was about to unfold, he cradled her soft, naked body in his solid, sturdy arms and lowered her slowly, lovingly, onto the bed.

As he lowered himself gently over her, he brushed the hair back from her eyes and searched them for the permission he so desperately needed from her. He wouldn't go any further without it. He wouldn't take from her what she wasn't completely ready to give. She paused as a cliff diver pauses before they dive headfirst one hundred feet into the unknown depths for the very first time. She inhaled and nodded almost imperceptibly. "Make me yours," was all she said. It was all she had to say. Peter kissed her lips tenderly, hesitated for a split second, squeezed her hands as they lay above her head on the downy pillow, and dove with her into the abyss of the carnal universe, branding her as his forever.

She cried out once but bit her lip to silence herself. He kissed her lip again where it was bit and didn't move another muscle. He stayed still and allowed her body to relax. "Breathe," he whispered softly as he kept his eyes locked on hers and kissed her fully to take her mind off the discomfort of the assault. Their bodies were pressed together so that every available nerve ending was stimulated, and their eyes never left each other's. As she relaxed, she felt her body answer the ancient rhythm with a will of its own. Little by little, the world fell away, and all that was left was she and Peter. As their bodies moved in cadence with each other, their union reached a pinnacle, and they floated through time together until they landed safely in each other's arms back on the bed.

Their bodies stilled, and they just lay there, tangled together in the soothing night air and dreamy blue light from the moon, their skin damp and their breathing ragged. After several moments, when their pulses slowed back to almost normal, he lifted his sleepy head to face her. He was afraid she'd be disappointed or regretful. Her eyes were closed, but there was a faint smile of satisfaction on her lips.

"Em?" he prompted. The nickname was whispered with concern.

"Yeah?" she sounded drunk.

"Are you okay?" he asked.

She looked at him slowly, her smile broadened and her eyelids lifted drowsily, and she said simply, "Never been better."

They lay there for a few more minutes as he caressed her and kissed her.

"Did it hurt?" he asked apologetically.

"A little, but just for a split second," she admitted. They were both quiet for a few moments and then,

"Show me," he told her.

"What?" she asked as if she hadn't heard him properly.

"Show me how much it hurt, slap me or pinch me or something," he instructed.

She lifted her head off the pillow to look into his face and see if he was joking. Nope. He was dead serious.

"Peter, you're being silly." She laughed lightly.

"I wanted it to be perfect for you," he said guiltily, not facing her.

Typical Peter. In his passion, he feared that he wasn't gentle enough with her. She touched his stubbly dimpled chin with one finger and turned his face toward hers,

"Peter, I love you, and it was perfect. Especially the ending," she added shyly.

At mention of the climactic ending, Peter smiled and teased, "Yeah, what's up with that? Women don't usually, uh, have that kind of 'success' their first time."

"Well, then, I'd say we're off to a pretty good start at the whole sex thing, you and I, huh?" she joked. "Can we do it again?" She didn't joke.

"I am forever your sex slave. Your wish is my command," he said as he bowed his head mockingly. "I love you, Em," he whispered closely in her ear as he scooped her closer to him. Then they both fell into a satisfied sleep, still wrapped in each other's arms.

He had a desire and need in his kiss that made her dizzy. Every time he took her in his arms and their bodies melted together to become one, he brought out an answering passion in her that she never knew existed. He had a way of being gentle and beastly carnal at the same time. She, in turn, felt completely safe and wildly adventurous all at once under his sexual tutelage. There was nothing he wasn't willing and happy to do to please her, and he did, night after night after night. Their physical relationship was very rewarding. It was a rare night that they didn't make love and they never tired of each other for five years. It was almost fairy-tale like until...about two months after he took the chief residency position.

But all good fairy tales have demons.

As chief resident, Peter came home night after night absolutely exhausted. All he could do was fall into bed and sleep. There was so much paperwork involved. And the politics of the hospital were overwhelming, especially to someone like Peter. This was not the career he envisioned. Insurance companies seemed to have more say in the treatment than either he or the patients, and the hospital was run more like a business than a medical community. He started working longer and later shifts. It was obvious that he was unhappy with something at the hospital. He gave short answers when she asked him, not seeming to want to talk about it, so she didn't push. She tried to keep herself busy with work so she didn't notice the long evenings she spent alone, and she tried to not take his foul moods personally. She tried very hard.

She was paired up with another journalist at the paper, and they worked late on some of their pieces. Doug was a more seasoned journalist; she was learning a lot from him, and he was becoming a good friend. It made Peter's absence a little easier to take for now. His year as chief resident would be over soon, and they would be married and fulfilling all the dreams they had planned over the last five years. She would just have to hold on a little while longer.

So close, and yet so desperately, heartbreakingly, tormentingly far.

Everything seemed to change on a dime when he was halfway into that first chief-resident year, and she started acting uncharacteristically distant and preoccupied. He questioned her occasionally, but she was a brick wall all of a sudden. He knew his frustration at work had been affecting his mood at home, but she must have known it had nothing to do with her. He'd told her about how unhappy he was as chief resident, hadn't he? Why was she such a clam all of a sudden? Not only would she not open up, she actually seemed angry at his probing. She was slipping out late at night when she thought he was asleep and had unexplainable absences at least a few afternoons a week. No matter how nice he was to her, she just got testier and testier.

One day, she had cut herself with a kitchen knife. It wasn't a bad cut, but it just would not stop bleeding. He wanted to take her to the hospital for a few stitches, and she threw an epic fit, stormed out of the apartment, and didn't come back for hours. She grew more and more tired looking, with deep circles blooming under her eyes. Her face was growing weary from the late outings, and her demeanor was growing evermore aloof. He asked her more than once if she wanted him to leave the chief-residency position, move up their wedding date, and start making plans for the future, but she would always spit out a hurried and contrite no. It was during one of these conversations, when he had just mentioned their impending marriage, that her left hook of an answer landed squarely on his right eye and took him out—flat on the mat past the count of ten.

He raked his hair. "Let's just get married this June, and I'll leave the hospital and open a private practice," he practically begged.

"No, Peter," she answered like a one-two punch.

Uh oh, *Peter?* Not *Pete?* Here comes another one-sided argument.

"Speaking of the wedding—I want to call it off," she kept her face hidden.

"Call it off?" he exclaimed incredulously.

"Yes, call it off...you know, not have it—ever," she replied with a hiss in her tone.

Dead silence for a full three minutes as the standoff escalated and their faces got redder and redder.

"Em? Please tell me what's going on. Did I do something? Did I not do something? Is there someone else? I don't understand what's going on. Please."

The beseeching tone of his voice at his last word tore her heart out. Good. She needed to be heartless now. She would mentally replace her heart with a steel box and a big fat padlock so she could get this over with and never have to feel this pain again.

"Peter. I'm not happy anymore. I have to leave you. There's nothing you can say or do that will change my mind. I have to go and be my own person. I've given this an immense amount of thought, and this is what I have to do. You have the chief residency and a brilliant career ahead of you. You'll meet someone else, and I want you to pursue a relationship. I hope we see each other again someday and can be friends, but I can't promise that, and I don't want to you to wait around for it. You are an unbelievably great guy, and you deserve every happy moment life has to offer. I'm moving out of town and into my own place this week"—a dramatic pause and then—"I've already put down my first and last."

The last statement might have been a metaphor, but he was pretty sure she was referring to the traditional first and last month's security deposit on an apartment. It was as if she had written this speech last week and spent every moment since then carefully and painstakingly memorizing it for a perfect delivery. Well, if so, job well done.

He crossed the room to take her hands in his and look directly into her face, no hiding this time, "Emily, look at me and tell me you don't love me," he dared.

She closed her eyes, steeled herself, reopened them, summoned everything she had, reminded herself that this was for his own good, lifted her head and placed him in the crosshairs, steadied her aim, and pulled the trigger.

"I don't love you, Peter." Her voice sounded robotic and cold.

What more could he say? She had emptied the last chamber straight into his heart; the fatal bullet hit its mark, and the room seemed to be filled with the smell of sulfur. She was packed up and moved out by the next afternoon. She left him with such an air of finality that it would haunt him every G—dforsaken day of his life since.

———

CHAPTER 6

Peter sobers from his reverie, places the empty baby bottle on the nightstand, and looks down into the sleeping innocent face that is shining with daybreak. It's still raining outside, but the sun is fighting to fill the room and take away the melancholy. The sun is his comrade, and he joins the cause as he concentrates on the miniature being he is holding and shuts everything else out. He mentally devotes every ounce of his emotions to the infant and leaves nothing for anybody else. What choice does he have, anyway?

All this reflection has made Emily realize that she hasn't been back to Charlottesville in three years and she has some additional unfinished business to attend to. There are old friends and ex-coworkers littering memory lane who all deserved a call or a visit at the least, if not a full explanation for her mysterious absence the past three years. She makes up her mind to busy herself with those tasks, not completely knowing what she'll say to those people when she talks to them. Then she plans to visit some of her old familiar haunts. Today is Sunday. Peter plays again at the Ends of the Earth on Wednesday. She feels the plan coming together, and it makes her smile for the first time in a long, long time.

The rain that began on Saturday night, as Emily waited in dismay for a cab outside the bar, had not stopped since. Throughout the week, she needed the protection of an umbrella everywhere she went. This dependency lent itself to the anxiety and uncertainty that she was feeling as she anticipated Wednesday. At times, it is a blowing, fierce, scolding rain, and at other times it is a steady, gentle, admonishing rain. The gloomy weather had caused an even more somber mood to the tearful reunions Emily made that week.

She chose just two of her closest friends to see. She had preferred squaring things with Peter first, but things don't always go as planned. Caroline and Amy were shocked, thrilled, furious, aggrieved, and finally humbled and thankful, all in that order, to be reunited with their long-lost dear friend. Emily spent most of her purgatory from Sunday until Wednesday visiting with her old friends, and it gave her a false expectation of success in her upcoming second attempt at seeing Peter. She had sworn Caroline and Amy to secrecy about her plans and her whereabouts and mostly about the past three years. They both understood and completely agreed that it was between Emily and Peter, and neither of them had seen him in a few years anyway.

Wednesday has finally arrived, and she muses about how it came sooner than she thought it would. As she dresses and applies makeup she runs nervously through some possible phrases she might open a conversation with. She prepares herself for the fact that Peter may be even more reluctant to speak with her. The night is waiting for her, and she steels herself for the second round. *Ding ding.*

———

Peter was due to play from eight o'clock until eleven o'clock. Emily sees no need to rush and be there by eight only for him to tell her to leave again. After changing several times and redoing her hair, she realized she's stalling but can't help it. It gets later and later. A little later turns into even later and later. She starts to worry that she's lost her nerve to give it another try. The clock is ticking, ticking, ticking. Nine o'clock, ten o'clock. Five outfit changes, three hairstyles, and a few panic attacks later, she jumps into a cab trying not to think too much. It's 10:15 p.m., and she can't believe she's finally going through with this. Once bitten, twice scared to death.

Her own voice sounds strange to her as she tells the cabbie to take her to the Ends of the Earth. She giggles nervously at the double meaning—to the bar where Peter is playing or as far away as possible? The cab ride is disconcertingly short, and her heart is pounding against its steel cage. What will she say? What will she do? As the rain comes down in sheets, Emily is preoccupied with what-ifs and steps nervously out of the cab and onto the curb absentmindedly, without paying the cabbie or opening her umbrella. She is leaning into the open passenger window, sorting out the fare when she senses someone behind her.

Maybe it is telepathy, or maybe it's the cabbie's gaze over her shoulder that makes her skin prickle and her heart rate quicken. After thanking the cabbie, she turns as if in slow motion toward the door of the bar. She had prepared and prepared, mentally and physically, all week. She just spent hours on her appearance. She so desperately wanted a fresh start at this. She had some phrases picked out, some things she thought it most important to say. Her makeup was perfect, her hair was done the way he used to like it, though it was shorter and thinner now, and she was wearing a dress that she thought said "Truce." So much time and effort had gone into this moment wasted.

Now her mouth hangs open and mute, her hair is plastered to her head with rainwater, and her makeup is running in ugly black streaks down both cheeks as she stands in the rain staring dumbfounded at him. She looks anything but confident. Not the opening statement she had planned to make, but things don't always go as planned—again.

Peter had finished his set a little early, packed up his guitar lovingly, and exited the bar quietly and alone. He hasn't felt like chatting with anyone for the last few days. He's still licking his wounds from Emily's unexpected appearance the other night. As he pushes the door open to leave, he drops his head against the onslaught of rain, but something catches his eye. A yellow cab at the curb. A slender figure in the rain. His heart skips a beat. Could it be?

He is standing under the awning in the doorway, unmoving, guitar case safely in hand, face like he's seen a ghost. They both stand motionless that way for a few moments, blinking at the brutal impact of reality, each afraid to move first. He looks somehow changed since last week, a little broken, a little lost. It instantly makes her feel guilty and sad. She knows that she has to say something; it's her turn to go first.

Her mind searches for the perfect words but all it finds is, "Peter."

Her voice cracks slightly and holds more emotion than she planned, and she feels she has shown her hand, but she no longer cares. She pleads with her eyes, brows lifted against the torrent, for some reaction from him. The cab pulls away slowly, and she feels slightly deserted. He is silent and still. She is instantly exhausted. So very tired. She closes her eyes for a brief respite from the situation. Her head drops slightly, and her shoulders slump. She looks like she has given up and all the air has been let out of her.

"I…I was just leaving," he manages after clearing his throat, raising his guitar case slightly as a gesture of proof. But he doesn't make a move to leave. It's obvious now. He wants to communicate with her. He wants to interact. He wants something. She can tell, and it's enough for her right now. She lifts her head slowly and reinflates somewhat. She has to be cautious as if he's a small animal in danger that she has to coax to her for safety without scaring him away.

Their eyes are like lasers, piercing each other and searching for truth. She can see a million unasked questions on his lips. She feels an urgent need to let him know that she won't hurt him this time. She cautiously moves closer to him so they can both stand under the small awning, out of the downpour; at least she tells herself that's why. He takes this as a gesture of engagement and sets his guitar case down but near—in case he needs to make an emergency exit. He stares at it, thinks for a moment, drops his head in acquiescence, then looks back at her through squinting eyes as if he can't take in too much of her at once. As with a slow toxic poison that eats its victim's insides until there's nothing left, she must be ingested very gradually.

Her own eyes are watery, from rain? She won't last much longer before the dam breaks. A man walks by; neither gives him a passing glance. They're magnets now. The space between them grows smaller without them knowing it. Their eyes are locked in an embrace that is impenetrable.

"Hi," she starts very quietly. "I just wanted to see you…to hear you play," she continues softly.

At her gentle tone, he looks at the ground in apologetic regret for the things he said and did the other night. He doesn't know what to say, and he doesn't trust his voice. She understands his silence for what it is and speaks for him. She goes for broke and reaches for his chin to gently lift his gaze back to hers. She has to see his eyes as she talks to him so she can gauge his response. That was always where the truth was—in his eyes, the windows to his soul. Her fingers burn as they meet the stubbly skin on his face. His eyebrows shoot up as if ignited by her touch; as if he is coming back to life out of a long, deep slumber.

"I'm so sorry, Peter, about everything. I mean sorry not only as an apology, but as deep regret, also. I only wanted…" She's not sure how to finish that sentence.

A tear escapes from her lower eyelid and finishes the sentence for her. As it runs down her frail cheek, it mingles with the runny mascara and the rain still dripping from her hair. She looks so incredibly fragile right now. The look on her face mirrors the deep regret she obviously feels. And there's pain and something else written on her face. But maybe that's just what he wants to see. In either case, it's more than he can bear, and he reaches up with his right hand, as if in a trance, and wipes at the tear with the pad of his thumb. Slowly. It turns into a caress. She has him. She knows it, and the knowledge is too much.

The tears fall in rivulets now. She doesn't try to hide them or stop them. She simply matches his gaze bravely and honestly. He impulsively takes her hands in his to complete some sort of connection. As he does this, her head falls to allow her eyes to see their hands joined together, and he senses a restrained slight sob from her shoulders.

"Don't cry, Emily," he whispers in a soft voice, hoarse with emotion. *Oh to hell with everything*, he thinks. His heart has played a pair of aces against his mind's two kings, and he leans toward her as if in preparation for a kiss.

The nearness of him makes her a little dizzy, and she has to close her eyes to steady herself. She makes no move to withdraw, nor advance—just holds her ground for dear life. Just as she thinks he might actually kiss her as in her imagined scenario, he straightens, blinks, and shakes his head to clear it. He pauses as he regains his composure and searches her face for answers to his unasked questions. None. He doesn't accept or reject her apology for now, simply acknowledges it with a sad smile and an almost imperceptible nod.

He can't deny his heart at this miraculous second chance, so he asks her if she'll go into the bar so they can get out of the rain and maybe have a drink. There's the old Peter. She doesn't answer audibly, just smiles shyly through her tears, and nods. The sign over the door reads Ends of the Earth. She smiles as she follows him in and thinks to herself, *How appropriate.*

CHAPTER 7

Without discussing it, they choose the same table in the same dark corner of the room, where just a few nights ago she had sat as he all but physically threw her out. In direct contrast to that, Peter is now pulling out a chair for her to sit upon, as if trying to right a wrong. They've both learned a good lesson about regret since then. He helps her out of her wet coat and joins her at the table. They avoid eye contact for a brief moment to gather their chaotic thoughts.

Emily is dabbing at her makeup when a waitress comes over and asks disinterestedly what they'd like to drink. Happy for the distraction, they both answer at once and laugh nervously at their verbal collision. Peter indicates with a nod for Emily to order first.

"Just water, please," she says quietly.

She's doing this without an aid, Peter thinks to himself. Brave. Peter orders a scotch.

With that out of the way, they are forced to face one another and say something. Anything. The last time they sat companionably with one another, they were two young lovers out to conquer the world together. Emily rubs her arms and shivers slightly. They're both chilled from the damp weather and from all the things left unsaid. Peter asks if she's cold and offers her his sweater. All she can think is that this is such a nice difference from last week.

"No, thanks. I'll be fine," she answers.

Peter is looking at her closely now. He's no longer avoiding looking directly at her. He has a quiet calculating look on his face.

"Are you all right? I mean, how have you been, Emily?" he asks with genuine concern.

Her eyes widen slightly in surprised reaction to his question, but she waves her hand dismissively and assures him she's fine, just tired. "It's been a really long week, and all this rain doesn't do much for a girl's appearance, you know?" she says rhetorically.

His eyes narrow in suspicion, but he leaves it alone for now. Something's not right. It's more than the runny makeup and the drenched coiffure. He realizes it's been several years since he's seen her, but now that he takes a good look at her, he senses something's definitely not right. The apprehensive look in his eye makes her hurry to change the subject, and she quickly asks how he's been and how his mother is. She carefully avoids asking after his father.

They exchange the normal, benign inquisitives about mundane things for a few minutes before there's another awkward silence. Emily is tentative to broach the next subject, and she starts out weakly,

"Peter, what…" She pauses and restarts, "After—" She changes her mind and takes a side road. "I read that you've been to Somalia with Doctors without Borders. That's how I found you here. There was an article somewhere on the internet about your work there, and then it explained that when you returned, you decided to take a…brief…hiatus from your medical career while you pursued your interest in music." She pauses for a response.

His brows knit together with obvious unspoken emotion at the memory of Somalia.

She adds, "Somalia must have been heartbreaking."

He stares at her silently, weighing the purpose in her intention at this new line of conversation. Did she know more than she was letting on? Did she genuinely care about his welfare? Is she really sitting across from him making a reference to heartbreak?

"Heartbreak?" he sneers, as if to say, "What would you care if my heart were broken?"

She immediately realizes her blunder, but thankfully, the waitress arrives just then and sets down their drinks. Without pause, Emily looks up at the waitress and orders a dry martini, neat after all. Peter gives her a "Thought so" smile and mentally ticks a point in his favor.

He decides to let this one slide and answers further, "Somalia is a desperate example of human existence. I'm very grateful that I was allowed an opportunity to do whatever I was able to do to help as many as I could. It wasn't nearly enough, and I would have liked to have stayed longer, but they only allow you to stay for a year."

"I'm sure there's a very good reason for that," Emily reminds him.

"I suppose it was very emotionally draining, which could eventually affect the quality of any physician's care, but there's still so much that needs to be done. Anyway, I'm back now, but a little of me is still there, I guess," he adds with a melancholy look on his face.

He's obviously reliving some sad memories, and Emily doesn't want to intrude. The waitress returns with Emily's martini and brings them both back to the conversation.

"I wish I had been with you over there," Emily thinks out loud, again, before remembering that they are still carefully weighing every word they say as a jeweler weighs his gold. *Oops.*

But it is out, and she can't take it back.

Peter's eyebrows raise, his mouth purses, and he looks her dead in the eye. "Yeah. Me too, Emily. Me too."

Oops. Oops. She takes a big swig of her martini. It burns. She coughs. Her face reddens. Her eyes tear. Peter's face is stone.

When she can breathe normally again, she simply and unemotionally says, "Well, I had no choice."

The look on his face tells her that he isn't buying what she's trying to sell. She realizes then that there is no safe subject besides the weather, so no matter what she says it will be an oops. Not only is there a very large elephant in the room, but he's wearing a pink tutu and doing the rumba. There is just no getting around this, so she may as well go straight through the stormy middle. She doesn't quite know how to best begin this uncomfortable conversation.

As she is formulating an idea, she starts to feel the effects of little sleep, no food, high stress, and alcohol. Not to mention the pharmaceutical potpourri she's ingested today. The familiar feeling of bile rising in her esophagus begins. The tightening of her abdomen muscles is next, the quickened pulse. She knows what's imminent, and she needs to get to the bathroom quickly.

"Excuse me for one minute, Peter. I'll be right back," she says as she stands to hurry herself away.

He sees her enter the restroom, and he is irritated a little by the interruption at an inopportune time. He downs the remainder of his scotch and orders another.

Emily returns to the table about five full minutes later. Her face almost imperceptibly pale but flushed at the cheeks, and she's wearing a misleading smile.

Trying a little too hard, he thinks.

"Everything okay?" he questions.

"Yep. Where were we?" she diverts.

"You desperately wanted to be with me in the luxury resort destination known as Somalia but were otherwise engaged and sadly 'had no choice,'" he recaps with a sarcastic tone of exaggeration. The scotch is kicking in.

She switches back to her water and abandons her martini.

"Hey, you wanna hear a little tune while we're sitting here trying not to say everything we really want to say?" The scotch has definitely kicked in.

"Sure," she answers with a purposeful lack of enthusiasm. This is not going how she had hoped. What a shock. Does anything?

He opens his guitar case and gently lifts his guitar to his lap. At least she's able to observe his tender side for a moment as he holds the instrument like a child. Though she thinks his timing is a little strange, she relishes being out from under his scrutinizing, judging, accusing stare for a few moments while she ponders her next move.

He tunes a few strings, and it sends her back to 1999 when she made that first shy request. She wonders if he even remembers how they met. Then the undeniable first few notes of "You've Got a Friend" fill her ears. He only strums the melody but doesn't sing. She wonders why. She loves his voice so much—it had the color of mahogany, the texture of velvet, and the warmth of honey. She was transported by it.

He doesn't look at her until the song is completely over. On the last note, his guarded eyes meet her blurry eyes, and he tosses her the pick, just as he had done all those years ago, although this time with a slightly accusing look. She catches it in her palm, tucks it in her pocket, and smiles back tenderly, just as she had done all those years ago; she had forgotten that part. *Touché, Peter.* She is encouraged by this.

They're quiet for a few moments of unspoken truce, reliving those warm memories when their world was heartbreak free. The lines on their faces smooth slightly, and there's an undeniable eye of the storm sort of calm.

Then Emily's stomach churns. She needs food if she wants to avoid the mad rush to the bathroom again. And she thinks he could use a little something to soak up the scotch he's imbibed.

"Hey, Peter, wanna go somewhere to grab a bite?" she offers softly.

"Sure. Why not?" he responds, feeling the need for a change of scenery.

He stands up first, his guitar slung across his back arbitrarily, like an ever-present security blanket thrown protectively over a child's shoulder, and extends his hand to help her from her chair. She reaches for it, happy for the excuse to touch him. They're both trembling a little, but her hand fits in his like a sparrow in its nest. She grabs her purse and coat, and he leads her out of the bar and into the cool, fresh night air.

CHAPTER 8

The rain has finally passed for the moment, and it has cleansed the air. She could almost believe that she is back at UVA, standing with Pete under the old moon and stars they used to stand under. The scene around them reflects the fresh start they're trying to make. The streetlights are shimmering off every wet surface, making the world seem jeweled as if in celebration of their reunion. The street is quiet except for the gentle dripping of leftover rain from awnings and gutters.

There's a general feeling of ceasefire in the atmosphere. They seem to be the only two people on earth at the moment. It's almost midnight—the bewitching hour. They let go of each other's hands at the awkwardness of the moment.

The silence is starting to become uncomfortable, so she breaks it boldly. "Where should we go from here?" She chances the metaphor.

He pauses as he searches her face for a double meaning. "There's a place I like just a few blocks away," he offers as he nods down the street in the direction he starts leading her. Both of them slide their hands in their pockets protectively, but they continue talking and smiling hopefully.

She is encouraged by his agreement to grab a bite to eat with her. Her foot is in the proverbial door. They stroll easily along the empty sidewalk. They seem to own the world right now, and it's comforting. The night air has sobered him a little.

"I want to apologize to you, also, for asking you to leave like that last week. It's a self-preservation thing. A knee-jerk reaction, I guess," he says, ashamed. "I just haven't seen you in such a long time. You surprised me." His voice is thin, and his face is shielded.

The night air has refreshed her, and she accepts his apology with a warm smile. Her smile does things to him. It always did. He is in purgatory right now. He can't act normally, as if nothing ever happened between them, and he can't act angry because they're past that now. And he can't throw her down and have his way with her right there on the sidewalk like he wanted to because, well, that would be weird.

"I'm sorry I didn't warn you that I was coming, but I had no way of getting in touch with you to let you know. I really didn't mean to cause all this drama," she says as lightheartedly as possible.

"How in the world did you know I'd be playing at the bar?" he questions.

"There was a brief bio about you on the bar's website. That's the article I told you about earlier."

"I didn't know I was so famous," he jokes.

They both laugh halfheartedly. It's a forced laugh, but at least it's an attempt at civility and familiarity. It feels good, like sliding into a favorite sweater on the first cold night after a long, hot summer. It's an olive branch extended to each other simultaneously, and they both take hold of an end as if it's a life preserver.

"I've been trying to find you for months, so I searched the internet, and finally, last month, I found that story about your time in Somalia, and it included your performance schedule at the bar," she sums up neatly.

"I see. And what else did the article have to say?" he asks—with feigned nonchalance, she thinks.

Maybe it was just the journalist in her, or maybe he was hiding something, but something is definitely strange about his tone. She thinks for a moment, twisting her mouth in concentration and looking upward as if her thoughts were hanging from a tree above her, ripe for the plucking.

"Really, not much else. You were in Somalia, you came back, and you're performing a couple times a week at the bar while you settle back in to American life. I know MSF performs debriefings on the physicians as they return to their homelands. I also read somewhere that MSF has a peer support network that helps with counseling and de-stressing when the aid workers return home. I assume there is a period of readjustment followed by evaluation before you reenter the medical community at home? Thus, the hiatus. Correct?" she asks, proud of her research and summation.

"Yeah. Pretty much sums it up," he nods and smiles. He is secretly relieved that she has supplied all the answers for him. *Quite convenient, that journalist's mind she possesses*, he thinks. No further explanation is required, and his secret is safe for now. He isn't ready to start answering questions about the baby just yet, especially from her.

She is just as relieved that the article hadn't mentioned a wife. And she sees no wedding ring, so she feels safe.

————

Small victories on the battlefield of love.

————

He slows his gait and, with his hands still in his pockets, indicates via a pointing elbow the door to the cozy-looking all-night coffee shop. There is condensation on the windows, which suggests that it is warm and probably laden with the homey scent of baking goods inside. She smiles her approval as her stomach growls, and he reaches for the door.

A cheery-sounding bell jingles as they open the door. It seems to mock their good nature at being with each other again. A few heads swivel automatically toward them at the sound, vacant eyes resting briefly on them before the heads swivel back almost robotically. She feels a little conspicuous for a split second, but her anonymity was back in place almost immediately. They pause in a brief search for the perfect table and find a snug booth in a corner. There aren't many patrons there at this time of night, just enough to allow them to blend in. The lighting is dim, the background music is soothing, and the décor is comforting. It is perfect. In the strategy of confrontation and territory, this place is the Switzerland of coffee shops.

A short, plump woman bustles over to greet them and hands them menus. She herself looks like one of the cupcakes in the bakery case window. Her cheeks are as red as cherry jam, her apron is dusted over with flour, and her white hair is whipped up on top of her head like frosting. She offers a pleasant,

"Welcome to Mimi's. What can I get you folks to drink?"

They order tea to warm themselves up and tell her that they would look over the menu and decide on the rest of their order in a few minutes. She smiles and nods and is off in another bustle to fetch the tea. Emily squints and thinks for a moment and makes a childish face of concentration.

"Let me guess," Peter says with a glint in his eye as he recognizes the face she made. "Alice from *The Brady Bunch*?" It feels good to talk about familiar things with her.

"No," she retorts, a little embarrassed and uncomfortable at his reading her mind, "Aunt Bee from *The Andy Griffith Show*."

He raises his eyebrows in judgment and finds himself impressed. "Good call." He nods.

She laughs. She couldn't believe he remembered her little game of name the TV character. First the James Taylor song and now this. She thought she was the only one who remembered every gesture, every nickname, every look, and every moment of their life together. It was starting to seem as if he had hung on to everything as well. This is definitely encouraging.

The teacups are placed neatly on saucers, which are lined with delicate doilies. The steam from the hot tea rises up as if to entice and beseech, "Drink me." She feels her mouth water and the emptiness in her stomach at the sweet scent of the tea. She realizes then that she hasn't eaten since morning and becomes instantly ravenous and a little light-headed. "Let's order, okay?"

"Sure." Peter chuckled as an adult would placate a child.

They silently analyze the menus while "Aunt Bee" stands poised with pencil on pad. Peter orders an orange scone, and Emily orders scrambled eggs, bacon, and a biscuit. Just like old times. She could always eat him right under the table. *How could she possibly have become thinner if she eats like that?* Peter wondered to himself. There's still something nagging at the back of his mind about her appearance. Her metabolism was a thing of wonder. He couldn't help but snort a small laugh through his nose at her order.

"What? I'm hungry, all right?" she defends herself.

He just shakes his head and smirks.

They are sitting opposite each other, and neither one can believe that they are together. It feels so good to both of them to be that near one another. As they sit, the silence becomes awkward again. So much to discuss. So many questions. Where do they start? Nothing left to do but talk. There were no stalling tactics left. Should she get right to it and tell him the truth about why she left and why she came back?

Before she can say anything, he starts to speak.

"Before we say anything else, I want you to know that it really is so good to see you, Em. Weird, but really good," he admits.

"You too, Peter," she says softly.

"It's been a long time," he begins cautiously.

"Close to three years," she agrees, nodding.

"You seem to know all about my life in the interim. What about you?" he tries to sound only politely interested and not accusatory and desperate for information. *Why in the world did you leave me?* he thinks to himself.

"I've been writing short articles for a local paper out in San Francisco," she answers.

"San Francisco?" he asks leadingly. This is his first breadcrumb on the trail that will lead him to enlightenment, finally. His mind turns it over and over, savoring the tidbit of information as a starving dog chews furiously on a bone.

"Yeah, I moved out there," she says a little cryptically. She doesn't want to make up some lame excuse for going to San Francisco, but she doesn't feel the right moment has come to tell him the truth. Man! This was going to be a lot harder than she thought, doing this face-to-face. Maybe she shouldn't have come. Maybe she should have written a letter and had it forwarded to the bar instead.

"Are your parents still out there?" he asks as he stirs his coffee to avoid looking like he's trying to gain information that she may not want to give out.

"Yeah, I've been staying with them for a while," she answers vaguely. There is a thoughtful pause.

"So have you been staying with them this whole time, or was there someone else for a while?" Peter finally asks softly, his eyes darting back and forth, giving the appearance of a frightened fish caught in a net.

At the look in his eyes, she felt another ping against the steel box in her chest. She wants to put her hand over his and confess everything right there and then, but she has to remember to go slowly. It was going to be very, very difficult to explain why she left without making him angry, and she had to think it all through very carefully before she spoke. She can see the pain on his face, though, and has to say something,

"I've been with them most of the time and on my own the rest of the time." She slices open the net and lets him swim to safety.

"Em?" is all he says as he keeps his eyes trained on the spoon with which he is still stirring his tea superfluously.

Before he can ask her anything too heavy, she takes a slight detour, interrupts, and delves, "What do you plan to do next, back to the hospital or private practice?"

He seems a little irritated that she had steered the conversation away from her, but only a little.

"Not sure," he replies. He doesn't want to admit that he may have burned some bridges in the local medical community. Even though she seems to be up to speed on everything, he gives her the blow-by-blow of the last three years, of course, omitting the news of the newest member of his family,

"Well, right after you...your...uh, I mean about three years ago, I started working double shifts in the ER to gain more experience"—*to keep my mind off of you*—"I decided not to go into private practice because I enjoyed the challenges and rewards of treating the broad span of patients I saw at the hospital"—*because I had no reason to develop my personal life once you left.* "After about a year and a half of that was when I went to the recruitment meeting in New York at MSF, Medecins Sans Frontieres, because I wanted to help the neediest of people"—*plus I needed to get as far away from here and away from everything that reminded me of you.* "They sent me to Somalia for a little over a year. Then I came back here a few months ago, and here we are."

As he sums up the last three years, images fill her mind of a lonely Peter boarding a plane with a suitcase full of the things that he couldn't bear to part with for an entire year. She wonders what those things were. Was there a picture of her in that suitcase? What about his father's watch? His dad had died while she was away; she knew from her mom that it had torn him apart. It pained her terribly that she wasn't there for him during his grieving. Did he bring his cherished guitar?

Those long months must have been life changing for him. Of course she'd seen all the footage in the news about the war and disease in Somalia. G-d, how she wishes she could have gone with him and been at his side during such a challenging time. The devastation must have been unbearable to witness, but if she knew Peter, he was probably knee deep in the middle of things, weary and spent, trying to make as big a difference as one human being possibly could.

To have been there with him covering his efforts from a journalistic point of view and bringing awareness from around the world would have made her feel as though she could help in some way also. She would have loved to have been able to help the world as he does and to help Peter. But she gave up that right when she walked out that apartment door. Not that she really had any choice. She couldn't have gone anyway. She thinks for the millionth time over the past three years about how cruel fate could be.

"Were there any journalists there with you covering the story?" she wondered innocently out loud.

He rakes his hair—his trademark. She assumes that it's because this is a touchy subject.

"It's okay, Pete. We don't have to talk about Somalia if you don't want to," she offers.

The dam breaks, and his head snaps up at the old familiar sound of his nickname on her lips, and he can't help but lose his fragile restraint. At her incessant questions about Somalia, he thinks he finally realizes why she has abruptly entered his life again. She's a heartless, thoughtless bloodhound—not a woman.

He clenches his teeth slightly, lowers his voice to an ominously low decibel full of warning as he spits out, "Is that what your sudden reappearance is all about? You want the story? Always the journalist. Always chasing that Pulitzer. I can't believe that you would come here after all this time and reopen all these old wounds, just to pour salt in them by selfishly looking for a story. Is anything you've told me even true? Or are you really involved with someone else too? "Boy, you're good. I'll give you that." He snickered. "You should be going after an Oscar, not a Pulitzer. You want a story? I've got one for you. How's this? 'Doctor Loses Control in Coffee Shop and Injures Woman with Hot Tea.'"

He leans forward in his seat to emphasize his seriousness and continues. "Emily, three years ago we were in the perfect relationship. We were happy, we were committed to each other, and I thought we were totally in love. At least, I know I was. Then out of nowhere, you tell me you're leaving me? You need to be on your own? You need to make a life for yourself? For Christ's sake, you were moved out in two days! You wouldn't talk to me. You wouldn't see me. When I called your parents to try to find you, you'd obviously told them to keep your whereabouts a secret."

He looks down at the table and pauses to collect himself. When he lifts his head and looks back at her, his eyes are bloodshot with restrained emotion and his voice is raspy. "You didn't even call when I needed you most, Emily. That was the shot that hurt the most."

She knew exactly to what he was referring—his dad's passing. Her head drops in shared pain. The look on his face and the hurt in his voice is killing her slowly. She leans toward him to begin to defend herself but sits back speechlessly as she realizes she can't address all that just yet. She has to start at the beginning in order for him to fully understand and accept the decision she made three years ago.

As she collects her thoughts to try to organize an intelligent and unemotional response, he takes her lack of response for undeniable proof on his side. "You disappeared into thin air, and then I disappeared too into Somalia. That's the only information on Somalia you'll get out of me."

Emily's face is stricken. She feels cornered and confused. She didn't expect that attack at all. He made her sound so cruel and callous. And where was this crazy idea about a "story" coming from? She's done enough investigative work to know that he's acting like someone who is desperately hiding something. She is frozen with disbelief and a little afraid at his craziness and pseudo threat. Just then, the waitress comes waddling over, sets down his orange scone and her hot streaming plate of eggs with a flare and a habitual "Enjoy your meals," and is off. They both look at their plates as if they have no idea what it is. Emily looks back up to Peter and tries to begin a reply to this insane accusation.

She takes a deep breath and begins. "Peter, I can't believe that you really think everything you just said is true. Firstly, do you think I wouldn't be able to find an MSF doctor in San Francisco if that's all I wanted? Secondly, do you really suppose that I'm capable of the extent of duplicity that you're accusing me of? I know that I left suddenly, and badly, but it's not at all what you think. When I found about your dad…well…I just couldn't talk to you at the time…oh, if you only knew the truth. I want to explain it all to you, Peter. Just give me a minute—" She stops midsentence.

She knows she's not making sense. Her nerves are getting to her. Panic is licking at her heels. The look on his face is getting colder and colder. She feels like she's losing him all over again. She places her hand over her mouth to hide her discomfort and suddenly feels the familiar churning in her stomach. Her face takes on a greenish hue. Her free hand clutches her stomach, and her eyes close tightly in pain. The smell of the food is unbearable.

Coupled with the stress and emotion, she feels the infamous sensation of rising bile again. She breaks out in a cold sweat. She can feel the dampness above her upper lip. Next will be the dizziness and the shaking. She has to get out of there fast.

She grabs her purse, spits out another "Be right back" more urgent than the last time back at the bar, slides out of the booth, and runs for the bathroom like Cinderella from the ball at midnight. Only there was neither a golden coach that would turn into a pumpkin, nor fine white horses that would turn into mice. Her fate was not so fairytale-like. She runs into the ladies' room.

Peter watches as the door swings shut behind her with a frustrating thud.

Now what? He tosses his white napkin onto the table, surrendering to no one, disgusted with himself. *Why did I have to go and attack her like that?* He berates himself. Things were just starting to feel pleasant and civil between them. He couldn't even believe that he was sitting across the table from her. He shouldn't have let his anger and suspicion get the best of him. She obviously wants to talk about their separation. He had thought of this moment often over the last three years. It's what got him through the hell of Somalia. As he waits for Emily to return from the restroom, he reflects on that hell. He hears her words again. "Somalia must have been heartbreaking." Well that's one word to describe it. He could think of a few others.

———

Man's inhumanity to man sometimes seems boundless.

———

CHAPTER 9

JANUARY 2006

The landscape of Somalia was becoming more and more defined in the tiny porthole of a window he was looking through on the Antonov An-24RV Russian-built aircraft. His flight from Djibouti to Mogadishu, the capital of Somalia located in the southern region on the coast of the Indian Ocean, was very short. Final leg of his long journey. He was very tired, and he felt smaller and smaller as the hours passed by. He wanted to feel small—small and insignificant—so that maybe he could take control over himself again.

From 8000 feet of elevation, the outskirts of Mogadishu looked pretty in a biblical way. Roughly two thousand miles from Bethlehem, it reminded Peter of stories from the Bible. There were ancient rocky hills, oceans of sand, and miles of shoreline along the Indian Ocean on the east. As the plane made its sluggish descent and neared the city of Mogadishu, the topography seemed to change little by little. At two thousand feet of elevation, he could discern buildings that looked evacuated, a stadium that looked neglected, and vacant mosques shining proudly in the sun. There were virtually no cars on the debris-laden roads, and he couldn't see any signs of life. As the plane descended, to one thousand feet, the runway was within sight. It was little more than an asphalt strip in the middle of the sand. It ended about one hundred feet from the Indian Ocean. No room for error.

He had left Charlottesville for Richmond almost forty-two hours ago. Then he flew to Kennedy airport in New York. From there, he flew to Heathrow in London, then to Djibouti, then to Mogadishu. He had been on two taxi rides, three busses, and four airplanes, and he was exhausted. He felt beaten and drained, but to be fair, he felt that way before he ever left Charlottesville. In fact, he'd been living like an automaton since the day she left.

The MSF briefed him on the conditions in Somalia as well as provided the necessary vaccines for typhoid, yellow fever, hepatitis A, and hepatitis B. The floods from the tsunami had wiped away thousands of homes and lives. The 9.0 earthquake that triggered the 2004 tsunami was centered on the west coast of Northern Sumatra. It had ignited flooding of epic proportions. Drought and famine have punctuated the region for at least the past three years. Added to this was an intense political scene that pitted Islam extremists, ICU (Islamic Courts Union), who were reported to be backed by al-Qaeda, against Somali liberals. The death toll was rising at an alarming rate. Fighting was escalating, and projections of an all-out war were imminent.

Peter had always been interested in the humanitarian effort of the MSF and took this opportunity to devote 100 percent of himself to the cause. He wanted to get as far away from his deserted, abandoned life as possible, and this really fit the bill. Instead of getting over her, he had grown more and more withdrawn since Emily's departure. There were no more friendly drinks with co-workers after work, no Monday-night football with the guys, and no signs of life—only work. He went on a couple dates after she left, mostly out of spite, but his brooding disposition eliminated many repeat dates.

Famine is poverty of the body; loneliness is poverty of
the soul.

Immediately following Emily's aberrant departure, Peter decided
to play it cool. If she wanted to leave, let her. He wasn't going to
chase after her like some lovesick puppy. He had made it perfectly
clear that he didn't want her to go, that he wanted to work things
out, but she left anyway. Her punishment was that he wouldn't
pursue her. He would wait. That lasted exactly one week. And it
was torture. He realized he wasn't the waiting kind.

So he got on the phone and started calling everyone they
knew. No one knew a thing. She had very thoroughly covered
all her tracks. She sold her car privately for cash, canceled all
her credit cards, left no forwarding address anywhere, except
maybe at the paper, but they were not legally permitted to tell
him anything. She definitely did not want to be found.

He knew her well enough to know that she wouldn't cut
off her parents, so his next course of action had been to call her
parents. They wouldn't tell him anything except that she was okay
and apparently wanted her space. They neither confirmed nor
denied her whereabouts. Though, they did counsel him not to
look for her. Wherever she was, she didn't want to be found. The
coldness and determination in their voices convinced him not
to try.

He begged and pleaded with them to tell him anything
they knew. He was so confused. He needed to know what went
wrong, and of course, he suspected that there was someone else.
But no matter how earnestly he beseeched, they were a vault. He
believed their sincere empathy for him when they told him they

wished there was more they could say. They had always liked him very much and assumed he would be their son-in-law someday. They apologized for her and assured him that she'd call when she was ready.

He just didn't get it. What could have motivated her to leave? How could she not care about her career? How could she have so coldly dismissed her friends? How could she have completely abandoned her life? But mostly, how could she have so heartlessly forsaken him? All arrows pointed to an affair, but something in his heart or his soul just couldn't accept that. He guessed that's probably what every man in love would think, though. She had pulled a total Jekyll and Hyde, and he had no one left to ask, no stone left to turn, no hope left on which to hang.

—

It was about three weeks after she left when Peter reached an emotional rock bottom. The phone rang at 3:00 a.m. It's never, never good news when the phone rings at 3:00 a.m. The person on the other end was so emotional that he couldn't make out what they were saying.

"Slow down, slow down." He tried to calm them down so he could understand. "Take a deep breath, and start over."

His first reaction was panic for Emily. Something happened to her. *She's upset or she's hurt or she's dead.* His mind was running red lights.

"Peter," the voice said after a long pause for thin control. "Your father's had a heart attack."

It was his mother. She was at the hospital in Florida. Alone. He was up and out of bed and halfway to fully dressed before she even had a chance to breath after the next rounds of sobs.

"I'm already on my way, Mom. I'll be there this morning. What's his status?" Peter tried to keep a clear head until he had all the information.

"Not good, Peter. Not good." And she was crying again.

"But more specifically, Mom?" Peter's voice rose with panic.

"He's gone, honey. He's g…" Her sobs took her voice away again.

Peter sat slowly on the edge of the bed and sank gradually to the floor. Animalistic instinct is to get as close to the ground as possible in times of severe stress or threat to life and limb. This seemed to be all three. *Gone? His dad? Couldn't be.* Denial. He actually considered asking her if she was sure. Maybe there was a mistake. Maybe it was one of those rare instances when the attending physician pronounces a patient deceased, but there's still a faint, faint heartbeat. He'd read about it in medical journals. His mind had to take this small detour so that he didn't have to face the finality of it all at once. But of course, he knew that his mother would never have called him and told him this dire news if she weren't "1,000 percent" sure.

"Peter?" his mother searched after a few full minutes of silence.

He sniffed, cleared his throat, and answered, "I'm here, Mom." His voice was frayed with emotion.

"I'm so sorry to have to give you this terrible news over the phone, honey," she cried on.

"I'm sorry you're there alone, Mom. But I'll be there this morning. I'm on my way. Did you call Michael and Jennifer yet?" he asked as he gathered his wits.

"No. Not yet. I will," she answered vaguely.

"I'll call them, Mom. Don't worry," Peter assured her.

After a few more emotional words, they hung up, and Peter began making the necessary phone calls and arrangements, all the while feeling the absence of Emily even more severely. She should be here with him at a time like this, he thought. She had loved his father dearly. He was instantly furious with her all over again.

On his flight to Orlando a few hours later, his mind kept wandering back to Emily. She should definitely be notified at least. Even though she did leave, he should at least get word to her. Whatever she did with the knowledge would be up to her. As he drove to his parents' home, he gave Emily's folks one last phone call. He told her mother what had happened and, of course, received immediate and heartfelt sympathy.

Avery Waters was a caring, kind, thoughtful soul, and he could hear that in every word she uttered. Avery promised to get word to Emily for him and asked if donations in her father's memory to the American Heart Association would be acceptable in lieu of flowers.

Peter told her thanks for both and hung up with a feeling of having sown the earth, planted a seed, watered it, and was now waiting to see the tiny green sprout pushing valiantly toward the sun. Would Emily call? Would she come to the funeral? If this didn't stir her to call him, nothing ever would. A cold chill passed through his blood at the train of thought he just had.

Three days later, Peter stood at the gravesite of his father as the casket was lowered respectfully into the waiting earth. Standing with him was his mother, brother, sister, other family members, and close friends. No Emily. No call. No show. No nothing. The casket was fully lowered, and the dirt was being shoveled back into the gaping wound. Along with the remains of his beloved father in that deep dark hole in the ground, Peter buried any hope or desire of ever seeing Emily again.

Peter received a sympathy card from Emily a couple days after the funeral when he got back to Charlottesville. It seemed sincere, emotional, genuine, and straight from the heart. It rang of the old Emily. He could tell her heart was broken for him with every word. He even imagined her tears. Well, he didn't care if her bloody, beating heart had been sealed in that envelope along with the card—too little, too late. He thoughtlessly tossed the card into the trash, and along with it the envelope, which he knew had to have born the postmark that indicated where the hell in this meaningless world she was at the moment.

———

There is nothing scarier than the unknown; sometimes nothing sadder than the truth.

———

Every morning he woke up, and for a split second, she was still there next to him, breathing softly in her sleep, waiting for him to kiss her awake and give her a proper good morning. Then he'd remember everything, and it was a fresh wound all over again. Each day got worse and worse instead of easier. Each night was more painful than the previous until he thought he'd go mad. He had to find a new life.

It was four months after Emily left when he finally went on the first date. The first date he went on resulted in an angry and brief episode in bed. It didn't bring him the relief and comfort he thought it would. He attempted dating a few more girls over the next few months. He had drunk sex, more angry sex, and eventually empty but necessary sex. Her leaving had changed him. He was becoming bitter, lonely, and cynical. He felt barren and empty, with no purpose. The war-torn, ravished, hopeless landscape of Somalia matched his mood perfectly.

CHAPTER 10

He was told he would spend at least one year in Dhahar. His plan was to stay in Africa, out of reach of Emily's shadow, for as long as possible and help in as many countries as he could. He hoped to be given an extension and relocated at the end of his mission in Dhahar, but they limited the tours because of stress. In his mind, he rolled up his sleeves, strapped on his boots, and began to save lives before they even touched down. He didn't realize that through trying to save others, he was really saving himself. He thought he was avoiding his own troubles, but he was actually working through them. He'd been that way his whole life. It's what made him a dedicated and respected physician. To him, his patients weren't just another case on a clipboard. They were an extension of himself. He was part of the human race, and they were part of the human race. The connection to him was intrinsic. He was determined to save every single man, woman, and child who needed saving, no matter what the cost to himself.

The faster and further we run from our troubles, the
closer we get to them.

As soon as he filled his lungs with fresh African air, he could feel the change within. This was so much bigger than anything he'd ever done or been through. His heart ached for the people who were merely trying to exist in this mess. The literacy rate was 37 percent, and the life expectancy was forty-eight years old. Infant and maternal mortality rates were among the world's highest. The under-age-five mortality rate was 22 percent. The main causes of death were diarrhea, respiratory infections, and malaria. These things were all so painfully simple to correct in the US. Peter couldn't even imagine the senselessness of these deaths.

Less than 30 percent of the country had access to clean water. Malnutrition was rampant. Regular immunization programs were impossible due to the fleeing of the frightened citizens. Measles and cholera were serious threats, against which few had been vaccinated. School enrollment was only about 13 percent for boys and only 7 percent for girls. Due to the fighting, about 375,000 people had been forced into tenuous living situations, where they faced hunger and human-rights abuses. His life would now most certainly have purpose. His own troubles were more than dwarfed by the tragic situation these undeserving victims had fallen into. He had his work cut out for him. Surely, the memory of Emily couldn't overshadow an entire nation of despair? Surely.

After the marathon journey from the US to Mogadishu, Peter had about an hour to collect his belongings, including his trustworthy guitar, and get on a decrepit, questionable-looking bus heading for Dhahar. The first thing Peter noticed was the armed guard who would be traveling with them from Mogadishu to Dhahar. The MSF had explained to him that all aid workers must have armored protection when traveling from one area to another. Being warned of this in the safety of an office back in the US and actually experiencing it were two completely different things. The sight of the austere guard with his weapon held at his chest sent shivers down Peter's spine.

There was only one other passenger joining them on the bus. His name was Eduardo, a priest from Italy. They introduced themselves, sat in opposing seats, and rode most of the way in awkward silence. The priest was a small, quiet man whose head was permanently tilted slightly up and back, giving him an air of arrogance. He looked at Peter as a professional chef might look at an onion, scrutinizing its worthiness for use in his main dish. Peter attempted small talk.

"How long will you be here on your mission, Father?" Peter asked politely.

"However long the good Lord needs me and deems me of value to this region, son," the priest, who was about the same age as Peter, answered condescendingly, with only a slight Italian accent. He must have been educated in England. Then he returned his attention out the window.

Since the priest didn't ask Peter any conversational questions, Peter had to assume the conversation was over. He didn't care much for the priest's answer to his question, either. Why do some religious leaders feel the need to hide behind their religion when they don't know something? Couldn't he just say, "Probably a year or so, then we'll see"? Whatever. They each dozed now and then, until a large rut in the abused pavement would wake them with a start.

Dhahar was a small village due north of Mogadishu about five hundred miles. The bus trip would take about nine hours. The scenery from Mogadishu to Dhahar was punctuated with small stick-frame huts covered in plastic sheets rising up out of the sand as if they were flags of testimony to a will to survive.

As they approached Dhahar, Peter saw wild horses running freely, with their manes and tails flapping defiantly in the wind. Their wild freedom and thriving health contrasted harshly with the images he saw of human suffering due to famine and the devastation from war. *If only humans could be as resilient and free as wildlife, but we're too smart for that,* he thought ironically.

The one thing that sets us apart from all the other animals in the world is greed. Greed will end up being man's most evil predator of all. People fear disease, people fear nature's wrath, and people fear the unknown, but it is the greed hiding in the hearts and minds of humans that has always caused more death and destruction than any other disaster in history. Never will one see a wild horse, a lion, an elephant, or any other "unsophisticated" animal take more than he needs to live. Only humans, at the top of the proverbial food chain, have that weakness. And everyone pays the price for it.

By the time he arrived at Dhahar, he was beyond exhausted. It was very late, around midnight. His new world was hushed and dark. *Perfect,* he thought. He found the small one-room dwelling that the MSF assigned to him. Without even inspecting his quarters or changing his clothes, he entered the insignificant cinderblock structure, collapsed onto his cot, and fell into the deepest sleep he'd been in since he couldn't remember. The long, arduous trip had finally brought the mind-numbing, soul-battering, bone-weary bliss he had been seeking since Emily left. Thank the Lord.

When he awakened, the first thing that struck him was the heat. It was 5:30 a.m., and the heat was already suffocating. He lifted the mosquito net off his cot and climbed out. His dwelling was very basic, but sufficient, four gray block walls, cement floor, cot, four drawer-dresser, chair, small desk, a single bulb screwed into a socket in the ceiling, and little else. A sink, but no toilet or shower. Home sweet home for the next year, at least. From what the MSF had told him, he was lucky to have running water at all, but wasn't going to consider it potable.

What the hell did I get myself into? zipped through his mind fleetingly and was gone. He was committed wholly to this project and anxious to get started. He exited his quarters and entered the oppressively hot world of Somalia without trepidation.

It had been dark by the time the bus reached Dhahar the night before so he couldn't see his new surroundings very well. Now, in the light of day, all he saw was insurmountable desolation all around him. He heard a jet engine overhead, squinted, and looked up at the airliner in the sky as it made its getaway. It made him feel even more isolated in this strange place to see the modern jet fleeing away at about five hundred miles per hour. His head automatically searched around him as if weighing whether to remain there or chase after the plane for dear life. Then he simply shook his head, smiled, let out a brief humph at himself, and marched onward into the searing heat.

CHAPTER 11

Dhahar was a sparsely populated city made up mostly of very small cinder-block dwellings, not unlike his own, and few basic concrete buildings that looked like they would be condemned back in the States. The streets were sand, or if they were paved, they had been covered over with sand, and there were a small number of municipal structures. The most common mode of transportation among the villagers was of the four-legged variety, rather than the four-wheeled. This added to the sanitation problem, which was already almost insurmountable.

Utilities such as running water and sewage were practically nonexistent, and unsafely antiquated where they did exist. Telephone service and electricity were available in theory. He saw utility poles and electrical and telephone wires but doubted very sincerely that they led anywhere; maybe they did at one point in time. The MSF provided a few generators and a satellite phone for the medical center and mess hall as backup. The air smelled of stagnant water and refuse. Flies were infinite. The sun was brutally relentless.

This society devoid of Western world traffic and commercialism was eerily mute, like in a *Twilight Zone* episode. This corner of the world gave the impression of being forgotten, forsaken. Peter was right at home.

He walked down the sandy path and joined the other physicians in the mess hall for some coffee and bread to begin his day. There were five other doctors, three nurses, and about a dozen various workers at this location right now. These people have all braved the elements, the hostility, the threat to personal safety, and the threat of disease to be here helping these victims. He was in good company.

"New guy?" a tired-looking middle-aged man addressed Peter with a lifted motion of his coffee cup.

"Yes, just arrived last night," Peter answered as he filled his own coffee cup.

"John Barrett. Nice to meetchya. Peter Daniels? We've been expecting you. Heard good things, heard good things," he greeted as he extended his hand.

Peter smiled and returned the handshake. "Thank you. Good to meet you too, and happy to join your team."

"You're from Virginia, right?" asked John.

"Yes. Charlottesville actually. You?" inquired Peter with a slightly surprised look. This guy's done his homework.

"I hail from Iowa, Des Moines. Well, it's good to have you aboard. I've got to get out to the clinic. See ya out there." He smiled and was gone.

As Peter sat at the table, a few more comrades walked in and introduced themselves. There was Tom Campbell from the United Kingdom, Melissa Bennett from Great Britain, Miranda Thomas from New York, Jan Hegstrom from Sweden, and Seamus Kelly from Ireland, though he didn't meet them all that morning. Some had traveled to neighboring villages to administer care. They were from various countries. John and Miranda were the only other US physicians at the moment, but that changed monthly as missions ended and new missions began.

John and Seamus, or Shay as he liked to be called, had known each other for long time, having met on a previous mission years ago in India. They had formed a very close working relationship and often were found working together in hushed whispers on matters that seemed confidential. The others didn't question their activity. Everyone was so thankful to have an extra pair of capable hands; politics was kept to a minimum. That, at least, would be a welcome change from the hospital back in Virginia.

About a half hour after Peter, Father Eduardo walked in and nodded politely to the others but made no introductions. As Peter drank his coffee and ate his bagel, he looked around at the others as they came and went. He wondered what motivated all of them to come there. For most, it would have been the desperation of these third-world countries. For others it could have been seeking experience in extreme trauma situations. He wondered if any of them had any personal baggage that teetered the scales in the MSF's favor, like himself. Peter had always been very dedicated and devoted to helping those most in need but joining Doctors Without Borders took a very special sort of commitment. The working conditions, the risk to personal safety, and the lack of financial gain did not entice many physicians.

From all the information the MSF had briefed him with, he was prepared for the horrendous conditions he found when he arrived. He knew already that there were not enough resources, professionals, supplies, etc., to properly care for the population in this area. He wanted to engulf himself in a worthy endeavor that would leave nothing left at the end of each day with which to worry about his small troubles. He wanted to spend every breath, every pulse, every ounce of available energy he had on helping and saving people who would certainly suffer or even perish otherwise. He had definitely found the place.

As soon as he walked out the door into the increasingly oppressive heat, the blazing sun assaulted his corneas, and the self-sacrifice began. It felt great. The more exhausted, hungry, worried, and weary he became, the closer he felt to emotional freedom. If he could just drain everything from his body, there would be nothing left with which to feel. He was a world away from the source of his despair. He was at the far end of the earth. His only concern was that Emily had stowed away somewhere in his soul.

Miranda Thomas took him around the village and helped him get acquainted with his new surroundings. Miranda was the quiet, academic, serious type. She had joined MSF straight out of her residency to help pay off her student loans. They don't pay much in the way of salary, but student loans are forgiven according to the amount of time you serve on the mission. Every little bit helps when the student loans are equivalent to five times more than a first-year physician's annual income.

"What do you think of your new home away from home so far?" Miranda inquired as she used a damp handkerchief to wipe sweat off her brow.

"Same as you, I'm sure. It's not the Ritz, but it gets the job done," Peter reasoned with a friendly smile.

Miranda nodded in agreement. They passed many people as they walked through the village. All of them looked malnourished. Dental hygiene was poor. Their eyes showed signs of bad health, with jaundice and malnutrition being most prevalent. Most were dressed in rags and children were everywhere—except in a school.

He couldn't help but think over and over about how the tiny detail of where and when you're born decides your fate in this world. Peter himself could have just as easily been born into this unforgiving village instead of where he was born, in the western world with all its opportunity and excess. He could just as easily have grown up without a formal education, enough food to eat, or a safe place to live and play as a child. The thought made him feel very connected to these people, almost responsible for them.

One thing he noticed about each and everyone was the smile they greeted him with. They looked at him and Miranda as if they could wave a magic wand and solve all their problems. It unnerved him a little to be so revered. Some of them even gave them small handmade gifts. It reminded him of ancient civilizations where people left offerings at the foot of a worshipped statue. Voodoo. Witch doctors. Peter accepted all with a smile and a nod and hoped that he would live up to their reverence.

Just two months after he arrived, the worst fighting in decades had erupted. Seventy people were killed in one attack alone. They were fighting a losing battle. It had already been impossible to keep up with the wounded and sick they currently had, let alone the additional wounded from resumed clashes. There were several occasions when all the MSF staff had to be evacuated, and Peter had to spend a few days in a "secure area" for safety.

The secure area was basically a questionably fortified hole in the ground. There had been threats made to US officials. They were told that US physicians in the neighboring country of Ethiopia were being sent home and humanitarian efforts were being halted. They were disheartened to hear that but understood the reason. Some felt that the presence of aid workers from developed countries caused more harm than good in certain cases. The insurgents realized that where there was aid, there was money or drugs or supplies—all very good commodities on the black market. They became sitting ducks to any extremists looking for a quick way to raise some cash.

⌣

One day, as the sun continued to beat down and drain the energy out of everyone, he checked in on an elderly woman of only fifty-two in her hut-like, earthen-floored home. She lived in a one-room structure with her grown daughter, son-in-law, and three grandchildren. She hadn't been doing well, her breathing was shallow, and she wasn't eating. He knelt down beside her, pushed aside the mosquito net, greeted her, and started to evaluate her heart and lungs with his stethoscope, but she held his hands still and shook her head slowly in refusal. Her face was etched with years of suffering and worry far beyond her years of age. Her rheumy eyes held the sort of knowledge that only a hard life can teach.

Peter looked questioningly at her, unable to discern her meaning. Her eyes searched about the room for an alternative way to communicate her thoughts. She pointed with a crooked finger to the small broken table at her bedside, which held six wooden bowls, one for each member of her family. She reached over and took the top bowl off the stack. She held the bowl tightly to her chest and pointed to it, then to herself, then to the sky. She looked back at him with a sad courage and pleaded with her sorrowful eyes for him to understand. She kept making the same gesture over and over, pointing to the bowl, herself, and the sky.

At first Peter thought that she wanted him to collect rain in the bowl, that somehow she thought he could make it rain. He motioned with his fingers like rain falling from the sky into to the bowl, and she shook her head and closed her eyes in response. Wrong. Then he thought maybe she was just losing her mind. But her eyes were serious and intent.

It took him a while, but he finally realized that she was asking him not to help her, but to let her go to Allah so that her family would not have to worry about filling her bowl from their meager collective dinner. He patted her hands gently, removed the bowl from her grasp, and added it back to the family's stack. He shook his head slowly, but smiled to let her know that he respected her wishes but wasn't able to fulfill them. He continued with his examination for a few minutes, dispensed medication, held her hands to indicate friendship and caring, and then turned to leave.

As he was exiting the tiny home, he heard a clatter behind him. He turned back around to find that the old woman had picked up her bowl again and had thrown it on the ground. Her eyes held his in a challenge but softened a little as one might look upon a naive child before she closed them slowly in search of rest.

That image stayed with him all day. He was a physician, a healer. It was his duty to use his education to treat physical illnesses and conditions with the intention of healing and curing. It was not his place to make judgment calls on the value of a life. He understood logically as well as the old woman that her family would probably have a better chance at survival individually if she passed on. But that was not part of his job description or his personality. The rules he lived by were rules of the Western world. The rules that applied in Africa were completely different. Living in Somalia, he sometimes felt like he was trying to play basketball by following the rules to soccer.

As he passed by the old woman's hut later that day he saw Father Eduardo emerging from the inadequate doorway, a little disheveled and hunched over. He had the look of a chastised child on his face and seemed quite out of sorts as he brushed dirt from his shirtsleeves. He turned his head from left to right as he looked about nervously in search of something.

Peter threw out a friendly, "Good day, Father. Can I help you with something?"

"No thank you, Dr. Daniels," was his sharp reply. And he walked off in a huff in the opposite direction from Peter.

Later, Peter heard that the old woman had tossed dirt at the priest as he was saying a prayer and waving a crucifix over her. No one had been able to translate at the time, but it seemed the old woman didn't care for the priest's brand of "aid."

Peter tried to see the situation from the old woman's point of view. Her family was starving, she was ill, her country was in a tragic state of upheaval, and this man, with his superior attitude and foreign tongue, was chanting strange words and waving a strange religious idol around her home uselessly. He shrugged and guessed he would probably have reacted the same way as the old woman. He didn't fault the priest though. He was only doing what he thought was best for the sick and dying. Does the end justify the means, or vice versa?

———

Day in and day out, Peter vaccinated, medicated, sutured, fed, hydrated, and regretfully, too often, buried patient after patient. He came here to escape his private unkind world and found a living hell. He felt some small satisfaction at the number of people he was able to help but wondered how long their recovery would last. He realized that he could only mask their suffering for a brief time. In these conditions the same patients/victims were going to be right back where they were in about two months. The malaria medication would eventually be stolen, the mosquito nets would stop coming, the clean water supply would run out, etc. All of his efforts started to seem in vain. Even the births, usually such a joyous occasion, had the overwhelming aura of doom.

Of the live births, at least 12 percent would be stillborn. And what were the surviving babies being born into? What sort of chance did they stand? He was becoming even more of a cynic then he already was, and he didn't like it. Emily would be disappointed in him. At least, he had broken the shell of self-pity he had formed around himself. He still had so much sorrow and anger, but instead of being for himself, it was directed at the unfortunate, ill-fated people of this seemingly forgotten land.

CHAPTER 12

In April 2006, Peter met a seventeen year old Somali woman by the name of Aya, who was pregnant with her first child. She had been married young at the Somali average age of fifteen. She had been working with the aid workers since she was small. She was bright and intelligent and eager to learn. Their efforts would not be nearly as successful if not for her. Peter didn't know it yet, but this incredible young lady would change his life forever.

Her husband, Nadif, was living in Mogadishu, and her family was from an agricultural region of Somalia. Her husband had stayed back in Mogadishu to work in order to support his family and Aya. His work consisted of sifting through the rubble of the demolished US embassy with his bare hands in order to exhume the steel rods from the original construction. He could sell these rods at a profit of six US cents per rod. It took him twelve hours a day in the searing heat to retrieve twenty rods. He could have netted twenty US cents per rod, but he had to pay the gunmen who patrolled the ruin of the embassy not to shoot him. She said he didn't mind the work, but he would just like to not have to worry about the gunmen. Anarchy, at its best.

Aya weighed ninety-five pounds and was relatively healthy by Somali standards. She had been fascinated by the aid workers from foreign countries since she was very small. She didn't remember a time when she wasn't helping out at the clinic or by a doctor's side as they vaccinated or even operated. She had a natural intelligence that enabled her to learn very quickly and the physicians, and other aid workers would take every opportunity to teach her English, reading, writing, and math. The education she received by way of conversation, situation, and pure life experiences rivaled any private school in the US. Though her English was broken, it was quite understandable and made her an excellent assistant and translator.

She had become a permanent fixture at the clinic and often went out into the field with Peter. They spent long hours together, and Peter had come to feel a familial attachment with Aya. Her parents must have been very proud of her. Her bravado in the face of all this misery and her insatiable thirst for knowledge against all odds endeared her to him with a force he hadn't felt in a long time. She never complained about the conditions or her life. This world was the only world she had ever known. She often spoke fondly of her family, which had included a mother, father, two brothers, and three sisters at one point in time. All had perished by her thirteenth birthday either from malaria, malnutrition, or stillbirth, a typical story in Somalia.

In any city in the US, this brave, intelligent, hardworking young girl would be attending a university on a full-ride scholarship. The typical American teenager falls apart if their mp3 player gets stolen or their cell phone breaks. In direct contrast, Aya was so far removed from the triviality of these items that the comparison seemed ridiculous, even ludicrous. Peter couldn't help but think that Emily would be so impressed by her.

Peter innocently asked Aya one day if she ever thought about leaving Somalia and pursuing an education.

Aya's face grew thoughtful, and she replied, "Dr. Peter, I have pursued education all my life. You don't have to change your location to do that. There is a lot to be learned from everyone and everything on the earth. I do have dreams, though. I want to be in a place where the people don't suffer, where they rejoice at new birth instead of burying two out of ten babies that are born. I want selfish things too, like to spend the whole day just reading a book. I want to see a film in the cinema and to eat at the McDonald's." She giggled at this, because in an effort to bring levity to the situation in Somalia, the foreign-aid workers often joked about picking up McDonald's one night for dinner.

"I want to see the place where food is everywhere, water is clean, and medicine is always available to the sick ones. I dream of going to the place that is peaceful and where I could walk to the village market and wave and smile to my neighbors on the way, without fear of the bombs or the guns. I want a big, beautiful, safe home to bring my baby into when it is born. But in my dreams, this place is called Somalia. My home. I will never leave it. I will die here and be buried near my family."

Peter made no reply. His plain American words, even if he had spoken the queen's English, not broken English like hers, would have paled in comparison. Aya was a queen herself. Being a queen is, or at least should be, not in how you speak, but in what you say, and not in what you possess, but in what you give. The genuine love she had for people and the compassion she showed in the face of her own desperate need is what made her a queen—a queen, not by birth, but by divinity. How could someone so young be so wise and perceptive? She was like a mystic or a guru. She astounded him.

—◡—

Into this life go bravely, compassionately, and generously;
it will bring you peace.

—◡—

By the last week in April after he arrived, the death toll had quintupled and the capital where he landed that first day, Mogadishu, had been overtaken. All hell broke loose at that point, and the opposing clans held rallies all over that brought much attention from neighboring countries like Kenya. Refugees were no longer allowed to cross any borders, and that put a lot more strain on their efforts in Dhahar. There were more and more patients each day, and some of the physicians had to leave due to their visas expiring. Three new physicians were due to arrive soon. All three of them were from the US. Peter had been working several shifts a day, burying more people than he could stand, and trying even harder not to lose hope that all their efforts weren't in vain.

———

Later that week, the reinforcements finally arrived in the form of Robert from Chicago, Steve from Dallas, and Erin from Los Angeles. Robert and Steve were both internists. Erin was an OB. Everyone was very thankful when they arrived. Their help was desperately needed. There had been an uprising in a nearby village where Peter had been working more than twelve hours straight. When he pulled into Dhahar, he was exhausted, covered in filth and blood, unshaven, and a little wild looking. He jumped out of the jeep and was in dire need of coffee and something in his stomach to soak up the bitterness of despair he'd had to swallow all day.

As he crossed the compound seeking refuge with his comrades, he noticed several of them carrying boxes, moving medical equipment, and milling around a central figure who was blocked from his view by all the hubbub. He wondered what sort of project they were up to now. As he neared the crowd, the ringleader came into view. Her image stopped him dead in his tracks.

Wow. No wonder everyone was happily doing her bidding. Peter stood there for a full fifteen seconds as he drank in the portrait of a tall, slender but shapely woman dressed in a pink silk designer blouse, snug-fitting jeans, and plenty of estrogen. This very attractive newcomer seemed to be orchestrating the whole affair with a simple wave of her elegant hand. He shook his head to clear it and continued his pursuit.

Peter had come to be respected as a senior member of the staff over the time period he'd been there. He had worked very hard at renovating their triage system from the UK standard to the US military standard, which better fit the hostile environment they were working in. He wasn't completely sure, but from where he stood, it looked like this drill sergeant Barbie was undoing some of his hard work in the triage area. He was tired. He was hungry. He was downtrodden. And he was not in a welcoming mood. Peter didn't get irritated very easily or very often, but he was very irritated by all this. He stomped over to the irritant and demanded to know what the hell she was doing.

The unfamiliar woman swung her head around to face him with a level gaze, looked up and down Peter's entire length, turned her head dismissively back to the others, and continued with her interrupted conversation. When she faced him, he could see the dynamite sparking in her eyes. He hid his reaction as best he could. She barely even acknowledged Peter's presence.

This did not help Peter's mood. He moved so that he was physically standing between the woman and her minions, got right in her perfectly symmetrical, high-cheek-boned, flawless skin-toned face, and nearly growled, "Who are you and what are you doing with my equipment?"

The woman gave him an answering glare, casually turned over the object in her hand, read the MSF identification label out loud, looked him in the eye, and walked confidently away to continue her mission of rearranging the medical equipment.

Peter was left standing there with his mouth hanging open and the anger welling up inside him.

Too tired to fight and clearly not getting anywhere with her, he went to the mess hall where he found Tom and some much-needed coffee. Peter asked him what the scoop was on the new arrivals, particularly the shrew in pink. Tom laughed and said that her name was Erin. She was from LA but he couldn't recall her last name. She was an OB, and he had heard that she wasn't very pleased with the setup for female patients. She had started making some changes almost as soon as she had arrived.

"Of that, I am painfully aware. She must really be missing Beverly Hills about now," Peter remarked as he looked around exaggeratedly.

He decided to get some food into him, get some rest, and have a talk with "Barbie" in the morning. A quick shower in the bathhouse they all shared and he was asleep almost before his head hit the pillow.

All too early the next morning, he awoke to the sound of construction nearby. He threw some clothes on and followed the sound, with a strong feeling of what he'd find at the source. Sure enough, his nemesis was directing as individual cubicle-sized exam rooms were being constructed in what used to be a storage building. The building was the smallest of them all, but perfect for storing all the necessary supplies. *Boy, this woman had balls*, Peter couldn't help but think to himself.

Washed, clean shaven, and rested, Peter approached Erin for a second time in less than twelve hours. This time, he extended his hand in welcome and introduced himself over the noise,

"Hello again, we didn't formally meet last night. My name is Peter, Peter Daniels. And you are?"

She hesitated for a telling split-second, illustrating her suspicion at the drastic change in his demeanor.

He picked up the signal that she was a little apprehensive and added, "I was really beat up last night. Long day. I guess I was a little testy. I apologize." *You can catch more flies with sugar,* he thought to himself.

Without letting down her guard, "Erin Reid," was all she said as she shook his hand.

They stood in the blaring early morning July sun and sized up each other silently, hands clasped in greeting, polite smiles, and guarded eyes. Her hand was surprisingly soft and warm, for a drill sergeant, thought Peter. The hard lines of her face seemed to soften slightly at his touch. Their hands stayed joined for a fraction past awkward, and they both let go quickly at the same moment as when you reach for the light switch and you get a shock. Something about the exchange rankled Peter's subconscious.

A couple throat-clearing ahems and nervous shifting of the feet, then Peter slid into, "So, exactly what is your goal here?" as he waved his hands around to indicate the construction and the relocating of *his* equipment.

By the look on her face, any progress he may have made in impressing her with the recent apology was lost immediately upon his ill-disguised interrogation. Peter never was very good at pretense, straight shooter, all his life.

The cool exterior was back in place instantly. "I'm setting up a proper OB clinic. Female patients need to feel comfortable enough to come to me before they progress into an unrecoverable situation. More than half the women here are pregnant before the age of eighteen."

Peter immediately thought of Aya.

"And I'm sure you know the infant mortality rate. HIV, gonorrhea, syphilis, chlamydia, herpes, etc. etc. Do I really need to lecture you? Modern medicine scares them enough without being surrounded by men and disease while they're being examined and treated. I'm hoping to educate several of them as midwives. There is a dire need for appropriate female medical care here, in case you haven't noticed," she challenged with laser-like eye contact.

He stumbled for only a nanosecond before he regained his mental stance. "Well, I happen to have spent a very long time organizing everything since I got here. It's taken me many hours to set up the clinic exactly how I wanted it. And we don't necessarily have the resources for all these modifications."

She started to turn her back and walk away from his criticism.

"This isn't Cedars-Sinai, you know. In case *you* haven't noticed," he threw out accusingly.

He could almost feel her skin prickling. She halted, turned slowly back toward him with narrowed eyes, as the picture all started to come together in her mind. She hadn't told him she was from LA, where Cedars-Sinai is a very popular hospital among the rich and famous. He already knew where she was from, so he probably already knew her name as well. This led her to the assumption that his mock introduction and apology was merely a charade intended to soften the opposition for the impending attack.

She looked all around her with feigned surprise, as if in a panic, then breathed out dramatically, "Oh, damn! You mean my limo won't be here any minute to take me shopping on Rodeo Drive? What? No Spago's for dinner? Oh, whatever will I do?" she added with her head tilted back and the back of her hand dramatically pressed against her forehead as in old Western dramas. Just before she would have fallen to the ground in a fainted heap, she dropped the act and gave him a dirty "Now get the hell out of here, I'm busy" look and busily got back to her mission.

Round 2 went to Barbie. As well as round 1. Damn. There was no time to worry about all that now, though. One thing about aid work in an African country at war: no rest for the weary. Peter had to be at the clinic by 7:00 a.m. UNICEF was due in today and would be administering polio vaccines to the children of Dhahar. He needed to be available to assist with examinations prior to dispensing the vaccine. Thanks to UNICEF, there hadn't been a reported case of polio in over a year. He wouldn't finish with this project until well after suppertime, a long day in the African sun, and what a delightful start, thanks to his new friend, Barbie, he thought sardonically.

First thing, he entered the main clinic, where Erin had done the most damage, and inspected all his equipment and supplies. The rooms were rearranged slightly, more economically actually. Curtains were hung as dividers. Additional closets were fashioned out of cabinets. And upon further inspection, all the necessary equipment and supplies were stored systematically and behind locked doors when appropriate. He looked as hard as he could for a mistake or a flaw but found none. *Uh-oh.* Crow doesn't taste good. Neither does humble pie. Well, he still had to check out the storage-building-turned-OB-center. Maybe he would find a major screw up there, hopefully.

About midday, Peter noticed Barbie walking with some others to the mess hall, probably for a noon coffee and meal. That should keep her busy for at least a half hour. He had a few minutes to himself while they prepared the next group of children for the vaccines. He moved down the line of children as they tossed a small ball back and forth with him as he made his way closer and closer to the new OB building.

He walked stealthily to the entrance. When he walked into the tiny structure, the first thing that struck him was that the space actually looked larger from the inside than from the outside. How'd she do that? There were four separate exam stalls separated by thin fiberboard. That must have been all the noise he heard that morning. Supplies and equipment were all neatly and economically organized to make the best of the available space. It was all exceedingly clean as well. He recognized a few pieces of equipment from the main clinic, mostly things that strictly pertained to the gynecological side of medicine, nothing that he would need now that she was here. Damn. He raked his hand through his hair, demonstrating his frustration at finding everything flawless.

At that moment, he heard a sterile hello from behind him. He turned quickly to find, of course, Barbie standing just inside the tiny doorframe, holding an apple from the mess hall in her hand. Busted. At a loss for what to say to cover his actions, he blurted out honestly and simply, "I thought you went to lunch."

"Obviously," she muttered down her nose, with her eyebrows held high in disapproval. She ignored him as she passed by him to pick up a clipboard with a stack of patient-history forms. As she exited, she threw over her shoulder, "Continue your investigation, Sherlock," and she tossed the apple over her head, without looking, for him to catch it.

He found himself, yet again, mouth agape, looking at her back as she walked away, this time with a shiny red apple in his hand. He couldn't help but laugh at the situation. She was, if nothing else, very spirited. He left the small building and headed back to the polio vaccines. He took a big bite of the apple as he walked. He didn't notice Erin watching him with a knowing smile spreading slowly on her face.

CHAPTER 13

Peter bumped into Father Eduardo again on Sunday of the next week as he was visiting some of the villagers who were the weakest. They had set up a temporary "ward" to house those whose prognosis was poorest. Most of them were suffering from Typhoid Fever. Antibiotics cure more than ninety percent of patients with typhoid, but not where there is so little uncontaminated food and water. Salmonella was rampant, and the malnourished condition of most of the population made them perfect targets for infection. Once their bodies are weakened past a certain point, other infections occur such as pneumonia, diarrhea, etc., and they make it almost impossible to recover.

The priest was praying for these poor souls to be accepted into heaven. He was speaking to them, this time through a translator provided by the church, about accepting his Savior before it was too late. Anyone could see in his face that he was earnest and passionate in his sermon. However, the tired, suffering patients were obviously not interested in his speech. They closed their eyes and prayed to their own savior. The predominant religion in the area was Sunni Muslim, and they were a religious group.

Peter watched the interaction between the priest and Muslim patient, and something felt oddly familiar about it. He was not a deeply religious person, having made a life from science, but he wasn't completely without his spiritual beliefs. Peter felt that a person's religious beliefs should be honored on their own merit. He didn't really see how sending a Catholic priest to this part of the world to convert Muslims on their deathbed was really in anyone's best interests.

Still, the churches were a huge source of aid and donations to the area, and Peter was very respectful of that fact. A lot of lives were saved each year through the commitment by the Catholic church, Methodist church, Lutheran church, etc. But when they consistently kept trying to convert the villagers to their own beliefs, there seemed to be invisible strings attached to the aid.

Peter realized at that moment what seemed familiar to him, and he suddenly felt a small kinship with the priest, though he didn't agree with him most of the time. It was his experience a few months ago with the old woman who threw her bowl down. She had made her beliefs and wishes clear to Peter, but his culture, his education, his Western world ways prohibited him from complying. He realized with an epiphany that he wasn't all that different from the priest. They both believed that they were helping this impoverished group of people who "didn't know what was good for them." There is a very thin line between helping and hindering. Peter would remember this moment always and try not to let his own beliefs, no matter how strong and seemingly right, belittle the beliefs of others. Help is only help if it's welcomed.

———

As usual, Peter was very busy for the next few days, with hardly a moment to himself. The OB clinic was a raving success as word spread from girl to girl and woman to woman within the village and nearby villages. Erin was inundated with patients and worked mostly eighteen hour days and went to bed each night exhausted. They didn't see much of each other except in passing here and there for about a week.

Peter noticed a few of the men flirting with her hopefully. She was very attractive but seemed completely uninterested in flirting back. He knew she wasn't married. He also knew that her commitment to her work was very serious. She wasn't here to play around. What Peter learned from a distant observation of Erin is that she was hardworking, dedicated, compassionate, very skilled, and strikingly beautiful.

Others who had talked with her had informed him through idle conversation that she had an impressive career to this point. She was even awarded a prestigious humanitarian award for her volunteer work at the Mae Tao Clinic in Thailand, where medical services are performed for refugees from Myanmar. He had definitely underestimated her upon their first meeting.

Every male within a three-mile radius noticed her. So why did all this aggravate him so much? He assumed that it was because she seemed full of herself and she seemed to presume that she would always get her way. His annoyance certainly couldn't be because he actually had feelings of attraction for her, feelings that he had buried and held funeral services for a few years back—when Emily left. He had vowed to himself that he was through with relationships forever. He wasn't going to tee up his heart for the next woman to pull out her driver and send it into oblivion—again.

It was several weeks after Erin had arrived. She had proven herself to be a very competent physician, tireless aid worker, innovative thinker, and a true friend to everyone in the village. Peter wouldn't admit it to himself, but he was more than impressed by her. As they passed each other throughout the day, they nodded politely and smiled economically to one another, a pseudo-truce, so to speak. They just stayed out of each other's way. At least there were no more accusations and harsh words.

One night, as the full moon hung low in the African sky, illuminating everything below with an eerie blue truth, Peter and Erin crossed paths unavoidably. Erin had been tending to patients in the surrounding area when she arrived back in Dhahar very late. Peter was just finishing up in the clinic for the day when they both entered the mess hall at the same time. He had avoided her completely since "the apple." There was an awkward silence as they just stared at each other, unable to come up with appropriate words and unable to move a muscle. Peter finally forced a smile. Erin politely smiled back.

They each grabbed a few remaining rations of dinner, sat at different tables, though they were the only two in the room, and finished at about the same time. The silence between them resonated so loudly that it made their ears ring. Erin stood to leave first. Every atom in Peter's body was at full alert as she passed by. Somehow, he figured she knew this—planned this. She was mocking him. He knew it. He worked very hard to ignore her. Once she was out, he waited a reasonable amount of time and then left as well.

It was so damn hot that night, hotter than any night he could remember. The sweat poured off him like a faucet that was neglected and left running. He pulled his shirt over his head as he took the dark path from the bathhouse to his quarters. As he rounded a narrow corner where two buildings were built too closely together, he nearly bumped into a shape walking toward him in the obscurity of nightfall.

"Pardon me," he said reflexively. As he brought his eyes up from the ground he recognized the shape, and what a shape it was. Erin, of course, in a tight tank top that clung to her body with sweat—creamy white glossy skin glistening in the moonlight— and shorts that redefined the meaning of short.

"Jesus," he breathed to himself, but loud enough for her to hear. His eye movement became involuntary as he couldn't stop himself from covering the length of her several times with them.

"Nope, just me," she commented as a superioresque smile spread unabashedly across her face.

"What are you doing? Where are you going?" Peter asked angrily. "It's dark out here! And it's hotter than hell!" he unreasonably accused.

"I'm heading to the bathhouse, if that's permissible, and I can neither control the dark of night, nor the heat of day, Peter," she answered patronizingly with the kind of calm with which one speaks to a person on a ledge, a very high ledge.

"Well, you should be in your room, not walking around out here!" This sounded ridiculous even to him as he heard himself say it anyway.

"Humph. It seems that I can't even manage going to the restroom properly. Well, I'm so sorry to have once again disappointed you, Peter," she apologized mockingly.

He totally deserved that. He knew it, but it enraged him anyway. She said his name twice in their conversation, and the sound of it on her lips quickened his heartbeat. And that enraged him even more. Why couldn't he control his reaction to her? He was just staring at those lips now, her full, soft, slightly parted lips.

The word *carnal* kept flashing through his mind in red letters. He tried to blink it away, but it was branded there. He started to pant. His vision tunneled. And those lips got closer and closer. How did they keep getting closer? He didn't even notice himself moving toward her until he could feel the heat from her body and smell the salt in her sweat. The harder he fought off the physical attraction, the more attracted he became.

The lips smiled welcomingly, knowingly. His eyes were trained on those luscious red lips as they beckoned him to them. His own lips parted as he got even closer. He could feel her breath on his face. He was a goner. No force in this universe could have stopped what happened next. Not time, not space, not a splitting atom.

His mouth covered hers and brought out a groan from somewhere so deep within him; it sounded dangerous and feral. Her mouth answered every movement of his as if in a dance. Their lips parted, and the shock of their tongues meeting ripped them apart like a lightning bolt. As they searched each other's eyes for answers, permission, control, punishment, something, anything, their breathing got heavier and their bodies molded together. He could feel every inch of her hot, sweaty body against his, and he knew it would leave permanent scars all over him, but he didn't care.

Without one word, he pushed her forcefully up against the cool cinder-block wall with his whole body, cushioning her head with both hands as he pulled her closer and pressed his lips even harder against hers. Instead of stopping him, she kissed him back, openmouthed and hungrily.

"Peter," she moaned as he devoured her.

He lost all ability for verbal communication and answered her with only a caveman grunt. He was like a caged lion that had just been set free. And she answered the call to freedom. They had both been locked away from passion for so long, and they couldn't deny it any longer. Their passion was like an unruly beast, demanding and ferocious. He tore his mouth away from hers, and she whimpered at the sudden loss.

He looked dangerously into her eyes and groaned, "You're so...so...I can't control myself when I'm this close to you."

She held his challenging glare and simply answered, "I don't want you to, Peter."

She suggested they go into one of their respective rooms. Without one more word, panting heavily, he slid his hands down her sweat-soaked arms, took her hand in his, and led her to his quarters.

The room was hot as they stumbled in the dark to his cot. By the time they fell into it, they were both undressed and caressing every inch of each other, learning one another. Still not a word passed between them. Erin responded to every overture Peter made with passion. Peter felt awakened after a long, bad dream. And he awoke with a burning hunger in the pit of his soul. Their bodies became one in a flash of fire.

———

And out of the ashes, arises the phoenix.

———

Peter and Erin lay in his cot together for several minutes as they tried to catch their breath. When normal respiration returned, they dared to look at each other.

A sly smile grew on Peter's face and he teased, "Well, it appears, Dr. Reid, that we've found *something* you can do right after all."

Erin, speechless for a millisecond, opened her mouth wide in shock, laughed out loud, and slapped him in affected anger, as he smiled and laughed with her.

When their laughter ebbed, Erin teased back, "I heard you really did have a great personality and were a fantastic guy underneath all that callousness. You know, a simple 'How are you today?' would have sufficed to convince me. You certainly didn't have to go to all this trouble." She indicated their sexual encounter.

They talked on into the night with ease. The awkwardness was gone. The anger was absent. They were surprised to find that apart from being very compatible in bed, they had a lot to say to one another. Erin told him that she had learned all about him the first day she was there before she met him.

At one point, Erin asked him about previous relationships because she had heard the rumors about his bad breakup. She herself had been divorced and was a few years senior to Peter.

Peter hesitated before telling her about Emily. His hesitation was more to protect himself rather than to protect Erin. He decided, though, that he would be completely truthful so there would be no false expectations. He wasn't going to pretend he was over that part of his life. Always a straight shooter.

She listened as he summed up the years since he met Emily, and she watched his face closely when he spoke of her. She knew that Emily would always occupy his heart. It didn't really matter to her. She was totally focused on her work as an aid worker now. Nothing else interested her. She only wanted to be his friend. She wasn't looking for a soul mate. She didn't want any commitments or promises. She'd had those, and her heart was still broken. She explained to him that she just wanted a true friendship and someone she could share passion with once in a while. They were merely two people who shared a common emptiness. They talked until they were weary and unburdened then drifted into a peaceful sleep.

CHAPTER 14

Peter and Erin fell into an easy routine, and their friendship grew deeper every day. They didn't discuss the future, and they didn't dwell on the past. They just enjoyed the time they spent together in the present, whenever their busy lives allowed them the time. When they weren't swamped in Dhahar, they were traveling to other villages to offer aid. There was more need than there were resources, but yet they persevered.

Peter was preparing his supplies for some upcoming work in nearby Eyl. There was a total solar eclipse in the forecast. Peter found this to be of minimal scientific interest and forgot about it as soon as it was observed. The other aid workers felt the same. However, the Somalis felt quite differently. Prayers were being chanted, offerings to the sun and the moon were being made, and a desperate feeling of impending doom was growing throughout the village of Dhahar. Of course, Peter and his comrades did not participate in the rituals of the natives. The day came and went. As the sun set on the horizon that night, Aya encouraged Peter to take extra care due to the solar eclipse, but he scoffed. He was not superstitious.

The next day, the sun seemed to beat down with an even greater vengeance for having been concealed the day before, as if making up for lost time. *The villagers would probably see this as an omen also*, Peter mused to himself with a sardonic smirk. It was unusually hot, even for that region, and sweat was soaking his shirt by 10:00 a.m. They had a few rounds to make in Dhahar, then he had planned on making the journey down to Eyl on the coast. They had heard about an alarming increase in hepatitis A.

Miranda and Aya were supposed to travel with him, but the roads between villages were not well paved, mostly just sandy paths and the Jeep was not very smooth. The jostling would not be good for Aya in her condition. Aya would have to stay behind, and she was not happy about it. She had been uneasy about the solar eclipse and about Peter's careless attitude regarding it.

When she failed to convince Peter to take it seriously, she started in on Miranda. Aya and Miranda had grown very close over the few months they'd known each other. Miranda was the youngest member of the MSF team, and Aya felt a kinship with her. They looked very much alike also. Both had dark skin, large curious eyes, and were petite in stature. They both were caring, intelligent, strong young women, but Aya couldn't convince Miranda of the potential danger from the solar eclipse, either.

To Aya's dismay, Peter and Miranda headed out right after lunch. They were making pretty good time, until unfortunately, fate had other plans for Peter. After about an hour on the road, they met the devil himself, and Peter had to sacrifice a piece of his soul in the name of righteousness.

The capital of Mogadishu had been under heavy fire, and the Islam courts had taken control of the city and imposed Islamic law, Sharia. The fighting had intensified and was moving northward from Mogadishu. More and more clinics had been shut down and evacuated. The fighting had not reached Dhahar, and there was a relative, deceptive calm surrounding them. Peter and Miranda had loaded up the jeep with medical supplies earlier that morning.

Several factors contributed to the demise of the day. First, they usually received up-to-the minute reports of the hostility but had not received any that morning. Second, another MSF doctor was supposed to join them but had to stay behind at the last minute for an emergency. Peter should have canceled the journey then, but the reports from Eyl had been so desperate he decided to continue in order that he might prevent an all out outbreak of hepatitis A. Third, Peter always took the precaution of bringing the two-way radio with him when he made visits to patients in different villages. He knew he needed to stay apprised of the hostile conditions, and he heard no new reports since they left. But that was only because the radio wasn't working properly.

⸻

They had driven almost an hour in tranquility when they came upon an unexpected blockade. They weren't aware of it, even though they had a list of blockades; it was not included on the list. Peter and Miranda looked at each other in concern but had no choice now except to slow to a stop and hope they were allowed to pass through. Peter was very nervous, mostly for Miranda. The Muslim militia tolerated the doctors from MSF because they lived like parasites of the donations that followed the MSF. But they had no respect for women, even with the MSF.

Peter rolled the window down on the jeep as he approached the threatening-looking guard and handed him the identification papers he was required to have on him at all times. The guard said nothing. His face was ominous, and his eyes were covered by dark sunglasses. He had the undeniable air of a soulless, conscienceless, militant who shoots first and asks questions later.

He looked over the papers too briefly and threw them back at Peter. First red flag. He coldly motioned with his AK-47 for them to get out of the vehicle. Second red flag. This was not good. At the very least, they were going to pilfer Peter's supplies and medications for the black market. Damn! Those had just come in. Peter thought carefully before exiting the jeep and instructed Miranda to get out slowly and keep her hands away from her clothing so they didn't mistake her for having a weapon.

As Peter was reaching for the door handle, he stealthily picked up a small surgical tool from the pouch hanging on the handle out of the guard's sight and slipped it up his sleeve. He kept his hands above his head, the knife stayed in his sleeve better that way. He turned to look for Miranda and made sure she was okay. The guard indicated with the muzzle of his gun that he wanted them to walk over to the tent. Third red flag. The hair on the back of Peter's neck was prickling in warning. His whole body sensed that something dreadful was waiting in that tent. They couldn't run, and they couldn't fight an AK-47 so they had to go along with them for now.

As they entered the tent, it took a few moments for his eyes to adjust. The first thing that struck him was the acrid smell that attacked his olfactory sense—body odor, urine, rotten food, and stale alcohol. In the tent was another guard, even less friendly looking than the first, if that was possible. He was sitting in a folding chair with an upturned crate in front of him. On the crate, there were three empty bottles of whiskey and paraphernalia for drug abuse. They said some words to each other that neither Peter nor Miranda understood but could discern incoherence nonetheless. The first guard made some sort of joke, and the second guard showed ugly stained teeth as he sneered in Miranda's direction. It didn't take a genius to figure out what was going on here. Peter now wished that they would simply steal his supplies instead.

This happened occasionally. Some of the Muslim militia would get bored, drunk, or high, set up fake outposts, and rape young women as they tried to travel through, just for fun. Peter decided on the spot that this was not going to happen while he was still drawing breath. If his life came down to this moment, then so be it.

The second guard stood up and stalked toward Miranda, weaving and swaying as he went. He spoke to her with a snide tone and lifted her skirt a little with his gun. No doubt left, and no time to think about it. Since they were both under the influence of something mind-altering, it would give Peter the advantage; in fact, it made all the difference. Peter was not a big guy; he would have never stood a chance if they weren't inebriated.

Miranda was very scared. Her breathing was rapid, and her face was anxious. Peter tried to communicate with his eyes that she didn't need to worry. He would have to wait for the right moment, when they were least aware, which would probably make Miranda even more uncomfortable. But he only had one chance. He couldn't blow it prematurely, or they would kill him and Miranda, for sure. The only reason they hadn't killed him so far is probably because they didn't want to upset the steady supply of drugs and supplies from MSF, if they didn't absolutely have to. So many clinics had already been closed, and aid workers had been pulled out. Killing aid workers was like biting the hand that fed you.

The first guard tied Peter's hands behind his back. Then he tied his feet together and pushed him into a chair. The guard was so drunk that he tied the rope very loosely. Was he kidding? This was supposed to hold him? *Thank G-d for stupidity and insobriety*, he thought. As soon as the second guard started to undo his pants, Miranda, predictably, started struggling and begging. They liked that. They looked at each other and laughed conspiratorially. They were still holding their guns, but loosely and not aiming. They didn't feel threatened. Peter had to wait just a little longer until they were both completely distracted by Miranda. Unfortunately, he'd have to wait until they had her on her back so they would be completely engrossed in what they were doing.

Within minutes, the first guard predictably pushed Miranda down, stood at her head, bent and held her hands above her head, while the second guard, obviously his superior, was preparing to take first prize by pulling down his pants.

Then without hesitation, Peter, the shy Boy Scout, a straight-A scholarship recipient who literally never hurt a fly in his life, had already cut the pathetically tied rope from his wrists and begun to carry out his plan. His feet were still tied, but limply. At the precise moment, before any damage was done physically to Miranda, Peter leapt without hesitation from his chair with his feet together and slit the throat of guard no. 2. He efficiently used the body as a shield while slipping his hand into the trigger of guard no. 2's gun and shot guard no. 1 before the idiot ever knew what was happening. Done. He didn't waste time thinking about it. He scooped Miranda up, ran to the jeep, put her in, turned it around, and headed back to Dhahar.

Several miles down the sandy middle-of-nowhere road—after he finally exhaled, with his breathing exaggerated, his face sweating, his heart in his throat—he had to pull over to let the trembling in his hands subside so he could hold the steering wheel. He was by no means a trained soldier, a SWAT officer, or even a security mall guard. He was a quiet, gentle, reserved doctor from Virginia. He had never even been in a fight in his life. He had no idea how he planned and executed that whole scene so flawlessly and within the space of twenty minutes or so.

The whole thing was over so fast. The line between life and death, breathing and not breathing, was so terrifyingly thin. Peter pulled back onto the road quickly and drove back anxiously. He had always been a strong supporter of non violence so it was completely unnerving how fast he went from the pacifist he was to the involuntary killer he became. It shook him to his core.

That was the last time he would attempt making visits to villages in the south. Luck was on his side this time, as the guards' state of insobriety made them all but defenseless. Miranda shuddered and sat quietly for the entire ride. They didn't speak at all. Peter only asked once if she was okay, if she needed anything, and she only shook her head no.

When they finally got back to Dhahar, she simply said, "Thank you, Peter," without looking him directly in the eye. Then she got out and walked solemnly to her meager quarters.

Erin checked in on her before going to see Peter.

"What happened? Are you okay?" Erin asked excitedly when she found Peter in his dark room sitting on a chair, staring at nothing.

He roused from his trance and answered her vaguely, "Yeah, yeah. I'm fine. Did you talk with Miranda? Poor kid was pretty shook up."

"I just came from her. Physically, she's fine, thanks to you, I hear. Emotionally, it may take a while," she informed him.

They sat in Peter's room while he filled her in on all the details. She could see behind the guise of bravado and sensed his discomfort at having to do what he did. But they both knew it had to be done. They shared a few moments of silent meditation then brought up the subject of possible consequences to his actions.

Peter and Miranda had been traveling through a very desolate region about forty miles south of Qardho, basically in the middle of nowhere, when this occurred. So Peter had no fear of repercussions. No one would ever know who killed those guards. The secluded spot was probably chosen by the guards for its obscurity and isolation, which ended up working against them instead. The predators had become the prey.

Erin asked again if he was okay, and he assured her that he was. She told him she had to get back to the clinic, but she'd check on him later. He jumped up and told her there was no need. He had a lot of work to do as well. They both left that subject in his room and never spoke of it again.

The less obvious tragedy from the day's events was that Peter, for the rest of his life, would have to live with the fact that he killed two men. In Peter's world, there were two kinds of people—those who respected the inherent value in all life and those who did not. Primum non nocere —first, do no harm. He was constantly focusing on repairing, improving, or saving a life, never destroying one. He had the luxury of living in a world where he never encountered that fork in the road of having to terminate, purposefully and deliberately, one life in order to save another. But now the line between right and wrong was slightly out of focus. It was no longer simply black and white, night and day. Like the solar eclipse of the day before blending night with day, there was an homogenized version of sin and justice. Ironically, the warnings from the villagers regarding the omen of the eclipse had proved true after all.

Peter knew beyond a shadow of a doubt that they would have raped and, more than likely, killed Miranda. He was surprised with the speed of which he switched gears from healer to executioner. But something primitive and instinctive in him woke up and went into action. He no longer felt quite pure of soul and never would again, but that was inconsequential now, and he was certain that he would do exactly the same thing if it were to be done over. He realized that the privilege of living a life free from the choice between the lesser of two evils is something he left behind when he crossed the border into Somalia. Life's choices aren't always easy, but one does what one has to in order to protect the people they love.

Every day that passed in Somalia was a constant reminder to Peter of how incredibly fragile life really is. Sometimes, all that stands between life and death is a simple narrow yellow line painted on a highway or a handful of two-inch screws securing the railing on a twelfth-floor balcony or the nano-fraction of movement to the left or right with a scalpel. And sometimes, it's merely choosing between right and wrong, good and evil.

Erin and Peter were lying in his bed very early the next morning. They had the radio on and learned that a bomb had been detonated in Eyl. Every single man, woman, and child within a two-thousand-foot radius of the medical tents had been killed. Had they made it through to Eyl, this would have most definitely included Peter and Miranda. They were both too painfully familiar with tragedy to have felt any relief at not having been among the victims, but they also felt a degree of humbling from their high perch of personal grief.

"Maybe all that bunk about solar eclipses and omens wasn't just bunk," Erin admitted incredulously.

Then they held each other without speaking for a long time, each absorbed in their own thoughts. Erin was thanking G-d for intervening and bringing Peter and Miranda back safely. Peter was thanking G-d that he would live to possibly see Emily again one day.

CHAPTER 15

Several days later, Aya was carrying light jugs of clean water from patient to patient when she doubled over and clutched her belly. She was only five months pregnant, but she was experiencing bleeding and slight cramping. It was a wonder that she was able to conceive at all. But life knows no deterrent. It is strong and marches on through any conditions. Just as one lone courageous bright-green blade of grass will sprout up in the most unlikely crack of solid cement, so too will human life take shape against every disadvantage.

Erin examined Aya that day. She spent a long time examining Aya and asked her a lot of questions. After her examination, Erin deeply regretted having to tell Aya and Peter that her condition was called placenta previa, and it was unfortunately severe. It would most likely progress as her due date neared due to the growing fetus and the subsequent enlarging of her uterus. That wasn't good news even in a healthy environment, let alone in Somalia, where one out of every forty-eight women die from pregnancy or childbirth. Without proper nutrition and medication, this could result in death for Aya or the baby. Erin explained all this as gently as possible to Aya and told her that it was very important for her to rest as much as possible. She would be looking in on her every day, taking her blood pressure, checking her weight, and making sure the bleeding wasn't getting worse.

Privately, Erin was very distraught at her findings and let Peter know the true severity of the situation and the bleak outlook for Aya. They both were very fond of Aya and would do anything in the world to help her if there was something they could do. All he could do was to keep a close, watchful eye on Aya, making sure that she got as much care and rest as possible.

Each day, they grew closer and closer, even more so because of her condition. She spoke often of her husband until her sixth month of pregnancy. She hadn't mentioned him in a few days, so Peter asked if she'd had a message lately. Her eyes filled with tears, the only tears he'd seen from her besides the day of the attack. She explained that she had received news of his death. The gunmen. They liked to chew on a leaf called *quat*, which had amphetamine-like properties. The locals gave the gunmen this leaf as bribes. One day, while Nadif was working on the steel rods in the rubble, the gunmen got high and shot him for no reason at all.

In addition to her obvious sorrow at having lost her husband, the one person who was her family, she feared that the baby would now have nobody to raise it if she died in childbirth. She had never been scared before for herself, but she was now worried for her unborn child. Every day, she became more and more withdrawn. Peter kept trying to reassure her that he would be there with her when the baby came and he would watch over her. She understood perfectly what Erin had told her, and she also understood perfectly what her odds for survival and those of her baby were. She was too smart for Peter to try to convince her that there was nothing to worry about. She had seen too many tragic births and deaths.

He wearily sat down to a supper of bread and cheese with Aya and Erin one evening after ten straight hours of work. After his meager meal, he picked up his loyal guitar, pulled a chair next to Aya, and began to play. In his guitar, he could always find solace. It would never disappoint, hurt, or leave him inexplicably. And he hoped he offered a little solace as well. Just as he was starting to drift away, riding the notes he was playing as if they were a small sailboat traveling happily up and down over the light waves, Aya turned to him, looked directly into his eyes, and stated quite plainly and matter-of-factly that she wanted him to promise to find her baby a loving family to raise it after she died.

Peter's fingers stumbled and froze on the strings, making a queer noise. He returned her gaze with an openmouthed, empty, blank look of awe. He was speechless. He just looked into the face of this fearless young soul and tried to assure her that that wouldn't be necessary and she would be fine, but they both knew he couldn't promise that. After the necessary words of comfort, he just silently nodded his agreement. The depth of what he was beholding was very sobering, and they all just sat there in reverent silence together. Her prognosis was poor with the conditions they were living in. Cesarean section was not an option, considering her fragile physical state, and the baby's health was uncertain.

Aya was very intuitive. That's what scared Peter. If she feared that she was near peril, he wouldn't dismiss her concerns casually. She did not seem frightened, just concerned for the safety of her baby. After Peter's promise, Aya seemed more relaxed as she faced her probable fate. Knowing her baby would be loved and cared for was all she needed right now. Peter would probably never meet anyone as incredible as Aya the rest of his life.

Erin watched the whole conversation as if she were a fly on the wall. She didn't say a word. She and Peter shared a casual relationship, and she didn't want to overstep the boundaries of that relationship by offering advice that was not asked of her. As much as she felt for Aya, she had always been of the school of thought that you cannot get too personally involved with patients. It clouds the judgment. It affects the objectivity needed for rational treatment. It violates the Hippocratic Oath. But she was human, also. You'd have to have a heart of stone to not become emotionally involved with someone like Aya.

———

The days turned into weeks. Patients came and went. Clans battled each other. Diseases were spread. Lives were lost. Everyone was exhaustingly busy. Peter continued his work tirelessly as best he could. He had been in Somalia for ten months, and his visa was only good for one year. Aya had been getting weaker and weaker. She spent most or all of her days on a cot in the clinic. Erin had told her that if she could carry the baby until at least eight months, it had a much better chance of survival. So that had remained her goal. Her entire existence now was purely to give birth. When she was awake, she talked constantly, through her weak voice, about the baby. She also asked Peter many questions.

All of a sudden, she wanted to know what his home in the US looked like, if his parents were still alive, what the schools were like, and if there had ever been a woman in Peter's life before Erin. Aya knew that he and Erin were intimate, but she also knew that they weren't in love. Peter felt as though Aya was trying to escape, if only in her mind, from the sorrow all around her every day and imagine life in another world, far, far away from here and all her troubles.

He indulged her and answered everything very honestly. When Aya asked about his progress with finding an adoptive family for the baby, he wanted to reassure her that everything would be okay, but he also didn't want to waste what little time might be left of her life on empty promises, and he didn't want her to face the possibility of death with unanswered important questions weighing on her mind. He simply told her it was his top priority. Peter had seen the orphanages in Somalia. He had seen dog pounds in the US that were more sanitary. He completely understood Aya's concerns. She wouldn't rest easy until she knew her child would not end up in a Somali orphanage or as an orphaned refugee in Kenya where they commit heinous crimes against the weak and undefended.

When it came to the question of the woman in his life, Peter stopped and became pensive. He began again as if he had just opened a much-anticipated Christmas present. He tore at the ribbon and threw off the lid excitedly as he rambled on and on about Emily. He spoke of how they met during one of his performances, of how beautiful and kind she was, and of all the plans they originally had. He spoke for a long time. He hadn't let himself even think of Emily that much at once, let alone talk about her. It felt so good to speak from a happy heart rather than a bitter heart. He was so tired of being angry and hurt. He just wanted to concentrate on the good times.

It sounded to anyone listening like Peter and Emily still had a relationship. He didn't know why he spoke like that, but he couldn't stop himself. It felt good to be connected to Emily again, even if imaginary. He talked longer than he realized, and Aya watched his face as he spoke. She didn't miss a thing and knew exactly why he spoke that way of her. Aya told Peter that though Emily was far away, she was always very close in his heart. Aya also told him that those we love never stray too far. Love is a tie that binds us for eternity. It may take side journeys, but it always finds its way home again.

"Love is one of the strongest forces in nature," she told him. "As long as you always do what's in your heart, love will find you. Your guitar is in your heart, Peter. Always play it for the world to hear, and love will come back to you."

Something about the way she said all this made him shiver with hopeful expectation that he hadn't allowed himself to feel.

He realized that he still missed Emily terribly and probably always would no matter how much he tried to deny it.

⎯

The brain may be the engine, but the heart is the compass.

⎯

Peter had arrived in Somalia last January during one of the worst droughts in recorded history. Millions of people were being displaced in search of drinkable water. Innocent victims were being shot for a cupful of anything potable. The term "warlords of water" was being coined to describe the mentality of those who would just as soon kill someone than share their water source. And if the Islam extremists who overthrew the government were to be considered the "wolves" of the region, prolific killers as they were, then the Ethiopian troops who sought to reestablish order after the Islamists were removed were the "coyotes." In addition to a record-breaking drought, the friction between the clans and extreme political groups and the absence of a central government turned a horrific situation into a horrific situation of biblical proportion.

However, during the summer of Aya's pregnancy, the winds changed. As if someone had picked up the earth like a toy and turned it around, the storm clouds formed and the rains began. Monsoons fell onto the dry, cracked, unyielding earth and caused severe flooding. Water-borne diseases spread like wildfire. Refugee camps popped up on every high ground, and the people were again displaced from their "homes." As her perilous pregnancy advanced, the rains kept coming. The climate mirrored the turmoil within her womb.

By December, just as rivers all over Somalia were spilling over their banks, Aya's womb was also breeching its containment. As the baby approached its birth weight, she was losing more and more blood. She was very weak now and unable to sit up. Peter's heart was breaking for her, and he spent as much time as possible by her side. He had made a makeshift bed on her dirt floor from an old pallet and some discarded bedding.

He talked to her constantly when he was with her. He would read to her from some of the books that came in on the donation trucks. They were mostly medical books, but one was *Wuthering Heights*. She had never heard that story, and it became her favorite. It was a story of boundless love and heartbreaking devotion. What she loved most about this story was that love persevered beyond the threshold of death. It confirmed her belief that if she loved her baby enough, even death couldn't truly separate them. She had Peter read *Wuthering Heights* over and over.

And of course, he played his guitar for her. She loved his guitar and the person he became whenever he played it. She told him over and over that the guitar would always bring him happiness and good luck and he should share that talent with the world.

He wished over and over that there were something he could do and felt so frustrated. In a different time and place, he could have done so much more for her. He had never felt so helpless and useless, and it was very close to driving him mad.

Aya never spoke one word of regret, fear, or protest. Whenever she had the strength to speak, she only wanted to be reassured that Peter would find someone to care for the baby. He patted her hand or smoothed her cheek and told her not to worry, that everything would be okay. He didn't want to dwell on the morbid possible outcome of this pregnancy, so he always gave her quick, nondescript replies. Aya had lived with death all around her most of her life. She was not afraid of her own possible death, but Peter was.

They came from two completely different worlds. Peter's was a world where your life was measured by years. Aya's was a world where your life was measured by actions. She had told Peter once in an effort to comfort him, in her broken English, that everyone dies, death is unavoidable, but there is no more worthwhile reason for dying than to bring a new life into the world. Yep, Emily would have definitely been as awed by Aya as he was.

He had given the situation great thought ever since the first time Aya asked him to promise to place the baby. The flooding was getting worse and worse. Aya's family had all perished. The baby would have no kin. There was obviously no family in Somalia that was in any position even close to adding a member to their family. Each raindrop that fell was a reminder of the impending dilemma he faced. He had checked into adoption programs from foreign countries, but Somalia was one of the few countries that was not included in the Hague Convention of Intercountry Adoption. With no government in place in Somalia, adoption by a foreign country would be nearly impossible. In addition, Islam jurisprudence typically did not permit formal adoption of any sort. They believed that a baby belonged only to the family into which it is born and should be raised in that culture.

His prospects of securing this baby with a family other than Aya's were very grim, but he didn't let on to Aya. He was thankful each day that she never asked him specifically what he would do for the baby. She trusted him implicitly. He wondered why.

CHAPTER 16

It was late one night, and Peter was lying on his pallet in Aya's room, hovering somewhere between sleep and wake, listening to the deluge threatening to sweep the village away. As he slipped slowly into the still world of slumber, he pictured all the tents and stick huts floating on a huge river toward some unknown destination far, far away. He didn't know where the village would end up, but he was shamelessly enjoying floating, floating away from here. He had the innate feeling that any place was better.

As he drifted along with all the other aid workers, villagers, and refugees, he became more and more content with the journey. They gently floated up and over gently rolling waves. The people were all smiling and laughing and singing the native songs he heard so often since he'd been in Somalia. There was a collective feeling of happiness and relief.

Just when he let his guard completely down, the river slowed and now they were all collecting in a broad, wide pool of almost stagnant water. People were quiet now. No more laughing or singing. They were just floating slower and slower together. Then they all turned pleading eyes toward him. As he started to notice that the pace and temperament had changed, he heard a great rushing noise ahead of him. He turned his head in what seemed like ultra slow motion and realized with a panic that there was a hundred-foot waterfall right in front of him. Somehow he had leapfrogged to the front of the group and was just about to plunge over the edge to his certain death.

———

Peter woke suddenly to find four inches of water in the room, threatening to encompass his pallet. He jumped up groggily and shook his head to clear it from the dream. He instinctively checked on Aya before he opened the door to find standing water everywhere. Aya had to be moved to the clinic. It was the only dry area he could think of. He sloshed back over to her cot and gently touched her shoulder to awaken her.

She was breathing evenly, but shallowly. It was very difficult to rouse her. She made an attempt at lifting her eyelids, but they snapped back almost immediately. He didn't have much light in there, so he couldn't judge her condition. He bent down to his pallet and felt around for his MSF-issued waterproof flashlight, found it, and turned back quickly to assess Aya.

As soon as the light touched her face he knew. Her lips were pale, and there was sweat on her brow. He gripped the flashlight between his teeth and scooped Aya gently but firmly from the cot. She couldn't have weighed much more than one hundred pounds, and she was almost eight months pregnant. Her light weight sent a chill down his spine. As his hands adjusted the weight of her body evenly, he felt the warm, damp, sticky substance that he recognized immediately. Her water had broken, and it was bloody. She was in labor.

"Damn it!" he cursed under his breath. He had reacted to many emergencies since he landed in Mogadishu a lifetime ago. He was always methodic, coolheaded, and professional. Even though he lost about 15 to 20 percent of his patients to circumstances beyond his control, he had acclimated to the severe conditions and always performed flawlessly. He was in autopilot right now and knew that he had to get her to the clinic and get this baby delivered as soon as possible.

He trod sure-footedly but quickly toward the clinic only fifty feet away. He made it there, with Aya supported safely in his arms. She didn't wake until he set her down on the bed. Her eyes struggled to half mast, and she made an exerted effort to say something. He leaned down close to her ear and gently encouraged her to repeat her precious words.

"Don't let my baby die, Peter. No matter what." She barely breathed.

He didn't care if it was ethical or not; he would promise her the moon, the stars, and all that is holy right now if he thought it would comfort her.

"Shhh, Aya. I won't leave you. Your baby will be here soon, and you'll hold it and see it and kiss it. It will be the luckiest baby ever born to have such a mother," he whispered.

A very faint smile fleeted across her lips before her eyebrows knitted together in agony. The baby was getting close. Peter was a general physician, not an OB, but he could see all the blood escaping from her and knew what that meant. Not good. He ran over to the intercom system on the table and pushed the button for Erin's extension.

"Hey, it's Peter. I have Aya in the clinic, and she's about to deliver. I need you stat," he practically shouted.

Erin was there in less than two minutes, and she was already scrubbing up when he found her. She asked Peter a series of questions regarding dilation, heart rate, blood pressure, contractions, etc. He answered what he could while she gathered all the supplies she thought she would need. As soon as she was finished examining Aya, she turned grim-faced to Peter to tell him the status of the delivery. He already knew it wasn't good for Aya, but he asked specifically about the baby. Without the modern equipment like ones back home, there wasn't much she could tell about the baby.

Aya's face contorted slightly again. Another contraction. They were about one minute apart. The blood loss was significant. Erin needed to do a more thorough internal examination. She knew this would be very uncomfortable for Aya, but something seemed very wrong, in addition to the problems Erin was already aware of. The baby's heart rate was low. The labor was not progressing as it should. Erin gave Peter a look of "Stand back" and reached up into Aya's womb. After a few eternal seconds, she removed her gloved hand and closed her eyes in denial.

They moved several feet away in order to be out of earshot of Aya and spoke in low murmurs.

"She has a condition called vasa previa. In short, the fetal blood vessels are compromised, and the baby is in grave danger if it is born vaginally. We have to do a C-section like yesterday, or the baby will die," Erin regretfully announced.

"If we do a C-section, Aya will most definitely die. If not, she stands about a 10 percent chance of making it," Peter thought out loud.

"If we don't, she still has a 90 percent chance of dying anyway, and the baby will definitely die," Erin reasoned.

No time to think. Erin was absolutely right. Aya's last words were still in the air: "Don't let my baby die, Peter. No matter what." He had already scrubbed up in preparation. Erin robotically arranged the tools they would need. Peter kissed Aya's forehead paternally, told her he loved her, and prepared her for surgery.

He couldn't believe what this came down to: a choice between life for the baby and almost certain death for Aya. What kind of G-d would put a man to such a test of faith? Aya would surely die—and at his own hand. His feelings of morbid culpability gave way to logic and reason. Better one tragedy than two. As soon as the sedation set in, he performed the C-section with Erin.

Within moments, Peter was pulling a small, round, wet, but perfect, baby from Aya's womb.

———

The baby came to life with a force that rivaled the storm outside. Her screams for precious oxygen were primitive. She was very, very small, probably five pounds, but her lungs were definitely developed. As Erin stitched Aya back together mechanically in a futile effort to alleviate the bleeding, Peter cared for the baby, taking all her vital signs, cleaning her, etc. Then Peter handed the baby to Erin and attended Aya, stroking her temples and speaking soothingly in her ear.

She roused slightly from the meds and looked into Peter's face wordlessly in an obvious inquiry about the baby. Peter smiled and told her that her daughter was small but very healthy, breathing well, and was the most beautiful baby he had ever seen. He would have said that even if he didn't think it, but in this case, he didn't have to lie. She looked exactly like her mother and obviously already had her strength.

Aya asked almost breathlessly if she could hold her.

"Here she comes right now," Peter said as Erin approached with a whimpering, clean bundle.

Erin laid the baby on Aya's chest, over her heart, and stepped back to let them see each other. Peter's eyes blurred at this sight. He knew Aya didn't have very long. Her blood pressure was dropping, and her body was weakening by the minute. Aya's blood loss and weakened state to begin with were no match for the paltry supply of emergency medical equipment they had. Even if they had all the modern medicine from the Western world and the most experienced team of surgeons on the planet, he knew Aya's condition was beyond repair.

"I have a name for her," Aya said barely audibly.

"What is it?" Peter eagerly questioned.

"Ayanna," Aya smiled down at her infant.

"That's perfect. Ayanna," Peter repeated.

"But who will love her?" Aya didn't have the strength or time to choose words. This was the quickest way to arrange the question of who would adopt her and be her family.

That was the moment. The moment that defined Peter. At that question, from that brave, selfless, dying girl, in the face of the tragedy and sacrifice befalling her, Peter knew what his life was about. He knew what every moment of his whole life had led him to.

He stood very straight, took a deep breath, and very seriously stated, "I will."

Aya smiled weakly, but knowingly, and breathed, "I know, Peter." She said it as if she always knew that Peter would make this decision. She had just been waiting for him to realize it himself.

Erin and Peter watched Aya and Ayanna for almost an hour as they bonded for their brief relationship on earth. As Aya became weaker and weaker Peter helped support Ayanna in her hands. There was no way Peter was removing that baby from her mother's last embrace. Ayanna quieted as if in reverence to her mother's last moments in this world. Aya's breathing slowed, and with Peter's hands on hers, holding her child over her courageous heart, it beat its last—and then she was gone.

They stood quietly in the small, insignificant room, absorbing the enormous significance of the last few hours' events. After a respectable amount of time, Peter lifted Ayanna to his own heart, held her lovingly, and told her that he would never, never leave her. He leaned down to kiss Aya good-bye one last time on her forehead and pronounced her.

As he looked at the official clock for the date and time, he realized that it was December 25. Of course, that meant nothing at this far end of the earth, but to Peter, it was a sign that he should remember that there was a plan, a meaning to all that passes. Sacrifices have been made when necessary throughout eternity, and it is through these sacrifices that we learn faith and hope. Without faith and hope, what are we?

Erin gave him a look of questioning. It was not good practice to become emotionally attached to a patient is what the look intimated. What rules applied in this place? He had grown to love Aya as his own family, and Ayanna already felt like a part of him. Some things were bigger than rules, oaths, and laws. It would be a daunting and almost impossible task, but that baby was coming home with him—or he wasn't going home. Period.

Later that morning, just before dawn, when the night was at its very darkest, and Peter felt like he and Ayanna were all that existed in the world, he sat in a lonely room, cradling his new daughter. From the moment he had rescued Ayanna from Aya's failing body, he had felt the connection of parent and child. All the love he felt for Aya was instantly Xeroxed onto her baby. The room was empty, except for the rocking chair he was sitting in and a small table upon which rested a copy of *Wuthering Heights*. He rocked her gently as she sucked his pinky, and he stared at her face so that it would become engraved on his brain.

The rain had taken a vow of silence in honor of this sacred event, and the moonlight shone through the window and illuminated Ayanna's face. Peter could almost feel the light being reflected back onto his own face. He had a voice that many people had called a gift, but he hadn't sung out loud in a very long time, not since Emily left him. At this moment, it was the only possible thing to do. As he felt his heart becoming physically attached to the tiny human sleeping near, he began the only song that made sense to him at that moment.

Although this was certainly an hour of darkness in his life, it was also a time of great joy and new life. He had lived among these brokenhearted people and felt their loss deeply, especially the loss of Aya, whose answer to the world he held in his hands at that very moment. In the still night, he could hear Aya whisper her words of wisdom to him that everything will be alright. He knew he need not answer her whisper; he need only believe, have faith, and let it be.

It was as if Paul McCartney had foreseen this moment and written it just for them.

CHAPTER 17

The sky had resumed the torrent of rain by morning, and Peter hadn't slept at all. Erin came in to check on them and found Peter reclined in the rocking chair with the sleeping Ayanna protected in his arms. She spoke softly so she wouldn't wake the baby.

"How's Ayanna doing?" she asked with concern.

"She's fine. Sleeping quietly," was all he said.

Erin entered the room fully and let the door close behind her. She walked over to Peter as he cradled the baby and crouched beside them to get a closer look at her tiny little face.

"She's perfect," Erin whispered to Peter as she searched Peter's eyes for something. She kept her eyes on him and spoke as plainly as she could, "Peter, I…you…" She wasn't sure how to say what she was thinking. "I am awed and humbled by your act of humanity. When did you decide that you would take care of Aya's baby? You never mentioned it to me."

"I've actually had it in the back of my mind for a long time, probably since Aya originally asked me to find a family for the baby. I think Aya knew it too," he mused out loud.

"Ayanna is a lucky little girl," Erin thought out loud. "Hey, John has something he wants to talk to you about," she added.

Peter nodded his acknowledgment and slowly, carefully, stood up, handed the baby to a surprised Erin, and headed out to meet John.

"Hey, you look like crap on toast, pardner," said John.

Peter made a polite smirk at John's awkward attempt at levity, pulled a chair out next to him, and fell into it with a sigh. John slapped Peter fraternally on the back and let his hand rest there a moment in silence as a gesture of sympathy. These men had both seen more death and tragedy since they'd been in Somalia than a single man should see in a lifetime. But that didn't lessen the depth of grief at this moment. Everyone knew of the fond familial relationship that had grown between Peter and Aya. She was like a daughter to him, and they were all very affected by last night's events.

"There's going to be a ceremony for Aya this afternoon," John said in a soft voice. "Everyone who can walk will be there."

So many bodies were buried every day that they couldn't attend all the funerals. John was letting Peter know how highly they all regarded Aya and that they were all sympathetic to Peter's pain and loss.

"I hear from Erin that you've decided to take the baby back to the States with you?" John gently probed.

Peter cocked his head toward John at that question, as a gunman might cock his gun, daring him to say one more thing about it.

John was quick to recognize Peter's agitation. He put his hands up in mock surrender and said, "Whoa, buddy, I'm not trying to stop you. Just the opposite. I might be able to help you." He didn't lower his hands until Peter relaxed his posture.

"I'm sorry," said Peter as he lowered his face into his hands and "washed" the stress away from his eyes. "I'm so tired and so empty."

"I know, buddy. We don't have to talk about this all now. I just wanted you to know that I—we all want to help you, and we think that what you're doing about the baby is really great. You're a good guy, Pete," John consoled.

Peter just held his gaze for a moment then smiled weakly and muttered, "Thanks."

He placed his head in his hands with his fingers sliding into his hair and sowed multiple rows through his scalp to help cultivate his thoughts as a farmer might sow the earth to help cultivate the soil. He inhaled deeply. He had to think. He had an enormous task ahead of him and he didn't know how to begin.

John mistook Peter's expression for regret and asked, "Are you sure you want to go through with this? You were in a very emotional place when you made that promise to Aya. We all understand that," said John, almost conspiratorially.

Peter was so exhausted, so weary and beaten up with emotion. Maybe that's why he overreacted. Or maybe it was John's assumption that he would make a promise to a dying courageous girl that he had no intention of keeping. Whatever it was, it hit him with a vengeance.

"Is that what you think? Is that what you all think? That I would look into the face of a beloved friend as she lay dying at my hands after she's just given birth and say 'Yeah, sure, I'll raise your kid' as if I was telling her, 'Yeah, sure, I'll return your library books, no problem,' and then renege as soon as her body was cold? Let me explain something to you as clearly and simply as I can. I did not make that promise out of guilt, emotion, or duress." He took a deep breath to collect his thoughts and began with renewed calm. "John, I didn't merely make a promise—I was bestowed an opportunity. I'm taking Ayanna home because I want to, not because I have to. Understand?" he asked as if speaking to a child.

Peter suddenly realized that he was standing up, menacingly looming over John. John's neck was craned back, and his eyes were wide with shock. John's expression slowly transformed from surprise to comprehension. As the grin bloomed on his face, he started nodding in approval and stated with relief,

"All right then. Glad to hear it. It won't be easy to get the baby out of Somalia. We've got some figuring out to do."

The funeral service that evening was the most attended service in Dhahar in the past year. If a human is indeed judged by the number of true friendships they form on earth, then Aya will be welcomed with open arms at the gates of whatever heaven she believed in. It was raining lightly during the procession, and the ground was soft. The months of rain preceding had made the dirt yielding, as if it had been preparing to receive and embrace this treasured gift.

Aya had been laid in a simple coffin, which was carried by some of the village's young men, of whom she had earned the devotion. The long train of mourners consisted of all the lives she touched so dearly—the little girls whose hair she braided, the little boys whom she taught American baseball, the children whom she had begun to educate to read, the young men and women her own age with whom she had shared her childhood and her misery, older villagers whom she had nursed in the clinic and visited in their homes when they were too weak to come in.

The line seemed never ending and would have been five times as long had it not been for all the deaths preceding hers. It was awe inspiring, and it made Peter realize how incredibly lucky he had been to have come to Somalia when he did and had the opportunity to have known her. As usual, at each emotional moment in the past several years, he thought of Emily and how she would have been awed by the sight, as well.

There were two religious figures leading the ceremony for Aya. One was the local imam, or Muslim leader. The other was

Father Eduardo, the Catholic priest from Italy. They both spoke lovingly of Aya, mostly enumerating the many, many ways in which she helped her community. He didn't understand too much of the Muslim's leader's words, but anyone could certainly have easily recognized the compassion with which he spoke of her. She had been held in high esteem by everyone she had ever met and touched. The area's highest religious figure was no exception. He gave her the respect and admiration she deserved, which was not customary of the politics in that area. She was after all "just a girl."

Father Eduardo, surprisingly, spoke mostly of what he had learned from the eighteen-year-old Aya. He started out by explaining that he had been commissioned by the Roman Catholic Church to come to Dhahar for the purpose of saving and teaching the local inhabitants. However, over the course of the year that he'd been in Dhahar, and mostly due to Aya's gentle words and patient ways, he had been the one saved and taught. He told the emotional crowd that she had saved him from a life of narrow-minded imprudence and had taught him to open his eyes and take a good look at the vast world around him. He smiled at the irony of this young girl who had never been outside the 1,200 square kilometers of the Dhahar and Mogadishu regions yet possessed a knowledge of people and cultures and basic humanitarianism that rivaled his university-degreed colleagues.

Father Eduardo's eyes and heart had been opened by young, beautiful Aya, and his life would be forever changed for the better. He would continue his mission work, but he would put the needs and welfare of the people he met before the demands of any single religion. He vowed before all of Aya's mourners to commit the remainder of his life to trying to be as great a humanitarian as she was. Peter was speechless.

When the time came for him to make the eulogy for Aya, it came easily to him, though he kept it brief due to his emotions.

He told of how fortunate he felt that he was afforded the amazing chance to have known such an incredibly compassionate person. He also had learned so much from her, and she would remain forever in his memory and in his heart. He then made a solemn promise to all those people who witnessed this day, even though most could not understand him, to raise Ayanna to be educated, proud, and above all else, deeply loved. He pledged to ensure that Ayanna would know everything about her mother and how truly wonderful she was.

He ended by saying that though he wished G-d hadn't taken Aya away so soon, he thanked him for allowing her to be here long enough to touch each of their lives in such a loving way and to give them Ayanna so that she may carry on Aya's good name. Then he ended the service as he picked up his guitar and played it mournfully.

Miranda didn't speak at the service but sat in the front row and held Ayanna while Peter spoke and played. As a doctor, Miranda was not unfamiliar with death; she loved Aya like a younger sister and was more than deeply saddened by her passing.

The vigil went on long into the night. The rain couldn't keep her followers away. Peter walked back down the line of people, again remarking to himself at the number of mourners. *Not surprising*, he thought. A nurse was sitting with Erin as he approached her. The nurse was admiring the baby and asked what her name was.

"Ayanna," Peter answered proudly as he reached them.

"Hmmm, I like it," mused the nurse. "I'm interested in names and have learned the English meaning of most of the Somali names. I've heard *Ayanna* before. It means 'beautiful blossom or flower.'"

Peter contemplated the meaning and decided it was perfect. A beautiful bloom amid all this sorrow and despair to remind them all of what human perseverance is about. That Aya carried this child almost to term in her condition was nothing short of a miracle. He wondered if Aya knew the meaning of the name when she picked it. Probably, there seems to be little she didn't know. Peter asked the nurse if she knew what *Aya* meant.

"Bright one," the nurse replied.

Peter smiled in agreement.

CHAPTER 18

The next few days were intense. The hostility had escalated in recent weeks, and people were again fleeing Mogadishu in droves. Refugee camps were inundated with weary, frightened, hungry victims, mostly children. In addition to all the patients who needed care, Peter had been trying desperately to find a way to secure a travel visa for Ayanna. His own work visa was due to expire in two months, and he would need to have all the proper paperwork in place in order to start adoption procedures back home.

Flights from Djibouti were irregular due to the fighting. The first thing he needed was immigration papers so he wouldn't have any delays in Mogadishu, but this would be next to impossible. The biggest barrier to his efforts was the fact that there was currently no practicing government in the capital city of Mogadishu since they had been overthrown. There was no birth certificate being issued for Ayanna and no death certificates for her birth parents, Aya or Nadif.

Peter needed help getting Ayanna out of Somalia from every front, so he made a call to his mother back in Charlottesville from the clinic's satellite phone, explaining the situation and asking her to contact an attorney and get some legal advice about a way to get the baby home.

Phyllis was, of course, initially shocked at the news of his wanting to adopt the infant, but she was very supportive and proud of him as well. He had spoken to her only a handful of times on the satellite phone provided by MSF since he'd been in Somalia. At five bucks a minute, they were told to limit their calls as much as possible. So his mother knew only a little of the history to this baby. She had been just as impressed by Aya as Peter was and deeply saddened at the news of her passing. His voice on the phone when he called about Ayanna was reassuring, though. He sounded like he had a true purpose to his life now—something to hang on to, some glimmer of hope to bring back from hell. She promised him that she would do what she could and get an answer to him as soon as possible.

He would have to wait for his mother's call and do what he could from there in the meantime. They had limited internet access on the satellite phone, so he was almost isolated from any avenue of research, and he felt useless. He didn't feel hopeless, though. He knew his mother would find a way.

Sure enough, her call came in two days later. Not great news. What she had found out was exactly what he had discovered from his limited ability to investigate. The US did not like to get involved with foreign-born adoptions where the civil authority had been broken. The political upheaval that was being experienced in Somalia made it difficult, almost impossible, to acquire the legal documents necessary for adoption and immigration.

The only thing she could add that gave him something to work with was that she had learned, off the record, that immigrations in nearby Djibouti were very lenient due to all the foreign-aid workers that pass through there on their way to impoverished countries. They were a benevolent society that wanted to facilitate humanitarian efforts, rather than hinder them. She hoped that would help, and she'd keep working on it.

They hung up, and he hung his head. There was absolutely no way he was going to leave Ayanna behind, even for a day. He didn't care anymore if it meant breaking the law, either. He made a promise to Aya on her deathbed, and he was going to keep it no matter what. He would somehow have to get Ayanna out of Mogadishu and into Djibouti, but how?

He only had a few more weeks to figure it out. Ayanna's birth weight was low, but not terribly. He wanted her to be at least ten pounds before he attempted the long journey home with her. She was doing surprisingly well. Everyone was taking excellent care of her. She seemed to belong to the whole village, the same way her mother had. In a land of nothingness and need, it was amazing to see the generosity and love that was evoked by this small infant. It was a real lesson in humanity—among the many lessons he had learned since he landed here a million years ago— that he will keep with him forever and pass on to Ayanna.

Peter turned in fairly early, exhausted and weary from a long day's work and worry. Everything seemed so different since Aya was gone. Even the landscape seemed to change. He didn't hear birds, he didn't see sunsets, and he didn't even notice much wildlife. The flooding had persisted and was probably the cause for these absences, but it all seemed to begin with Aya's passing.

Just as he started to nod off he heard a voice.

"Pete?" It was John, and he was poking his head in to see if he was awake.

"Yeah?" Peter answered.

"Got a minute?" John asked.

"Sure." Peter rubbed his face to wake himself up. "Do you need a hand with a patient?"

"No, nothing like that," said John. "I've got Shay out here with me, and we just want to talk with you about something."

"Shoot," said Peter still trying to shake the sleepiness off.

They both stepped in, and each pulled up an unremarkable-looking wooden chair. The room was dark, except for what little light came in the window. Peter, dressed only in shorts, undershirt, and the gleaming silver MSF ID tag around his neck (which was a constant connection to the sane world), sat on the edge of the bed, face eager to find out what this was about. They both drew a breath, and there was a silent passage between John and Shay as they sorted out just how to begin.

Peter's eyes volleyed back and forth from John to Shay waiting for the first to speak. Anxious, he finally spat out, "Come on guys, what?"

John leaned back at that prompt and started speaking. "Peter, Shay and I want to help you get Ayanna out of Somalia. We have some ideas that might work. We've been doing some...um... uh...humanitarian side work, so to speak, of our own in the last few months. We have a little experience at getting visas that are otherwise hard to get—if you know what I mean."

They looked at each other to check the progress of the conversation, nodded in silent agreement over its success so far, and then Shay took over in his heavy Irish accent. "You see lad, there've been many a babe we've come across since we been here what needed some saving, and I don't mean only medical. We have several options for ya t' consider. Your main goal obviously is to get Ayanna out of Somalia and back to the States legally so that the proper paperwork is in order for you to adopt her. Right?"

He continued without waiting for a response. "There's only two possible ways for you to raise Ayanna legally. One would be to claim her as your own, and the other would be to have the necessary documents that are unattainable from the country of Somalia."

Without pause, John took over in a soft conspiratorial voice; it was as if they were speaking as one. "So first—and hear me out before you refuse, please—there were no birth, death, or marriage certificates issued for Ayanna or her parents. No one would question the baby's paternity, and certainly no one would demand a paternity test. So—"

Peter cut him off, "Are you guys insane? You're not serious! Claim that Aya and I had Ayanna together? Not only is that wrong on a very basic level, but the ramifications to MSF would be extremely detrimental. Can you imagine what it would sound like to have the victims in this region being impregnated by the aid workers who came here to supposedly help? Then to have them die in childbirth because of it? And besides those obvious things, I would absolutely never disgrace Aya's memory like that. No way!" He was disgusted by the suggestion and stood up as if to indicate the conversation was over and they needed to leave.

"Wait, wait, wait," Shay started, reaching up to Peter as if to physically pull him back down onto his cot. "We reckoned you'd have none of those shenanigans. It would've just been a hell of lot easier that way, but we have another way. Sit your arse down and relax. We've come to help ya, boy."

Peter looked them both squarely in the eye to try to read their thoughts before deciding whether to trust them with another one of their "ideas." He realized immediately how desperate he was for help when he sat back down on the bed, held his head in his hands, elbows resting dejectedly on knees, and sighed, "Okay, what?"

"We have a friend in Djibouti." John leaned forward and spoke even lower than before. "She's helped us a few times before. She's in a position at the immigration office over there to get things done. She'll have the paperwork ready to get you through customs with a counterfeit birth certificate claiming Ayanna as a resident of Djibouti and counterfeit death certificates for Aya and Nadif. She'll send the papers over with the next delivery of meds that come through customs. It will be a whole hell of a lot easier to adopt an orphan from Djibouti than from Somalia. In fact, I can pretty much guarantee that adopting a child, orphan or not, from this hellhole would be near to impossible.

"After you get Ayanna out of Somalia to Djibouti, you'll have to contact the office of Homeland Security and the US Embassy to file an I-600 and show proof of her being an orphan for international adoption. You may have to stay in Djibouti for a few extra weeks until Ayanna's passport and visa comes through. Do you have cash on you? It'll be about $350 to file for a visa for her. You'll have a little bit easier time since she's orphaned. They're a little more lenient with the kids who have no parents to claim them. You'll have to get an attorney to finalize the adoption in the US. It will take a lot of paperwork and a lot of time and a heap of cash to get it finished, but I can contact her tomorrow and get the ball rolling if you're interested."

"What's the risk?" Peter queried.

"Well, the obvious drawback is the counterfeiting and the repercussions that could bring. The other risk is that the ICU will take Ayanna from you in Mogadishu anyway, and you'll not know where she'll end up. They'll sell her as fast as you can blink an eye," Shay warned.

"There's always that risk. These bastards with the ICU are heartless and unpredictable. We haven't lost anyone yet, but we've heard of others," John answered matter-of-factly.

"What's the penalty for counterfeiting?" asked Peter.

"You'd be charged with forgery or unlawful production of a passport, under section 1543 of title 18 of the United States Code. Imprisonment of no more than fifteen years, plus a hefty fine, is the punishment. And worst of all, Ayanna would be deported to an orphanage in Somalia," Shay answered grimly.

"How many have you helped? How long have you guys been doing this? How successful have you been?" Peter asked in rapid succession and a little suspiciously. "How the hell do you know all this stuff?"

John and Shay looked conspiratorially at one another again and paused as if trying to remember the approved response.

"We've been here long enough to know that these people often need more than just medical care. What good does it do to heal a patient back from death's door, only to drop them off at the same doorstep weeks later? We've been able to rescue about a dozen orphans so far. We hope to save more. These are kids who have absolutely no family here to care for them. Like Ayanna, they've lost everyone. The Islam ideals prevent adoption, so these kids, as young as three in some cases, were on their own. You've seen the orphanages around here, right? Scary stuff. We have agencies in various countries screening adoptive families, and we carefully select a family to place them with. Our friend in Djibouti makes it all possible," John admitted, somewhat reluctantly.

He thought for a second and added with his head tilted slightly in a dare and his eyes narrowed for seriousness, "Peter, of course you know that what I've just told you is highly, highly confidential. We're all dead if it gets out, including a lot of innocent children. You know that, right?"

Peter paused at the gravity of all he just heard, as if weighing the right and wrong of it, and finally answered simply, "Of course, John, of course," and he added an approving slap on the shoulder to seal the promise.

Peter was not one to break the rules, but this was a lawless world of injustice, where the victims paid with their lives. And most of those victims were children. He had learned firsthand the extent he was willing to go to in order to save an innocent life that day traveling to Eyl. This was nothing.

Shay saw the conflict on Peter's face and reminded him, "You know what's a real crime, Peter? Being orphaned in a country where a quarter of the kids die by the age of five, terrorists have overthrown the government, deemed you unworthy of anything but a price, and sold you to the highest bidder. That's what's really scary."

"Can't argue with that," Peter agreed.

"There are no rules in this game, Pete. That's the definition of anarchy. We're doing the only humane thing we can do by getting these kids out. In addition to all of the existing problems and diseases here, TB is making a big comeback. They've already closed several of the MSF clinics to the south due to hostile actions by the ICU and have sent all those aid workers home. There's no national guard rushing in here to rescue anybody. There's only lawless men with automatic weapons and greed—a dangerous combination," John added.

"I know and I appreciate all your efforts guys, I really do. You make an excellent point. It is a risk, though. Ayanna's whole life is on the line here. Can I have the night to think it over? Make sure there's no other way?" Peter asked.

"Sure, lad, sure. We know it's a tough one. You won't be ready to leave for another couple o' weeks, and we'll need about one week for our gal in Djibouti to get your papers. So let us know in a few days after you've had a good, long think." Shay patted Peter understandingly on the knee a few times and stood to leave.

John added, "Peter, whatever you do, please pay attention to the fact that the ICU is on the move, and it's getting really bad in Mogadishu. Flights to Djibouti could get scarce. Whatever you decide, we're here to help you, but we have to move quickly, okay, buddy? Now you know why we suggested claiming paternity—hell of a lot easier." He laughed. "Worth a shot."

Peter smiled and nodded. His mind was distracted with worry. "Thanks, guys. It means the world."

Peter had some thinking to do. There was obviously no risk-free way to get Ayanna out of Somalia and into the US with the appropriate papers for a legal adoption. This was an all out dire situation that this little girl was born into. The more he mulled it over, the more he realized that the best option was John and Shay's confidant in Djibouti. The idea of having a fraudulent act in his past bothered him, but what choice did he have? He couldn't help but wonder what Emily would do.

CHAPTER 19

He was forced to make an early decision a few days later. Dhahar
was situated in an area of Somalia that was referred to as Puntland
and was still governed theoretically by the TFG, found in the
horn of Somalia, away from most of the fighting. Most of the
heavy fighting was centered in Mogadishu in the south, which
gave Peter and his group a false sense of security. In recent days,
that all changed. The clan rallies in the north had become violent,
and the evidence of the violence was uncomfortably close. The
clinic where they worked in Dhahar was being closed, and the
MSF workers were being evacuated. They were instructed to
pack up all the supplies and equipment and travel to Hergeisa,
instead of Mogadishu, to board a US military flight to Djibouti
in ten days.

The MSF almost never used military or United Nations
aircraft to transport their personnel, but the clans' fighting had
escalated so quickly that other provisions could not be made. It
seemed like the decision was now made for him. They all started
packing up immediately; there was a lot of work to be done.
The most important of which was Ayanna. She was almost ten
pounds now, but that no longer even mattered. Peter worked all
morning then went to find John and give him the go ahead for
the counterfeiting.

He was halfway to the clinic when he noticed Erin carrying her things from her quarters and loading them into the Jeep. They weren't supposed to move out until next week, so what was she up to?

"Hey, Erin," he called over to her. "What are you doing over here?" he asked as he approached her.

"Hey, Peter," she answered back distractedly, "I was going to explain all this to you tonight." She hesitated before she went on. "I'm leaving tomorrow."

"What the hell are you talking about? The plane won't even be here until next week," Peter asked even though he knew she hadn't made a mistake. She had something up her sleeve.

"Peter, I'm not going with you all to Djibouti," she informed him. "I have other plans."

"Erin, you don't have a choice. The MSF will not cover you and your visa if you stay," Peter said with anxiety in his voice. He knew from the months that he had become close with her that when she said something, it was final. She was staying behind no matter what he said.

As a moment of silence between them grew, Erin arranged her thoughts and began her answer, "You know, I've been corresponding with a doctor from Ukraine for the last year and a half. I first learned of her about three years ago. She is the most amazing doctor and human being I've ever known. She has been running a clinic for the women of Somalia for the past twenty-five years, with little outside funding, if any at all, at the risk to her own personal safety. She has grown children of her own, but she rarely sees her own family. At times, she has had to singlehandedly fight off the militia who come to seek retribution on their adversaries who are under her medical care for their wounds. She is not a young woman anymore.

"I joined the MSF with the sole intent of getting to Somalia so that I could eventually join her clinic outside Mogadishu after my mission was over in Dhahar. I never had any intention of returning to the United States. I didn't care if my visa expired. What meaning does a visa hold in the midst of all this insanity and suffering? You can't put a time limit, monetary limit, or political limit on saving lives. I don't want to go back to a life full of self-absorbed people who pretend they don't know what's going on in the rest of the world. It has become socially acceptable to stand by while innocent children around the globe suffer and die needlessly, but that doesn't make it right."

"At one time, not so long ago, it was socially acceptable to enslave other human beings against their will. That wasn't right either. I suppose we all have slavery in our ancestry if we search back far enough. I guess what I'm trying to say is that inhumanity touches everyone, either directly or indirectly. People think that it's someone else's problem, Somalia's problem, Darfur's problem, Afghanistan's problem, the cotton-plantation South's problem, Germany's problem. Sooner or later, as history has proven over and over, it becomes everyone's problem."

"Very few people understand this but, my friend in Mogadishu does. Joining her has been the only goal in my life that has had any meaning whatsoever. It's my way of doing whatever I can to really help, and not just talk about it. It became my North Star. I felt I had no other purpose in this world other than to be here, helping. I sold my home, my car, all of my material possessions before I left LA. I never told anyone all this, but I'm telling you all now because I want you to understand the significance of what I'm about to say. I'm going to Mogadishu to join the clinic there, and nothing in this world can stop me, Peter."

Peter had seen that look in her eyes before. It reminded him of Emily just before she left for good. The memory of that weakened his resolve. Who was he to tell her what to do? They had shared a few passionate moments, had become very good friends, and had grown to respect one another as physicians. If this was her life's ambition, he wouldn't try to stand in her way.

"I just want to be sure that you understand how dangerous this could be for you, Erin. You can leave with us now then return when it's calmed down a little," he offered halfheartedly.

"Peter, you know it will never calm down. It's been like this since the early '90s. Besides, they need more help when the fighting is at its worst," she reasoned.

She was right. He knew it and couldn't pretend otherwise.

He stared at her quietly for a moment then simply leaned in for a tight hug. She was remarkable, and he felt something very strong for her. He wouldn't call it love, but it was as close as you could get. When he released her, he looked emotionally spent.

"Erin, you're one of the most incredible people I know. Promise you'll stay in touch somehow," he ordered softly.

"Of course, I will, Peter. You're not so bad yourself, you know. Take good care of Ayanna. You're going to make a great father for her," she added warmly.

They agreed to spend her last night in Dhahar together and to part in the morning without tears or sorrow. He helped her finish loading the jeep then went to find John.

———

When he caught up with John that afternoon, he found him in a foul mood. He was sitting with Shay in the back room of the clinic, and he had his head down as if the world were a weight on top of it. His eyes were bloodshot, and he obviously hadn't shaved or slept in some time.

"What's going on, guys?" Peter asked with genuine concern. These guys didn't shake easily, and right then, they looked pretty shook.

"We've had some trouble. A little girl. She was only ten," John started but couldn't finish.

"It's not a fool-proof method," Shay finished for him with an emotional quiver to his voice.

"What exactly happened?" Peter asked with growing concern.

John looked up at Peter then and just shook his head as his face folded inward with pain.

"For G-d's sake, John, what happened?" Peter tried again, a little louder.

"She's made. The operation is shut down. Our girl in Djibouti is out. We were trying to place an orphaned girl from near Mogadishu with a family in London. It went sour. We've no idea where the girl is now. She was taken into custody at the border, and her chaperone was detained. They followed the trail all the way back to Djibouti, and our liaison is busted. We can't get you any papers now, Peter. It's over." And John's head was back in his hands in distress.

Peter walked slowly backward out the door without taking his eyes off John and Shay. He felt betrayed, like he couldn't trust them. He was counting on them. Now what? He knew it wasn't their fault, but he was panicking. How the hell was he going to get the baby out of Somalia? The only thing he knew for sure was that he wasn't leaving without her.

Ayanna was six weeks old. And already she has unknowingly faced the tragedy of losing her entire family and the misfortune of being born into the midst of a civil war. This poor, defenseless infant with no family and no home. The world seemed completely unbalanced to Peter, and he wanted to scream. He wanted to punch somebody. He wanted to fight the world and fate for putting this tiny being into such a predicament. She had no idea of the havoc descending all around her. He hoped he could keep it that way for her sake.

As Peter was contemplating what the hell he was going to do now, Miranda came into the clinic. She immediately became aware of the somber mood in the room.

"Bad news?" she asked as she joined them at the table.

Peter looked at John for guidance in how to explain the situation to Miranda. John and Shay passed a few conspiratorial glances between each other. Shay closed his eyes and nodded.

John began to explain cryptically, with his head still down in defeat, that they were having trouble figuring out how to get Ayanna out of Somalia and into the US. They took turns explaining the laws on foreign adoption, the lack of proper documents, etc. Without exposing their previous involvements, they let Miranda know how dire the situation was.

The more John talked, the clearer it became that there was almost no way of succeeding at getting the baby out of Somalia. Then after a long, silent break in the conversation, and without consulting Peter or Miranda separately, John decided something. He lifted his head slowly with renewed ambition, looked Miranda straight in the eyes, and proclaimed hopefully, "There is only one way I can think of to make this work now."

He waited for their reaction, but they were all silent, even Shay. They had no idea what he was thinking. They could tell by the look on his face that it was big and promising. They watched and waited as he put his thoughts together.

John turned to Peter and said, "Ayanna cannot leave Somalia if she is Somali, right?"

"Yep," Peter answered impatiently, because they had already covered this fact over and over.

"And relations between the Somalia and the US, Somalia and the whole world for that matter, are nonexistent, so an adoption is out of the question, right?" John continued as he directed the next question to Miranda.

"Yes, John, correct," she too answered impatiently.

"What's your point, man?" Shay got to the heart of it.

"And, kids, if Ayanna were instead an American citizen, that would be whole different story, right?" he kept speaking in an elementary-school teacher's voice, as if waiting for any of them to chime in any moment.

"Yep," Peter said redundantly, sounding a little irritated at this point. "But she's not, so what are you getting at, John?"

John didn't answer but turned his head exaggeratedly toward Miranda as a smile slowly lit his face.

"Why are you looking at me like that?" Miranda asked hesitantly. She could feel something cooking, and it wasn't supper.

"Well, Miranda, did you know that if a child is born to a US citizen while on foreign soil, that child has automatic US citizenship, dual citizenship in some countries, though not in Somalia," John added as if reading from a manual.

"Really?" asked Miranda nervously as she backed away from him instinctively.

"Yes. The mother and father don't even have to be married. They just have to be US citizens in good standing. You and Aya looked very much alike, Miranda," John continued as he looked back and forth between Peter and Miranda.

"Wait a minute...wait a minute," Peter interjected.

"Yeah, wait a minute," Miranda agreed shakily.

"You're not suggesting that we claim the baby as Miranda's and mine, are you?" Peter asked incredulously. "I thought I already explained to you that I don't want to jeopardize the MSF's reputation with sordid sexual misconduct and unplanned pregnancies."

"Yes. Yes, you did, Peter. And I have to say I agreed with you. It could be detrimental to the MSF program to have the aid workers getting involved that way with the patients," John said, seemingly defeated. "But"—he continued with a tone that imparted confidence in his new plan—"Miranda is not a defenseless victim of the crisis in Somalia, now is she? Who cares if a couple of crazy American doctors got it on while they were on assignment with the MSF? We all know how possible that scenario can be, don't we, Peter?" he asked snidely under his breath.

He stammered and blushed slightly but answered, "That may be, but it's too risky and too much to ask of Miranda," Peter complained.

"Well, there's always some risk in situations like this," John conceded. "But is it too much risk in order to save an innocent infant's life? Because one thing's for damn sure, Ayanna won't survive if you leave her here. When we leave, things are going to get a whole lot worse, and no one here could possibly even care for her now. I assume you plan on raising Ayanna in the US? Or did you decide to raise her here, in this land of opportunity?" he asked sarcastically. "And don't even think about staying with her in Somalia temporarily. Uncle Sam's coming for our asses, and he doesn't take no for an answer. If you don't get on that plane next week, you'll never practice medicine anywhere again, except in Somalia—a life sentence in the devil's backyard. Erin made that choice because she never plans on returning to the US, but you do, right?"

Peter was incapable of speech. John made some very good points. He admitted there were risks, but he also pointed out that it was the only way, and they had to do something. Peter had the look of having been painted into a corner. He kept looking back and forth from John to Shay to Miranda, waiting for someone to say something that would make this whole thing easier. He was also angry that John would put Miranda on the spot like that.

He himself had no problem with claiming to be Ayanna's natural father, but it wasn't fair to expect her to do the same.

He made this known. "John, you have no right to suggest this to Miranda. You should have talked it over with me alone first. You've gone too far—"

Peter was getting angrier and angrier, but Miranda interrupted his tirade before it got out of hand.

"Peter, settle down," she said in a calming voice. "John's absolutely right. I know there are risks. I know that it's a decision that bears a lot of responsibility. I know that this will have a huge impact on my life, but I also agree that this is the only way to get Ayanna into the US." She turned to John with conviction. "I can do this. I have to do this." Then she turned to Peter. "and I want to do this."

They all waited for someone to say something, for someone to refute her. No one did.

"John, tell me what I need to know," she said finally.

John ignored Peter's shock and began to answer Miranda. "It's very simple, really. We will declare that you two met here when you first arrived in Dhahar. You began a physical relationship at that time, which resulted in a pregnancy, and Ayanna is the result."

Miranda put her hand up in a halting motion as Peter opened his mouth to interrupt.

As he quieted, John continued, "Since you are both US citizens, she will automatically be a US citizen. Since there is no US diplomatic presence in any part of Somalia, and thereby no consulate to issue the necessary birth records, you'll file for Ayanna's birth certificate in Djibouti at the American consulate there. We're traveling there with the US military, so you won't need paperwork here at this end. It couldn't be more perfect. You'll travel to Djibouti together as a family, putting on a good show of love and affection, yada yada. You'll file the necessary forms in Djibouti. And you'll be back in the US with Ayanna in less than two weeks. See? Very simple. Whatever you do from that point on is up to the two of you."

"John, won't they require proof of some sort?" Peter spoke as if John had lost his mind.

"Just your passports, visas, and affidavits of residence in the US, which the MSF will send over. Since Somalia is currently without a government and considered to be in political upheaval, they won't expect any sort of formal birth records. In some countries, they require DNA testing, but not in Djibouti. Aya and Miranda practically looked like sisters anyway, and Ayanna is the same race as Miranda, so they won't question her maternity. Miranda will name you as the biological father. Whomever the mother names as the father is legally binding unless someone contests it, which no one will do. Shay and I can witness any documents that need witnessing. There's a sixty-five dollar fee. And the consular report of birth will serve as Ayanna's birth certificate. You won't have to go through any adoption processes or guardianship stuff or anything. She'll be yours and Miranda's, Peter," John summed up tidily.

"Sounds pretty damn good to me," Miranda said very nonchalantly.

Peter was not as nonchalant. "John, could Miranda and I have a moment to talk this over?"

"Sure, sure. We'll meet back up with you at your place in about an hour. We've got some calls to make. Come on Shay, let's get busy." John slapped Shay on the knee, and they headed out. John had complete confidence that Miranda would talk sense into Peter.

Peter turned to Miranda and said in an exhausted tone, "I don't know, Miranda. First of all, do you completely understand the gist of what you're agreeing to? To the rest of the world, Ayanna would be our child. Your family, your friends, your co-workers. For the safety of Ayanna, we wouldn't be able to tell anyone the truth. Loose lips sink ships and all that. She would even grow up believing that we're her mother and father. You will suddenly have a child, Miranda! I carefully, thoughtfully, and intentionally decided to raise Ayanna as my daughter, probably the moment Aya asked me to find a suitable guardian for her baby. But you haven't had time to really think about this. Miranda, please think this through. How would you handle the fact that you'd be returning home with an illegitimate child, with a veritable stranger for the father?"

Miranda was silent for a moment as she stared at the floor, collecting her thoughts for her response. She seemed to be weighing, deciding. When she lifted her head to face him, there was no trace of hesitation or indecision or in her eyes.

"Peter, what choice do we have? No, I'm not sure about all of this, but I am sure of one thing. I'm not leaving Ayanna here. I loved her mother like a sister, and I won't let her down, even in memory. I couldn't care less what people will think. This is much bigger than that. Their opinion is not even a speck on the radar screen to me. And as for having supposedly conceived an 'illegitimate child with a veritable stranger,' I couldn't think of a more suitable person to have a child with."

"That being said, I have no intention of living together as a family. I only want to do whatever I can to get Ayanna to the US to be raised by you. I'll do whatever you need to help you raise her and be a part of her life in any way I can. If you want me to stay with the two of you for a while, I can delay my career plans. I'll always be your very dear friend, but I'm not looking for a husband, Peter."

"I think we should explain it all to Ayanna when she's old enough to understand, but that won't be for a very long time, and we can think about that later. She'll understand that this was the only way. More than anything, I want her to know who her real mother was and how wonderful and brave she was, but she won't have a chance for that if we don't get her out of here, right? And this is the only safe way to get Ayanna out."

Neither of them said a word for the next ten minutes. They just held each other's gaze and let their minds digest everything that just passed between them. No matter what detour Peter's mind tried to take in figuring out an alternative solution to the problem, it always circled back to Miranda and him posing as Ayanna's mother and father. He hated to admit it to himself, but it was the most viable plan.

Peter had been a little concerned that Miranda intended to set up house with him and Ayanna when they got back home and was definitely relieved that she had other plans. He was slowly coming around to accepting this plan. He knew for sure that Islam law would not allow a Somali orphan to be taken to the US to be raised by an American. Not in a million years. Adoption was out of the question, and leaving Ayanna there was out of the question. So in the end, he had to accept that he and Miranda would be her parents—on paper.

Chapter 20

By the end of the week, everyone was finished packing up, having worked together long, exhausting days in the hot sun. The taste of defeat was bitter in their mouths, and the overall gloom that descended upon them was heavy. They did all they could as far as last-minute medical attention, preparing the villagers as best they could for their departure.

Peter's heart was heavy as the final day approached. He awoke on his last morning in Somalia with the slow realization that he could not change the world as he thought he might be able to. He had done all he could, and he had helped a good many people, but it didn't seem like enough somehow. He understood exactly how Erin felt about wanting to stay in Somalia. If he hadn't committed himself to raising Ayanna, he might be tempted to stay with her. As it was, instead of him staying there, he was taking a little bit of Somalia home with him. He would devote himself to doing the best job he possibly could of raising her. And who knows? Maybe, when she was grown, she would return to this region someday in the capacity to help and really make a difference in this world.

As his thoughts turned to Ayanna, he got out of bed and picked her up from her tiny makeshift bed in his room. The weight of her petite body in his hands felt somehow encouraging to him.

When he looked at her, he saw hope and possibility even in the midst of desolation, a fresh start, a new beginning, a clean slate. He would make sure she was highly educated academically, but also well educated as a humanitarian, like her mother. There was so much promise in that small being; she made him feel as if the world still had promise as well. She made him feel encouraged and optimistic—something that he hadn't felt in a long while.

The morning was blistering hot as usual, but Peter didn't really notice. He was taking one last look around at what had become familiar surroundings. As he stood just outside his small quarters holding Ayanna, he let his gaze move slowly around him as if imprinting the images on film in his mind. He wanted to be able to recall every detail when he someday told her about the place where she was born, the place where her mother and father had lived and loved.

Everyone was loaded on the bus and ready to leave for the airport. The good thing was that Hergeisa was much closer to where they were in Dhahar. They would have flown him into Hergeisa when they arrived, but the airport had been closed until recently from damage to the single runway. It had only reopened two months ago. Within the last twenty-four hours, Peter had helped to finish packing up all the supplies, made provisions as best they could for the persecuted souls who would be left behind, and prepared Ayanna for the trip.

He was saddened that it was ending like this. Somewhere in the recesses of his heart and mind, he really thought there would eventually be some small bit of happiness for these people whom he had grown to care so much about. He visited as many of them as he could, hardly sleeping at all, in the little time he had remaining there. They all cried and said their good-byes with desperation in their eyes. He instructed a few of them on some minor medical procedures as he had done the whole time he was there. He didn't want to leave them with no hope for caring for themselves. It would save some lives, but certainly not all.

In the middle of all that despair, a few of the villagers had actually made the effort to give him some small token of their gratitude. One was a handmade piece of jewelry made of sticks and stones and believed to have peaceful properties. What struck him about this was that "sticks and stones" in the developed world was a symbol of war, but here in this terrorized and victimized corner of the world, they viewed this symbol of war as a symbol of peace. Eye of the beholder. It made him think once again of how the time and place into which one is born makes them who they are.

Voltaire had once said that every man is the creature of the age in which he lives. Very few are able to raise themselves above the ideas of the time. To that, he would only add that if they do, they are the lucky ones, the truly gifted.

———

Selflessness and humanity are the gauges by which success as a human being is measured.

———

Hergeisa is the second largest city of Somalia. Even though the airport had been completely rebuilt recently, it somehow still seemed old, outdated, and uninviting. The drive took three hours, and they were all exhausted by the despair they witnessed through the windows of the bus as they traveled with heavy hearts to their escape. They all felt that they had accomplished only a fraction of what they had hoped to. Their effort over the past year had the distinct ring of a thimbleful of water being bailed from a sinking ship.

They pulled up to the terminal, which was little more than a cinder-block structure no bigger than a drugstore back in the States. The mood was somber. The guards were heavily armed and not a happy-looking bunch. Being with the MSF didn't win them any favor, either. They resented the interference from "peacekeeping" nations. In the city of Hergeisa, more aid workers were kidnapped and attacked than in any other area of Somalia. The only reason their exit was even possible was because Hergeisa was in the Republic of Somalia and had not been as heavily occupied by the ICU. Peter and the others disembarked the bus one by one and said nothing unless spoken to. His hands were shaking slightly, but not noticeably.

Peter and Miranda, with Ayanna safely in his arms, made their way to the tarmac where the C-27J Spartan aircraft was waiting. The sight of the twin-engine US military aircraft waiting faithfully on the pitted and neglected tarmac almost brought tears to everyone's eyes. From across the field, they could see the small emblem on the tail, blue stars with red and white stripes, smiling in the African sun, beckoning them home.

As they passed by the local authorities, they avoided eye contact and kept their pace even. They had all been instructed that this exit was prearranged and would not require any contact with the local authority, but they were expected to stay quiet and calm during the procedure. *Easier said than done*, thought Peter, as they passed by the AK-47 bearing guards. Peter had read some articles as he prepared himself months ago for his journey to Somalia. He had learned that some claimed that the Bush administration had some military dealings with the group in opposition of the ICU.

He didn't know whether he believed everything he read; he always tried to avoid politics and not let it interfere with his humanitarian efforts. And he simply didn't really want to know what the US government's interest in Somalia was. It didn't take a brain surgeon to figure out that it had something to do with oil. Although he had some far-right neurosurgeon friends back in Virginia who denied this emphatically. Politics.

In any case, he was happy to see the friendly metal beast because it made it a hell of a lot easier to get Ayanna out of Somalia. They may have needed paperwork otherwise. It was the fact that the US was transporting them that gave John the idea for Miranda to be Ayanna's mother in the first place. Fate had come through for them, and as they approached the airstair calmly and methodically, he gave one brief nod to the sky in thanks then climbed steadily upward toward the safety of heaven, with Ayanna held safely against his body and without looking back. As he lowered himself into the seat on the plane next to Miranda, he closed his eyes in relief, lifted his hand to his face, and smiled at the villagers' peace charm he'd been holding before kissing Ayanna on her soft head.

They were airborne within thirty minutes, and the once familiar details of the Somali landscape were slowly becoming obscured from the altitude. As their altitude increased and the terrain took on the vague lack of details with which he had first beheld it, Peter couldn't help but wonder at how fast his time in Somalia seemed to pass. The higher they climbed, the further away the last year became. As the terrain became blurred in its vastness, Peter also acknowledged how the past year had changed him. He arrived as an angry man drowning in self pity, and he was leaving a humbled man capable of living fully again.

He had learned more about life and the amazing nature of the human being from his time in this backward, desolate country, from these brave, spirited people, than he could have learned in twenty years at the university. Peter kept his eyes focused out the window until the war-torn, disease-ridden, flood-soaked, drought-damaged land he had just left became beautiful in its obscurity. *Beautiful* was how he wanted to remember it. That's how he would describe it to Ayanna one day when he told her of her extraordinary mother and the other brave, kindhearted, and noble people who were her people. That's how he would describe it to Emily—if he could.

They landed in Djibouti a short forty-five minutes later. The rest of his crew was continuing on to Paris in a few hours with all the equipment and supplies, but Peter and Miranda would have to stay put for as long as it took to get Ayanna a consular report of birth, known as an FS-240 form.

John and Shay had given him explicit instructions on where to go, who to talk to, and what to say. They had been instructed on the documents they would need in order to secure a birth certificate for a US citizen born abroad. They brought with them an official record of Ayanna's birth supplied by John, their own US passports, and affidavits of their residence and physical presence in the United States supplied by the MSF. Peter also had to swear in writing and under oath that he was the biological father and that he planned to financially support the child. Oh, what a tangled web we weave.

By the afternoon of their second day in Djibouti, all the necessary documents were in order, they paid their sixty-five bucks, and they were instructed that they would have the birth certificate in about one week. They would have to return to the American consulate to pick it up in order to expedite the process.

Ayanna then had to be physically examined by a local doctor and vaccinated according to Djibouti standards and US standards. Their week of waiting was filled with resting up after the grueling year they had just spent in Somalia. Exactly one week after they landed in Djibouti, they received Ayanna Daniels' birth certificate naming Miranda Lynn Thomas as the mother and Peter Howard Daniels as the father. The clerk at the consulate never skipped a beat. No questions asked. Slam-bang, "Thank ya ma'am." Jackpot. Bingo. Pay dirt.

They were on a flight to London the very next morning, then to New York, then to Charlottesville—home. Ayanna was a world traveler at the tender age of eight weeks old. Peter and

Miranda were her new parents. And the world was starting to look bright again.

CHAPTER 21

APRIL 2007

Peter sits impatiently in the sparsely populated coffee shop waiting for Emily to reappear from the restroom. As he comes out of his reverie about Somalia, he wonders what the hell is taking her so long. He probably scared her half to death. That door hasn't budged since she went in twenty minutes ago. He knows because his eyes were trained on it the whole time.

He starts to get agitated by Emily's lengthy absence. Did he upset her that much? She must have expected him to be a little angry at her. She couldn't have come back into his life suddenly after three years and not expect questions. She was a lot smarter than that. Emily was actually even downright clever, wily.

He begins to recall one time back at UVA, accidentally finding out that a certain Machiavellian professor of his was bent on "dating" Emily during their relationship and made an unsavory advance toward her. The professor made an implication that Peter's grade was at stake. It was his organic-chemistry professor, and he had to have at least a B in that class, or he wouldn't be competitive enough to be admitted into med school. The professor knew this, and she knew this. She didn't want to tell Peter about it because she didn't want him to make a scene.

He chuckles to himself as he recalls how she handled it perfectly all by herself. She didn't give in to the professor, she didn't report him to the Dean, and she didn't let Peter rescue her. She simply put together an anonymous article for the university's newspaper, an expose on inappropriateness of faculty-student dating, which included interviews with several female students, all of whom the same professor had propositioned over the semester.

Emily had done her research. She relished the opportunity, really. The professor wasn't named, but when he saw the article with all the familiar girls' names, he knew he'd been bested. Peter happened to find out about the entire incident when he overheard a phone conversation that ended with Emily telling the professor, in a strong, cold voice he didn't even recognize, that if he called her again or gave Peter a grade he didn't deserve, every one of those girls was prepared to go to the dean about him—with proof. He must have threatened her at that point because Peter heard her reply, "I couldn't care less what you do to me, but if you mess with Peter Daniels, you're going down, and you're going down hard." She didn't wait for a reply; she just hung up the phone with a slam.

Peter later told Emily that he had overheard the conversation and asked her exactly what was going on. She matter-of-factly explained every detail. He chastised her for not telling him at the onset. He told her that that's what a relationship was about, sharing happiness, joy, *and* hardships. But what amazed him most was how she never let on. She kept all of it so well hidden and put his well-being and career ahead of her own. He guessed that there was no length she wouldn't go to for him, and that was why he loved her so much—her unparalleled selflessness and courage.

He smiles to himself and muses at what other deep dark secrets she might have kept from him back then as his "big protector." Who knows what sort of disasters she thought she was averting or what impending doom she thought she was saving him from?

As he sits there, with her courageous heroism fresh on his mind, trying to sort out what made her leave him when she obviously cared about him so deeply, something buzzes in the back of his mind, the darkest corner of his subconscious thought. All at once, her image flashed in his mind. The short hair—she loved her long hair. Her grandma had always told her a woman's hair is her crowning glory. She would never have worn her hair short voluntarily. Her weight loss and sickly complexion. The dark shadows around her eyes.

His body starts to react before his conscious mind registers it. His heart pumps, and his eyes widen with the dawn of sick recognition. Why hadn't he thought of it before? It all adds up. *Oh my G—d, oh my G—d, oh my G—d,* he thinks to himself as the pieces all suddenly fall together. *That's it! That's the only thing that makes any sense! Oh my G—d!*

His mind is screaming, but his feet are cemented with fear in the dawning of recognition at this horrid reality.

———

His body finally catches up with the panic in his mind.

"*Oh my G———d! Emily!*" he shouts out loud as he jumps up and sprints to the ladies' restroom.

He bursts through the door only to find a weak and motionless Emily slumped on the floor, leaning against the cool cement wall, a pool of vomit at her feet.

"Emily?" he solicits.

She moans and lifts only her eyes toward him. He falls to his knees next to her and starts assessing her vitals. Pulse is okay, eyes are dilating normally, and there is no fever. That's all good. He scoops her up and carries her out of the bathroom. People look alarmed as he comes through the door cradling her in his arms. He asks Aunt Bee to grab a glass of water and some towels. He wets a towel and hands it to her. She thanks him, tells him he is embarrassing her by overreacting, and takes a sip of the water.

After a few minutes of silent inquiry between them, she sees in his eyes that he's figured it out and she asks in a weak voice, "I guess the jig is up, huh?" She attempts a laugh, but it comes out only as a nervous chuckle.

Peter has the immediate feeling of having seen behind the curtain, pulled off the mask. He had been so angry and so convinced that she was a selfish monster all this time. Now he looks at this waif of a girl, in her misery, trying to somehow lighten the situation with a weak attempt at humor, and his heart sinks to the ocean floor. He can't find the words.

He closes his eyes, shakes his head, and breathes, "Emily."

The depth of sorrow in his cracking voice is immeasurable. She had prepared for so long and so hard about how to tell him, and this had not been one of her options. She definitely did not want to have the obvious ensuing conversation in a crowded coffee shop, wet towel to her head, and vomit on her clothes.

She looks around nervously and whispers, "Peter, will you please take me to my hotel?"

After a few minutes, once her nerves and stomach are settled, he pays the check, grabs his guitar, and runs the three blocks to get his car while Aunt Bee sits with her. He carefully helps her into the car then he gets in, and she tells him which hotel in a weak, tired voice. He doesn't press her for answers yet. She isn't ready. He can tell now by all the signs that it was most likely cancer. He berates himself in his mind over and over. How could he, of all people, not have known? He had been so hurt and so angry that he never once considered something like this. He had been swamped with the chief-residency position, and she had become distant and spent an increasing amount of time with that guy Doug at work, so he was completely on the defense when she left like that. An illness never even entered his mind. He'd always heard that a doctor's judgment could be clouded by emotion, can't see the forest for the trees. The reason most doctors won't treat or operate on family members. Jesus. Emily. How in the world could he have missed this?

He drives deeper and deeper into the night in total silence. The rain has stopped and the clarity of the evening is sharp and illuminating. Until tonight, he hasn't shed one tear since the day she left, even in the face of all that had passed in Somalia. But on that lonely road, in that dark night, with this unbearable revelation between them, his vision blurs with three years' worth of emotion. He has to pull over until the emotion passes. He cuts the engine so he can completely concentrate on the situation.

Emily is still slightly green and quiet in the passenger seat. "Why did you stop, Peter?"

"I couldn't see where I was going anymore," is all he replies.

They sit in silence for some time, staring straight ahead at the stars out the window. They don't turn to look at one another, even when they speak. The gravity of what just unfolded is too much by itself. They can't bear to add the obvious emotion in each other's faces to the scene.

"That's why you left." This is a statement, not a question, and Peter's voice is very low and has a mockingly incredulous tone.

Her lips quiver; she inhales to steady herself, keeps her eyes straight forward, and answers in a whisper that cracks with emotion, "Yes."

"Should I be taking you to the hospital right now instead of the hotel?" Peter asks with concern, not having any idea of the current status of her medical situation.

"No, not at all, it's just a reaction to the medication. I've been busy all day, and I haven't eaten. That's all. It will pass in about twenty minutes," she supplies.

Another throat-clearing, emotion-gathering pause. "What… what form…what form of cancer is it?" Peter's voice cracks too with the strain of emotion pushing on the dam, and he has to restart the question several times before he can get the whole thing out.

Silence as she garners the courage to talk without breaking down.

"Leukemia," she breaths out, then hangs her head with relief from the infinitely overdue confession.

His hands quickly cover his face, and he shakes his head briefly as if he could shake reality off or choose to deny it. With his face safely hidden, his body becomes motionless and soundless for a full minute, then he breaks the stillness as his shoulders shudder in rhythm to his quiet sobs. He has no idea what her prognosis was. He just got her back in his life; he couldn't face the possibility of losing her again. After a long episode of emotional release, he rubs his red eyes, takes a deep breath, and braces himself for the answer to his next question.

He holds his breath with hope. "You're on medication. Are you in remission then?" he asks with his eyes straight ahead from under his bomb shelter.

Emily turns toward him with relief in her eyes—not for herself, but for being able to give him something good instead of bad—and says, "At the moment, and I have a 90 percent chance of making it to the first five-year waypoint. From there, we have to reassess." She's so glad that she had waited to see him until she could give him good news. Peter is visibly relieved.

His breath lets out quickly, his eyes close in a prayer of thanks, and he drops his chin and says under his breath, "Thank G-d."

They are silent for a few more minutes. He doesn't even know how to begin dealing with the myriad of swirling emotions in his head. He was up, he was down, he was up, he was down. And the peaks and valleys got steeper and deeper every time she opened her mouth.

In the end, he simply says, "Well then, let's get you back to your hotel."

He restarts the engine without another word. Emily keeps her eyes carefully diverted straight ahead and concentrates on the stars in the dark, distant sky.

CHAPTER 22

After they arrive at her hotel, Peter parks the car and helps Emily out. He supports her weak, spent frame to the elevator and takes her to her room—without one word between them. When they enter the room, she asks him to wait one moment while she goes into the bathroom to splash water on her face and rinse her mouth with mouthwash. She seems to be feeling better so Peter just sits and waits.

While Emily is busy in the bathroom, Peter's cell phone rings. It's Miranda. She wants to know when he'll be back. He apologizes for not calling, acknowledges the late hour, and explains that he bumped into an old friend and he'll be home very late. Miranda doesn't mind; she just wants to make sure he's all right and that he hasn't forgotten about their appointment with the Social Security office at noon the next day. He's been very strange and aloof all week, not himself. He assures her that he hasn't forgotten and he'll be home in plenty of time, and they hang up. Peter places the phone on the nightstand, distancing himself from the call, one drama at a time, too much to deal with at once.

He worries that Emily may have heard the call. He walks over to the bathroom door and hears the water still running. He's safe.

He has no idea how he's going to explain that whole situation, but he feels intuitively that it's too soon.

When Emily comes out, Peter is waiting right there at the door with a concerned look on his face. Without turning on any lights she walks over to the bed and gently lowers herself onto the soft mattress. She sits up against the pillow as she settles in for a long discussion, and he takes a seat in a chair across from the bed. The curtains are open, and the moonlight illuminates the room eerily. He fills a glass with water and offers it to her. She looks up at him as she reaches for the glass, and her eyes speak a polite, noncommittal thank you. She takes a few sips and wipes her mouth on her sleeve, looking like a vulnerable child. She has a few crackers and some fruit from the nightstand.

Peter just watches her quietly. He doesn't want to chance upsetting her or her stomach again. She looks better already. Her cheeks regained their normal hue, and her eyes are shining. They both sit in the softly moonlit room as their eyes adjust for what seems like an eternity. She remembers their first moonlit night of lovemaking, and her face softens at the memory. Neither one reaches for the lamp. They need the anonymity of the darkness to have the following conversation.

Peter has earned the right for the first word.

"How do you feel now?" he asks with concern as if he was judging whether she was up to the interrogation.

"Fine, almost completely over it." She smiles, feigning a one for the Gipper attitude.

"Good," he offers distractedly.

Another pause so they could decide where to go from there. He jumps off the high board first and lands with a small splash.

"Why, Emily?" he begged in a ragged whisper, hands clasped in restraint, shaking his downcast head in disapproval, staring at the emotionally empty, inanimate floor.

She remains silent while she collects her thoughts and prepares to do a back triple somersault off the board and join him in the deep, dark, bottomless pool.

Again, in a more beseeching tone, he asks, "For G-d's sake, Emily, why?" this time making eye contact through squinted eyes as if he can barely face her.

She has to say something, although she knows that nothing she could say would suffice. She has the look of intense thought. The air is electric, and she is trembling from the current,

"I…I…I just…I wanted. I didn't want you to watch me suffer for two or three years, only for me to die and leave you alone anyway. Then be left with what? A broken heart, no wife, no kids, maybe even a big dent in your career from all the time my illness would take away from your life? You were young, and you had your whole life ahead of you. Getting dumped is recoverable. You know damn well what it's like to be with someone who's terminally ill. You saw it every day of your life at the hospital. It ate you up to see patients like that. It ate me up to watch how it affected you—and those people were patients, not loved ones."

"I couldn't bear the thought of me being the cause of that much pain in your life. I gave it a lot of thought, Peter. I labored over the decision. Don't think I just casually decided to leave you. It was the hardest thing I've ever done to this day, including the three years I spent having chemo, bone-marrow transplants, and taking medication that makes you feel like death warmed over." She stops there because the memory of those events made her too emotional to speak. It had been a rough couple of years.

Peter takes the silent opportunity to say, "But it nearly killed me when you left, anyway, Em." He doesn't sound angry now, just broken.

"I know. I knew you'd have some pain from my leaving, just as I would if you had left me. But I figured it was the lesser of two evils, because you'd eventually get over it, meet someone else, forget me, and continue your life." The tears well up in her eyes at this notion. She wipes them away robotically, sniffs back any followers, and says bravely, "I hated leaving you. I hated myself for leaving you. I hated the world because I had to leave you. The only thing I was sure of was that I was doing the right thing by leaving."

There is direct eye contact and a challenging gaze as she says this last sentence. Peter relaxes his position consentingly, squints out the window as if he is tabulating something in his head, like maybe the score of this conversation. She has about three points, and he has only one, but he is going for the homerun now with the bases loaded. He turns his head slowly back to her and levels his stare.

"There's one thing you didn't consider, Emily, and that one thing was me. What I would have wanted. Not what you thought I'd want, but what I'd actually want. Your story sounds really noble, but I'm not buying it completely. Sure, you didn't want me to suffer, but I suffered plenty anyway, and you knew I would. I don't think the degree of difference was as big as you anticipated. And you're right. I do know 'damn well what it's like to be with someone who was terminally ill,' and it's definitely *not* like that. I should have been able to be at your side day and night, like I would have wanted. That should have been my choice."

"How about if you had died, and we didn't get this second chance? What then, Emily? Did you consider what that would be like? Here I am hating you because you dumped me for no apparent reason, then I find out that you really had cancer and didn't tell me, but now it's too late for reconciliation or forgiveness because you're gone and there's nothing I can say or do to get those precious last few years back! All I can do after years of missing you, blaming you, and desperately wanting you back is attend your funeral! You know what I think? I think you just didn't want to *watch* me suffer. You were protecting yourself as much as or more than me."

"I should have had the choice, Emily. I earned that much after all those years. Don't tell me that you thought I'd stay by your side purely out of obligation. You know that if I stayed it would have been because I truly wanted to, because I loved you more than anything in this world. And I did, by the way, love you more than anything in this world. I would have died for you. At times over the last three years, it felt like I did." Homerun. Out of the ballpark.

They are both drained. There is nothing left to say. They had both made very good arguments and still didn't agree. They sit in the dim silence and thank G-d silently that at least they were even able to be in the same room together, having this conversation. It is growing late, around two in the morning. They both need to sleep and resume this later. But Peter still has so many questions.

He rises slowly, turns toward the window, asks how she is feeling again, then he refills her glass with water. She thanks him, again, and tells him that she feels fine, again. The mood has the feeling of two boxers having returned to their respective corners for a brief rest before hitting the mat again. She explains that she is on a new trial medication, and it sometimes causes side effects, especially if she didn't eat properly. The martini didn't help, either. She should never have had a drink, but she had needed it badly.

"What is the medication?" Peter asks.

"Sprycel," Emily admits sheepishly as if she were still trying to hide something. Old habits die hard.

Peter turns to stare out the window again and to shield his face from her view. He reverts to the professional comfort zone. "Did they try Gleevec?"

"Yes, but I had liver complications from it and had to discontinue taking it," she explains. "I had been taking Gleevec and underwent yet another bone-marrow biopsy when I had some complications with bleeding."

She is quiet for a minute, and her face is clouded with pain and sorrow.

"I was in the hospital, hooked up to several IVs, recovering from that fiasco, when I got the message about your father, Peter. I was completely devastated. I want you to know that. I desperately wanted to do more than just send a card. I know you had to have hated me even more for that than when I left you. Your mother must have thought I was such a coldhearted bitch too. And I couldn't call because I'm a coward, and that's unforgivable, I agree. But if I had gotten on the phone with you at that point and heard the pain and misery in your voice, I would have broken down and ruined everything. I couldn't afford to do that at that point. My prognosis was not favorable early on, and I couldn't take that chance."

She can't say anymore as she sobs lightly at this recollection.

Peter watches her with thinly veiled reserve. Her anguish is genuine, and he can tell that that must have been the hardest part of her whole charade. The last vestiges of his reasons for hating her are melting away.

"Peter?" she prompts at his silence.

"Yes?" he keeps it short to hide his internal struggle and remains at the window with his back to her.

She starts out shaky and gains confidence as she continues, speaking to his back. "I won't apologize anymore because I did what I truly thought was best at the time. But I will say that I realize now it may have been a mistake to have left like that. It felt right somehow, though, to have control over something. I couldn't control my fate, I couldn't control my suffering, I couldn't control the cancer, but I could control whether you suffered or not. I just had to control something in my life. Better one tragedy than two, I thought." This sounded painfully familiar to him. "I actually felt it was a mistake after about the third round of chemo, but I felt like I was at the point of no return, at some far end of the earth. I felt so far away, so lost from you."

She feels that if she sums it all up, he might agree with her so she continues.

"The total treatment took about two years because they had to do a marrow transplant. I was so weak most of the time. I had no idea which way my progress would go. It was bad for a while, but then I started responding well. I was released from treatment about ten months ago, except for occasional injections. I tried to find you once I found out I was in remission. I missed you so terribly.

"There was no listing for you, your cell phone didn't work, and I didn't call your mother, brother, or sister because I wasn't ready to face them, especially until I had spoken with you. I called the hospital to find you, but you had joined the MSF. I knew you left the country, but I didn't know where you were—they keep that confidential. I kept trying to find you and was about to cave in and call your mom when I finally found the internet story about your solo at the bar. And that's where we are now," as if leaving it for him to take from there.

At his continued silence, she takes a new tack. "I came back for you. I came back to explain and apologize." There is a pregnant pause as she stands so she can move right behind him and say this close to his ear as if it were a secret. "And I came back to tell you how much I still love you, always loved you, never stopped for a second."

He can feel her closeness. He turns slowly back around to find her withered, gaunt face shining up at him hopefully, remorsefully in the moonlight. Her eyes, though shadowed with years of illness, are illuminated lanterns filled with unabashed love and desire, and they speak much louder and clearer than her words ever could.

She searches his eyes intensely with hers, decides to go all in, and repeats boldly as she moves even closer, "I'll always love you, Peter. Even if you hate me forever for trying to save you."

She reminds him of Aya just now, brave and proud and putting a loved one's needs above her own to a selflessly infinite degree. He realizes that it must have been a heart-wrenching labor of love for her to do what she did, whether he agreed with her decision or not. He pictures her scared and alone, facing all that treatment and her own mortality without him. He forgives her in his heart immediately but still has so much unshed anger within him.

Even surprising himself, Peter sweeps her up in his arms and kisses her with all the passion of the last three years. There is nothing gentle about this kiss, as in previous days. This kiss is demanding, reprimanding, avenging, and angry.

She doesn't pull away, though. She kisses him back with everything she has. If he wants to punish her in that kiss, she let him. If he thought he was taking back some control for all the years that were cheated from him, then so be it. They are hurtling through space, but at least they are together, and it felt wild and good. She has no idea where they would end up, and she doesn't care, as long as they are together for this moment—as long as the moment lasts. He is a wild mustang, and she has to hang on until he's broken. If she could just stay on long enough, she knew he'd break. She doesn't fight back, just hangs on.

He abruptly draws away, holds her at arm's length, breathing hard and fast, to question her with his eyes. They seem to say, "How do you like it? I'm in control now." Emily just holds his gaze calmly as tears run down her face and a smile of victory spreads across her face. This passion is better than indifference. She waited so long and went through so much to get here. She had to win him back. She knew now that she would win this. She could already tell that he was almost at the breaking point.

He kisses her hard one more time, more briefly, holds her away again, explores her eyes, then hugs her tightly like a beloved rag doll that had been tossed aside dismissively in childhood and suddenly, desperately reclaimed. He holds her as if he were holding on to a rope at the summit of Mt. Everest, twenty-nine thousand feet in the sky, as if his life depended on it. She doesn't realize it, but his life does depend on it.

"G-d, Emily. Three years! Three agonizing, heartbreaking, unbearable years. I was so lost without you. I was like a zombie at the hospital. I would barely talk with anyone. I was so desperate to forget you I left the country. I can't believe you did that to us. I'm so unbelievably happy that you're back and well, but so damned angry with you that you left. I want to strangle you and devour you all at the same time. Do you have any idea how much I love you? Do you?" he shakes her gently by the shoulders almost shouting.

She has to assume these questions are rhetorical since he is kissing her again before she can answer. Those words were the key—the key to the padlock on the cold steel box. It pops open and instantly disintegrates. All that is left is her own beating heart. The kiss is more gentle this time, but still urgent. Her tears of triumph fall like rain, but he never lets her go. She thinks maybe he really will devour her, and then she thinks, *That would be nice.*

He realizes with a force that he desires her, needs her, cares about her, and, finally, loves her even more than before she left. Nothing and no one in the past three years has made him change his mind, and he'll have no peace until he has her again.

After a long embrace that turned into a small waltz in place to the silent rhythm of their hearts, Peter leads her gently to the bed,

"I love you, Emily. I love you with everything I have to love.", no anger this time, no accusation in his voice. Just love—pure and simple. All the demons had been exorcised, and Peter is himself again. The gentle, tender, caring Peter she fell in love with almost ten long years ago.

As the world glows in the light from the full moon, Peter takes Emily to bed and makes her his all over again. Three years of longing and desire were threatening to unleash itself, and he has to concentrate on moving slowly. He touches her lovingly. He kisses every inch of her proprietarily. He caresses her soul with his tongue. Then he lowers himself lightly on top of her, covering her entire body with the warmth of his. She opens her body to him and beckons him with her hips. He pauses at the threshold of her world, looks meaningfully into her eyes as he strokes the hair from her face, and whispers how much he missed her, how much he loves her, how he would die if she ever left him again.

Then as he sank into her universe, she answers, "Never. I'll never leave you. I love you, Peter."

The last three years dissolve away instantly. His body is moving in time to hers until they both shatter into a million pieces at the exact same moment. They make the trip to euphoria one more time that night. And each time is like the first time, eight years ago.

They have been strangers to each other's bodies for three years but fall into each other like puzzle pieces. It is as if time had stood still. Emily is thinner and more frail looking, which only endears her to him even more. The journey of the last three years is evident on her body and face.

"It must have been hell going through that, Emily. I really wish I had been there with you." He isn't scolding anymore, only wishing.

"I wished it too a lot of times," she admits as they tangled their fingers together playfully. "I missed you with such a force that it was actually painful at times. I was so lonely. I never felt loneliness like that before. It scared me."

By dawn, they had talked until their voices were raspy. She had asked him all about his time in Somalia, to which he answered very ambiguously. He told her sketchy details about what a living hell it had been, how much he wanted to help those poor people, and how badly he felt having to leave them. That was part of the reason he just couldn't jump right back into his career at the hospital.

He didn't tell her the other part— about Aya and the new addition to his life that was, right now, sound asleep in her crib at his house. He had no idea how to tell her that he was, to the rest of the world, a new father. He would save all that for another time. *Too much drama already for one night*, he thought. After five minutes of hurried answers, he returned anxiously to the topic of her diagnosis and treatment.

Her story made his blood run cold.

———

Love is a tightrope upon which we are all struggling to balance.

———

CHAPTER 23

MAY 2004

It was an uncharacteristically cold afternoon in May when Emily walked into the doctor's office. She'd had a cough that she just couldn't seem to shake for a couple weeks now. She suspected allergies, but the over-the-counter pills weren't working, and she wanted to get some prescription strength allergy medication.

"Hey, Doc!" she exclaimed as he walked through the door. She'd been going to this doctor ever since she moved to Virginia and started her freshman year at UVA six years ago.

"Well, hello, Ms. Waters. What brings you in here today?" he answered in a grandfatherly tone. Dr. Crosby was a distinguished-looking man close to seventy, with very kind eyes and gentle hands.

"I have a persistent cough," she reported as she yawned. "Oh, excuse me. I'm so sorry. I've been so tired." She blushed as her eyes watered from the yawn.

"Have you now? Well, let's take a look, young lady," he instructed. He always made her feel like a little girl. She liked that. She felt protected.

He looked in her throat, checked her ears, shined a light up her nose, took her temperature, etc., all the usual goings-on at the doctor's office. All the while, she was making mental notes of what she needed to do the rest of the day. Grocery store, library, gas station, etc. She didn't hear what he said because she was a million miles away.

"Ms. Waters," he repeated, "may I ask how you got all these bruises?"

She looked down at her legs indifferently. "Oh, um, I'm not sure. I guess I'm just a clutz," she joked.

"Okay, Miss Clutz," he teased, "I'm ordering some tests. Take this paper down to the lab and wait for them to call your name."

"Are these allergy tests?" she asked innocently.

"No, these are blood tests. We'll call you as soon as we have the results," he answered cryptically. His tone had changed from before, and he kept his eyes on the floor and had one foot out the door. "Have a good day, and be careful driving, young lady." He didn't ask if she had any questions like he usually did, just left her standing there, staring at the back of the door.

Emily hopped off the table and went to the lab obediently. She was disappointed that he wasn't going to give her any allergy prescriptions. She'd been coughing and very tired, and it was starting to affect her work. She went to the lab, had blood drawn, went home, instead of doing all her errands, and fell fast asleep by two thirty.

Pete came home around four, woke her up, and ravished her body until she was delightfully weary. Then they ordered take-out because she was too exhausted to cook, snuggled on the couch under a blanket, and watched a DVD—because she was too drained to go out to the movies as they had planned, made love again, and fell fast asleep in each other's arms, all in all, a pretty great day. She didn't know it at the time, but it was the last great day she would have for the next three years.

At eight thirty the next morning, the phone rang. When Emily answered it, she was surprised to hear Dr. Crosby's voice. He asked if she could stop by sometime that day to go over the results of the blood tests. She agreed to be there by 10:00 a.m.

and hung up with a cheery "See ya later." She didn't even ask why. She didn't even question how he got the results back so soon. It had never even occurred to her to wonder why he called, instead of his receptionist. There were so many warning signs that bad news was imminent, but she carelessly and uncharacteristically ignored them all.

Emily was ushered into the doctor's office instead of an examining room and offered a seat across from his desk. Her pulse quickened a little as her subconscious finally registered the warning signs that she'd been overlooking. The doctor folded his gentle hands on his desk blotter and stared at them as he searched for the right words. He cleared his throat and began to explain as gently as he could. The doctor's soft, paternal demeanor gave her that false sense of security that set her up for the biggest fall of her life.

She was completely, almost criminally, blindsided when Dr. Crosby finally told her that the blood test results indicated that she may have chronic myelogenous leukemia but they can't be completely sure until they perform a bone-marrow test. He went on to explain that they'd like to perform the test as soon as possible. After a fleeting moment of hysteria, she calmed herself and decided not to panic until the final results were in. She scheduled the test to be performed in the doctor's office for the very next morning. Emily was instructed to not eat or drink anything after midnight and given a brief description of the procedure. So clinical. So calculated. So matter-of-fact. It didn't even seem real.

She went home and acted as if nothing had happened. She did not mention anything to Peter. He had arrived home very late that night anyway, so it was easy to just pretend she was already asleep. She awoke very early and was at the doctor's office by 8:00 a.m. They drew the bone marrow, and she was out of there by eleven. They told her it would take anywhere from a day to a week to get the results. Purgatory.

It was only two days later when they called her to come in and discuss the results. She had them call on her cell phone this time in case Peter had been home. She got dressed quickly and was at the doctor's office within a half hour.

Dr. Crosby's grim face said it all as she took the chair across from his desk. She felt like she was being given a sentence at a hearing. As he started speaking, she heard words like *I'm sorry, chronic myelogenous leukemia, blast cells, chemotherapy*. He kept explaining on and on, not knowing that he had lost her at chemo. Her mind was focusing on one big question of course.

"Will I die?" She was oddly serene.

He paused. He was stuck somewhere between hard truth and let her down gently. He tried his best.

"Well, of course, we'll do everything to prevent that outcome. We have to determine whether you're in the chronic phase or the accelerated phase," was the short answer as the doctor's brows knit together at her lack of reaction.

"How long do I have if I am going to die from it?" came the next obvious but disconnected question.

"That depends on your phase and how you respond to treatment. There are some new drugs out right now that look very promising…" He had a grim look on his face as he continued, and that's all Emily saw or heard—grim.

Then came the brick wall at one hundred miles per hour. She was somewhere else. She wasn't listening. She had gone to his office so unsuspectingly, believing naively that it would have all been a big mistake. She was dressed in a gray flannel miniskirt, stockings, white blouse, bright pink sweater and grey pumps. She remembered that very clearly. Funny that she would remember what she was wearing when she was handed a death sentence involving pain and suffering, with very little possibility for parole, no matter what her behavior.

Her very first thought, her knee-jerk reaction, was guilt and shame. It wasn't conscious. It was just the immediate feeling of, "Oh my G—d, what did I do to deserve this?"

All of a sudden the room got smaller, her adorable clothes seemed ridiculous, almost mocking, and she wasn't focusing on what the doctor was saying. She felt somehow that if she didn't focus on him, this would all go away. He was the person who brought her this horrible news, so ignoring him would make it all untrue somehow. He was speaking in a "Come off the ledge" tone now. It unnerved her even more for some reason. Why wasn't he freaking out with her? That would seem more normal.

The incongruence of his calm disposition, coupled with this disastrous news, seemed like something from a psycho-thriller film. He was too practiced at this. How many people did he give this horrible news to in a week? It seemed like a conspiracy all of a sudden. He seemed like an executioner all of a sudden.

She started to become very afraid. It couldn't be true. It had to be a mistake, that's all. She felt a short reprieve from her panic at realizing it really was all just a big mistake. But something still felt a little wrong. Dr. Crosby was standing up now and coming over to her to console her. But she didn't need a hug, because it was a mistake, remember? As he tried to hold her, she felt herself pushing him away. She didn't plan on pushing him, but she could feel herself pushing anyway.

She looked around the room nervously. It was so small all of a sudden. It was a cage, and she was trapped. She had to get out. She seemed to be outside of her mind now. She could hear her voice in her head—a high-pitched wail, but nothing came out. She could feel herself pushing someone, and she could sense the panic, but she wasn't doing it. She realized that she was on the floor now. She was scooting into the corner and curling up in a fetal position. She needed to stay low for some reason. She heard a buzzer, and some nurses came in. They tried to coax her up off the floor, something about it being dirty? Who the hell cared if it was dirty? She was angry now. *No! I don't want this*, her mind screamed, but it only came out as a whimper. They sedated her mildly and took her to an exam room to lie down.

A nurse stayed with her until she felt normal again— whatever normal was now. Emily had been talking and talking nonstop, though she couldn't really remember what she had said. The sound of her own voice comforted her for some strange reason. When she stopped talking, she looked at the nurse and saw tears in her eyes. She tried to tell Emily that Peter was such a wonderful guy, that he loves her and will help her through this. They all knew Peter from the hospital.

Emily realized that she had been talking about all the plans she and Peter had. At this realization, Emily jumped off the examining table and frantically told the nurse that no one from this office was ever to tell Peter anything about this. "Put that in my chart, right now! I want complete confidentiality! Peter is never to know!" She was practically hysterical all over again. They assured her, unhappily, that her file would be kept strictly confidential, and she calmed down immediately.

Emily never had another outburst or panic attack after that. Once she knew that Peter would never have to know about this, she felt in control of something again, and it gave her strength. She straightened her clothes, cleared her throat as if clearing her mind, ran her hand over her hair, and walked out the door, planning never to return. That office was now the scene of the crime, the scene of the tragedy that had befallen her, and she never, ever wanted to revisit that scene.

After she left, Dr. Crosby, for the first time in his professional career of over forty years, closed those kind eyes and placed his head in those gentle hands and wept.

CHAPTER 24

She had walked into that office a happy-go-lucky young girl of twenty seven and came out a fatigued old woman of about a hundred and one. She walked and walked and walked until she felt that all her nervous energy was spent. By the time she got home to their apartment, she had messages from the office asking where she'd been all day, messages from Peter asking if her cell phone died, and a message from her mom saying, matter-of-factly, that she just called to see how things were. She sat on the kitchen chair and stared at the answering machine as if it were judging her. "You have to tell everyone, you have to deal with a terminal disease, and you have to decide a course of action," it seemed to be saying.

Peter was due home in two hours. She had to be out. She couldn't face him. She bathed, changed, left him an ambiguous note about shopping, and headed to the library. The library was her church. The library was quiet and serene like a church; it was full of wisdom like a church, and its arms opened wide to anyone who believed in its purpose, like a church. She had felt that way her whole life, even as a small child. Peter had often teased her about it. Her grandmother was sure she would grow up to be a librarian. Now she feared she wouldn't have a chance to grow up to be anything.

As soon as she entered the vestibule, she could smell the musty pages and feel the warmth of the stories waiting to unfold, or the knowledge waiting to be learned. She thought about how she wished she could get the library in a pill form so she could take it any time she wanted and get that feeling of security. She found some books on different forms of cancers and scurried them to a quiet corner to digest hungrily. Maybe because she was a journalist, maybe because it all seemed so personal; she just wanted to take tonight to find out what she could on her own before hearing what the doctors had to say. What had he called it? Chronic myelogenous leukemia. She found it and swallowed every word like it was brussels sprouts, necessary evils.

What she learned was that there was hope—little—but still hope. She drew strength from the knowledge in these books and sat there almost until closing time deliberating over what to do. She needed to start treatment, and fast. That was obvious. But first and most importantly, she needed to decide what to do about Peter. It's all she thought about since the diagnosis. She tried to picture how she would tell him about her disease. She tried to imagine what words she would use. The pain she saw on his face in her mind made her stomach sick, and she felt as though she might vomit. If finding out about her illness was hard, telling Peter would be impossible.

No matter how many different ways she imagined telling him, it always resulted in her feeling the same sick, morbid, disgusting feeling. Would he view her as an executioner the way she viewed Dr. Crosby? Would he harbor some subconscious blame for her for ruining their life together? Would he waste his life and career away by her bedside during her long, arduous, excruciating treatment? And what about after she died, if she did die? Would he be able to pick up the pieces and resume his life and career, especially after several years?

She turned it over and over and over in her mind, and it always came up the same way. She couldn't abide the possible answers to those questions. She really didn't believe that she would live to accomplish all their dreams now, and she didn't want the next few years to be spent with him at her bedside while she slowly faded into oblivion, only to leave him broken and alone in the end. To be the source of that much heartache to him was more than she could bear—worse than the diagnosis itself. If he could achieve their dreams, even without her, then it would be something, rather than nothing.

The story of "The Yearling" came to her just then. When she was a young girl, she had read the book. She remembered being appalled that Jody would actually shoot Flag, his fawn, best friend, and confidante, whom he loved more than anything in this world. She was sick about it for days, and it made her hate the story. In her young mind, she couldn't understand that it was the only humane thing to do. She felt like poor Jody now, and she forgave him a little. Only, instead of a fawn, it was her relationship with Peter that needed to be put out of its misery before the real misery began. She would have to kill it mercifully so that Peter could live an emotionally healthy life and fulfill all of their dreams for her. That's what she wanted. He would be hurt by her leaving him, but he would eventually move on. *It's easier to move past a breakup than a death*, she reasoned in her mind. It was decided then.

She would formulate a plan for leaving Peter and head out to San Francisco to be with her parents. She would receive all her treatment there so that no one here, especially Peter, would ever know. The more she thought about it, the more sense it all made. If she went to San Francisco as soon as possible, she could start treatment right away, have the support of her parents, and have the added bonus of not having to face Peter's heart-wrenching reaction. Fight or flight, they say? She said flight. She would begin the withdrawal from Peter right away that evening.

She looked up a few more things on the computer at the library from the leads she had gotten in the books, left at nine o'clock, and arrived home at ten after stopping for some coffee and a snack.

Peter was camped out on the couch, watching a ballgame on TV and shouted hello as she came in. She barely responded but went into the bedroom and lay down. She was asleep by the time he came in, or so he thought. When he tried to ask her about her day, she didn't stir. Her back was to him so he just rolled over and went to sleep. She lay there awake and crying for an hour or so before she drifted off into a fitful sleep.

She felt a weight pulling her down toward the foot of the bed. She was sliding, falling—no, sinking down, down, down. Something was tied around her ankle very tightly. She couldn't shake it off. She kicked and kicked furiously at the thing, but it stayed on and kept dragging her deeper and deeper. She was in water now. Her long hair floated all around her head like a beautiful mermaid's picture she had once seen in a children's book. She looked up to see how far away the surface of the water was and found that it was getting further and further.

Then suddenly Peter was there, stroking her long flowing hair as it magically grew longer and longer and wrapped around him. He became entangled in it, but he didn't seem to notice or care. Like a siren's song, her hair was beckoning him down into the abyss with her. They were getting deeper and deeper, and she suddenly needed oxygen desperately. Her body ached for a breath, and with a panic, she realized that Peter also needed air to breathe. He still didn't seem to notice. He just kept smiling at her, naively, as he played lovingly with her long hair, all the while his face turning blue with deprivation.

Her panic for him intensified, and she tried to wave him away. Bubbles came out of her mouth as she yelled for him to swim away from her and to the surface. The bubbles reached him, and he played childishly with these, as well as her mesmerizing hair. She realized that he would never willingly leave her beautiful hair, the bubbles, or anything else about her, so she pulled out a knife from somewhere. When she saw the knife, she was terrified that she would cut him or kill him, but she merely swiped the knife around her head and watched as her beautiful hair floated to the surface, with Peter chasing after it.

As the water grew dark around her with her ever-increasing depth, she kept her eyes upward and watched as Peter made it to the oxygen-rich surface, just in the nick of time. She was immensely relieved even as her feet touched the cold, rocky, unknown of the dark ocean floor. Relief enveloped her like a warm fleece blanket. She had no strength left to try and shake the weight off her ankle. She ceased to struggle as she knew she was trapped forever at the bottom of the world and would probably die there unbeknown to anybody. But she was perfectly peaceful, knowing that Peter was safe at the top of the world.

———

In the morning, she reflected that that was the worst night of her life, so far. She suspected she was in for a lot worse over the next few months. She would keep up the aloof charade, no matter how hard it was. She planned to leave in less than two weeks, so she had to convince him that she wanted out. Little by little, he was getting the message. She would stay out late, go out in the middle of the night, and act short tempered with him. Peter would think it had to do with his new position at the hospital. Or maybe he would think she was meeting someone at night. She didn't care what he thought; she just had to make him suspicious of something, anything. She would deal with her emotions later. She was becoming adept at the art of deception.

She put her two weeks' notice in at the paper where she worked, and she called her folks. She had no intention of telling them the news over the phone, so she simply told them that she and Peter were going to concentrate on their respective careers before taking the big plunge and that she had an offer at a paper in San Francisco, so she was coming to stay with them for a little while. She had contacted a paper out there and got a part-time, freelance position, so it wasn't a complete lie. She would tell them the whole truth when she got out there, not over the cold, impersonal phone. She never allowed herself to feel anything. She stayed distant and detached so she could execute her mission flawlessly—and she did.

She had prepared her speech to deliver to Peter, and she had spent all those evenings out practicing it. It was a thing of beauty; those journalism and creative writing classes were really paying off in spades now, boy. The big event came, and she delivered a whopper of speech that left Peter completely stunned. She mentally removed her heart and implanted a little steel box with the lock. She tried not to look at him, turned abruptly, and walked out.

She sold her car to a used dealership, donated most of her things to Goodwill, and cancelled all her accounts and credit cards that could lead Peter to her. She cancelled her cell phone and began a new contract with a different carrier. She had grown away from most of her friends, but she had a few close friends whom she needed to explain her departure to. She didn't; she just blew them off. She was out the next day.

Peter was obviously broken, but she reasoned repressively that he would mend from this a whole lot faster than he would from her illness. She was almost home free. On her last day, she planned to be in the apartment with him as little as possible. They did cross paths once, and his face had the scars of betrayal and intense emotional pain. It was in his eyes, and it would haunt her forever. She was responsible for that, but fate had given her no choice. She very quickly averted her eyes and left, knowing that she may never see him again and that was the last image they would remember—him broken and she as cold as ice. She walked out of their life together and into the cruel future alone. By the time she made it to the airport, she had to stop the cab and vomit twice. Her stomach was the only part of her body she couldn't seem to control, and it bore the burden of the hell she was entering.

That was it. Cut and dried. How quickly you can kill a living, beating thing. A few well-planned words, a slamming door, and bingo! It's dead. It just seemed so unceremonious, so cold, and so painfully final to her. She felt as though she were in a war.

CHAPTER 25

Her flight to San Francisco was late that night. She was tired, tired from weeks of pretending, scheming, and sickness. As soon as she boarded the 757, she closed her eyes to the cruel world and tried to sleep. Sleep was an evasive creature these days. It was afraid of the person she'd become. It was getting harder and harder to coax it from its perch in the shadows. Right when she almost had it in her grasp, a man's voice loomed in her ear.

"'Scuse me, miss, but you've taken my seatbelt," said the voice.

Without looking at the source, she looked down, undid the seatbelt, dropped his on his seat, and rebuckled her own. Without a word, she closed her eyes again and concentrated on sleeping.

"I'm sorry I had to wake you, but the flight attendant made me. They won't even push back from the gate unless everyone's buckled," the voice apologized.

She ignored the voice and kept her eyes tightly shut. She definitely did not need conversation. She figured he would eventually get the idea. He did not.

"Are you going to want this blanket? There's only one, but you can have it if you want. I don't need it," the voice offered.

She was obviously going to have to be blunt, even blunter than dismissively handing him a seatbelt without looking at him and keeping her eyes closed as he spoke to her. That's pretty blunt. She looked at him finally and said, "I'm trying to sleep."

"Yeah, I see that. That's why I was offering you the blanket. It's freezing in here," he said.

She actually was pretty cold. He had probably noticed the gooseflesh on her arms. Maybe she could fall asleep after all if she was warm. She wasn't happy that he had a good point. Now she had to accept the blanket and thank him and be civil. *Ugh, people.*

"Okay, thanks," she said halfheartedly.

"No problem." He smiled. "Are you on your way home, or are you leaving home?" He tried to open a conversation.

"Leaving," she replied sadly.

"Oh?" he offered leadingly.

Oh, for G—d's sake, did she have to be downright rude?

"Look, thanks for the blanket, but I really don't feel like talking," she started. "I don't want to be rude or anything, but I've been really tired, and I just need to sleep, okay?"

"Oh, sure...sure...I'm sorry. Please don't let me bother you. Go ahead...get some rest," he stammered.

"Thank you," she said more softly, pulled up the blanket, and closed her eyes once again.

After thirty minutes, they were airborne, and her stomach was doing somersaults. The nerves, the illness, and the turbulence were all combining to nauseate her. As she lay there thinking of Peter, she felt worse and worse. She opened her eyes suddenly when they hit an air pocket and found the man next to her watching her intently. That was a little weird. She sat up quickly out of awkwardness and returned his stare. He looked away and pretended to pick lint off his slacks. He attempted to sneak a look back at her from the corner of his eye and found her seemingly waiting for an explanation.

"You looked really uncomfortable, like you were in pain. And you made some sounds, whimpering sounds. Are you okay?" He sounded genuinely concerned.

At that very moment, her stomach heaved, and she vomited, with little warning, mostly into the blanket and partially on him.

"Well, that answers that question," he quipped. "I'll get a flight attendant."

The flight attendant was over in a moment, and he told her what happened and asked her for a fresh blanket, some towels, and a can of club soda. When it arrived, he covered her again and offered her the drink to rinse her mouth. Then he cleaned his slacks with remainder of the club soda. He was blocking her from the aisle and asked her if she needed to get by him to use the restroom, but she didn't trust herself walking in the turbulence. He told her to let him know if she needed anything.

They were quiet for a while, then she said, "Thanks. I'm so sorry. I mean for being so unfriendly, and, you know, for puking on you."

"You weren't unfriendly." He attempted to make an excuse for her behavior. "You were just not friendly. And I'm already cleaned up—no harm done." He smiled with exaggerated friendliness.

They both smiled at that.

"Seriously, if you need anything, my name is Jim, Jim Serafino.

"Hi, Jim, I'm Emily."

"Do you usually get airsick?"

"No. Never."

"You look a little peaked. Do you feel like you might throw up again?" he asked, looking exaggeratedly around as if trying to find a place to take cover.

She laughed at the image of his being afraid of her. It was a genuine laugh for the first time in weeks, which seemed like years. Then she was laughing a little too hard and too long to be considered normal. It was like her body hadn't laughed in so long that its laugh meter was broken and it just couldn't stop. She was feeling a little embarrassed now, but she still couldn't stop.

As she tried to force herself to stop laughing, her eyes filled with tears, and her face crumbled. She was crying now, not just crying, sobbing uncontrollably. She covered her face with her hands and cried hard for the weeks that she had to hold back and repress. The emotional damn had burst, and the best engineering team in the world wouldn't be able to stop the onslaught.

As the moments passed, she became aware that an arm had wrapped around her and was patting her right shoulder tenderly. She finally stopped crying and wiped her face with her hands before lifting her head to find that it was Jim's arm.

"Having a bad day?" he soothed.

"Bad life, actually," Emily replied in monotone.

"Wanna talk about it?" Jim offered.

She hesitated. How could she explain without hurting his feelings that she didn't want to talk to a total stranger about her personal life?

He picked up on her obvious hesitation and quickly, but tactfully, supplied, "I'm actually *Dr.* James Serafino, PhD, in psychology, if that helps."

She stared at him with her red nose and wet lashes and joked, "What makes you think I need professional help? I always have a nervous breakdown after a good laugh."

Now it was his turn to laugh genuinely, including a backward tilt to his head. "You're funny, and that wasn't a nervous breakdown. It was technically only an emotional breakdown. Big difference."

"Sorry to disappoint. I can't even get my breakdowns right. I'll try harder next time," she joked again. She was on a roll now.

She was dabbing at her eyelashes with the corner of the blanket, and he handed her a napkin. She took a deep breath, sat up straight, and weighed how much she would tell him. She'd probably never see him again in her life, and they say unloading your troubles on a stranger can be very healthy emotionally, anonymity and all that psychobabble. She decided to give it a whirl. She didn't want him to think she was crying over nothing, anyway.

She thought for a moment on how to summarize, and in her best journalistic tone, she stated matter-of-factly,

"Well, Dr. Serafino, two weeks ago I was diagnosed with leukemia, very potentially terminal. I didn't tell my fiancé. I left him abruptly, allowing him to believe that I broke up with him because I don't love him anymore, and I am currently on my way to San Francisco for treatment."

He paused, looking straight into her eyes as if to judge whether she was being truthful, decided she definitely was, blinked, and blurted out, "Oh, is that all?" in feigned indifference, with a dismissive wave of his hand.

She stared back with an incredulous look, realized he was mocking her frivolous tone, and slapped him playfully on the arm. They both laughed easily, and at twenty-eight thousand feet in the atmosphere, a friendship was born.

It turned out that he was a practicing psychologist who lived just outside of San Francisco, and fate had the good sense, for once, to seat him in 9E and her in 9F. They (she) talked most of the way to California, mentioning Peter about a thousand times, and by the time they landed, they had exchanged cell phone numbers and promised to get together. Coincidentally, his office was not far from the treatment center she had chosen. He now knew all about Peter and her devotion to him. As a professional mental-health facilitator he didn't approve of her actions, though he had to agree that these were extenuating circumstances and there was no normal procedure. He encouraged her to reconsider telling Peter the truth but was met with a deeply rooted refusal. *Rome wasn't built in a day*, he thought. He'd work on that issue as their friendship grew.

Emily's parents were there to greet her at the airport, and she hugged them lovingly. This would be the last innocent, carefree hug before they find out about her diagnosis. She felt like an assassin, here to behead their happiness. She introduced her parents to Jim as they claimed her bags at baggage claim, then they headed home.

———

Her parents lived in a two-story townhome in the center of the city. She loved it. It was in the middle of all the excitement. She could walk to Union Square and take the trolley everywhere else. She had always loved San Francisco. She hoped coming here for treatment wouldn't taint it for her—if she was still here in five years to be tainted, she added mentally. That's how all the books categorized the success rate of treatment, by five-year increments. *Baby steps*, she thought.

They sat down in the living room to unwind with the fireplace going. Emily mixed them their favorite drinks and sat down for the "talk" she was dreading.

"Is Peter going to be out here for a visit then?" her mother tested.

Uh-oh. Avery Waters was not fooled easily. She wouldn't have become a managing partner of her law firm if she was. She knew something was up, which meant her father knew, too. Hugh Waters was a board member of a major insurance company. They were both forces to be reckoned with.

Emily sat down and smoothed her dress before she began. She felt like she was at a criminal interrogation and had to be flawless.

"I have something unpleasant to share with you. It's not what you think. It's probably worse," she began. "Two weeks ago, I was diagnosed with a serious illness." She didn't want to use the *L* word too quickly because of its gravity. "I've come here for treatment and should be here for a year, at least. I chose not to tell Peter about it but simply left him and let him believe I wanted a new life without him. I'm not proud of that decision, but I did at the time and still do believe it was best for everyone involved. I'll try to answer any questions that you have now."

If she could manage a perfect dismount off the settee, she'd get a perfect ten for that routine.

They both inhaled in unison and looked at one another with a silent communication born from decades of marriage. It made Emily a little jealous actually to see the closeness of a long-term relationship. She'd never know that now. She would never love anyone the way she loved Peter, even if she made it to the first five-year mark. The romantic part of her life was over, and she had held a tiny funeral for it in her mind and put the vestiges in the steel box before she locked it back up.

There was apprehension in Avery's voice as she asked, "What is the diagnosis exactly?"

"Chronic myelogenous leukemia." She closed her eyes at the term.

Her parents both got up off the sofa and walked over and flanked her on the settee. They silently hugged their only child, pressed their foreheads to hers, and cried with her for two full minutes. It was little wonder why Emily didn't want to deal with Peter's reaction; this was the sort of sterile, controlled environment in which she grew up. The love and affection was definitely there, but it was displayed economically.

After this rare display of emotion, they checked themselves and started figuring the logistics of her prognosis and the ensuing treatment. Emily had done her homework and had come prepared. She knew better than to arrive with unanswered questions. She would see a doctor at the treatment center first thing on Monday morning and have all of the proper preliminary tests performed to establish her exact phase of the disease. From there they would design a treatment program tailored to her situation.

On Tuesday, she would meet with the editor of the newspaper for whom she was to freelance. She had contacted them regarding writing some articles chronicling her illness, and they were enthusiastic about the idea. They commended her for her bravado and wanted to meet with her as soon as possible. It felt like she was shipping out to the front and would be covering the war from the battlefield. In essence, she was—the war on cancer anyway. Her parents were impressed, as usual, with her perfectionism and told her that they loved her, were very proud of her, and would do anything for her. She thanked them, of course.

With all that behind them, they resumed their conversation about Peter. Of course, they tried to dissuade her from excluding him but could not. Emily instructed them on her behalf not to give him any information when he called—and he would definitely call. They were simply to tell him that she'd begun a new life and will contact him when she's prepared, also that he should move on and not wait for Emily's call.

Emily didn't care whether they added a few sentiments of their own. She knew they truly loved him like a son and would feel some loss on a personal level. She understood that completely. Peter was a one-of-a-kind. She decided, however, that she would not think about him anymore. She really believed she could control her heart, or her steel box, anyway. She could do anything she put her mind to. In fact, Peter was the one who taught her that, she thought with irony.

———

When we're foolish with the heart, we only fool ourselves.

———

CHAPTER 26

The first round was just a complete physical, including an inspection of her spleen, and more blood tests. After the blood tests came back, the hematologist ordered a bone-marrow biopsy. The bone marrow biopsy was then examined by a cytogeneticist, and it was finally determined that Emily was on the edge between the chronic phase and the accelerated phase of CML. The determining factor between the phases was the percent of blast cells in the blood. Emily had 5.5 percent, which was at the high parameter for the lowest, or chronic, phase. This was exactly what Dr. Crosby had thought based on his examinations. There was still an ominous chance that she would not make the elusive five year mark. The prognosis was undeterminable until she actually began treatment and they could assess how she would respond. In other words, the enemy was evasive and needed to be flushed out of the jungle first.

There were going to be several factors in her treatment. They would include chemotherapy, new drugs such as Gleevec and Interferon, and probably a bone-marrow transplant. They started her with Gleevec. Gleevec is administered orally and has a few side effects. At her age and physical condition, they didn't anticipate any problems, but time would tell.

During the early phase of her treatment, just a few weeks after she left Charlottesville, she had a complication with blood clotting and had to be hospitalized for bleeding. While she was hooked up to several IVs and feeling very poorly, she got a message from her mother that Peter's father had died suddenly of a heart attack. She was grief-stricken and powerless. There was absolutely no possible way for her to attend the funeral, even if she thought she could. And a phone call to Peter right now would undo all the hard work she put into leaving. She was never going to forgive herself for this, but she finally decided that all she could do was send Peter a card, a cold, cardboard, inanimate card. Cancer had robbed her of her body, her heart, and now her soul. She cried all week over this. The doctor finally put her on Percocet to calm her.

About four months after the bleeding problem seemed to be solved, she developed abnormal liver function, one of the rare side effects, and they had to discontinue the Gleevec. This was a setback for the troops. Weary and discouraged, they would have to try alternative weapons that were a little more dangerous and unpleasant. Back to base camp, or the hospital as the locals called it, to regroup and debrief for the next plan of attack. From there, they moved on to traditional chemotherapy.

Emily had never stayed overnight in a hospital in her life. Her parents visited her every day, and she was happy for that. Jim also visited a few days a week. She was surprised to see him the first time but grew to anticipate his visits. The sounds, the sights, the smells, and the entire mood were as strange to her as the front line. She was in the infantry now, and she felt like she needed to keep her head low and her wits sharp.

Everything made her jump with surprise. The nurses and doctors all performed their missions tirelessly and thanklessly. They were the true professional soldiers in this war; she was only an enlisted, here for her tour and either discharged at the end, given leave for a brief period, or sent home in a body bag, a medical chart for her dog tag. There were no rules. Her fate did not depend on her behavior, valor, or purpose; it merely depended on being in the right place at the right time. Dumb luck. She was terrified but marched on with a primitive will to defeat her enemy and survive.

Because she was borderline accelerated phase CML, and they had to stop the Gleevec, the doctor ordered chemotherapy via intravenous drip. The first round of chemo was brutal. Lying there for hours, watching the poison slowly, stealthily enter her body, searching out the enemy and killing it on the spot, Emily was reminded of the period in history when leeches were popular forms of treatment. What would future generations, who hopefully are inoculated soon after birth against all forms of cancer, think of chemotherapy? She had heard that arsenic was the main ingredient in the latest and greatest fight against leukemia. Arsenic? That had to be the Agent Orange of the medical world.

There was collateral damage to every conflict in history. Emily's hair was the first to go. Then her face became hauntingly gaunt, with big dark smudges for eye sockets. Her reflection in the mirror confirmed her capture by the enemy. She had the thin, weak, sickly pallor of a mistreated prisoner of war. Somehow, she drew strength from the image looking back at her, made an about-face, and marched back the laborious three feet to her foxhole of a bed. Her long-term existence felt tenuous at best.

In the evenings, when the she was supposed to be asleep, Emily would lie in her lonely, sterile bed with her eyes wide open, staring at the nothingness that her life had become. This was when the whole floor was perfectly quiet, no doctors or nurses were poking or prodding her weary body, and there was nothing to distract her from her thoughts. Emily's mind would faithfully make its way back to Peter. Sometimes it seemed like she had to search through a thick jungle, turning here and there by instinct, climbing over tangled vines, swimming across great rushing rivers, but she would always find him eventually. He was never very far from her heart or her mind.

Meaningless, inconsequential tears would form dried salty trails on her cheeks by the morning, and she'd wipe them away to hide the evidence of her nightly trysts. She had come to look forward to the pain of reliving her memories with Peter each night. It's the only thing that made her feel alive anymore.

———

A nurse came in one day, uniform jingling with all the ID tags, smiley-face pins, and years of service buttons, and happily began changing the sheets. As she worked, she conversationally asked if the handsome man who always visited her was Peter.

Emily froze and didn't answer, feigning sleepiness from the chemo, but let the nurse keep talking. She supposed a part of her secretly wanted them all to think his name was Peter. It would make Peter seem near, and it was good to hear someone speak the name *Peter*, because she couldn't bring herself to say it these days. The nurse explained matter-of-factly that, on her worst nights, she had been calling for Peter in her sleep, so they assumed that was his name. Emily smiled a vague smile then closed her eyes in an effort to protect herself from the emotion that was stirred and never denied the assumption. The subconscious is a powerful thing. She better not underestimate it.

As the nurse finished her work and her chatter, Jim poked his head in and spoke softly, "Hey there, kiddo."

"Hi," Emily answered sleepily, happy for the distraction at the perfect moment. With Peter's image fresh on her mind, the look on her face was one of honest affection and it disarmed him a little. As the nurse picked up her supplies and started for the door to give them privacy, she smiled at Jim and said,

"Well, speak of the devil! Hi, Peter."

He froze, as if he'd been sucker-punched in the gut, covered up his reaction before Emily noticed, and entered the room. Then he sat down on the edge of the bed, asked how she was feeling today, and gave her several newspapers to read. He usually either brought newspapers, magazines, cards, or something for her to pass her time with. He never showed up empty-handed since she was admitted three weeks ago. Before she was admitted, they had met for lunch once and talked about their lives. He had been dating the same girl on and off for almost a year but told Emily, during one of their heart-to-hearts, that he just couldn't seem to commit to her. The girl didn't push him to, either. She was pretty much married to her career.

Now he had that look on his face. She was in for a lecture; she could always tell. After he handed her the newspapers, he just sat there staring at her with that tsk-tsk expression.

"Emily, I care very much about your well-being, physical and mental." He paused for "serious doctor" effect. "That nurse just called me Peter," he threw out with reproach.

Emily was lost in her own pain and embarrassment so she completely missed the personal injury on his face. "Well, Jim, why on earth did you tell her your name was Peter?" she teased, pretending to be looking at the newspaper.

"Emily," he seemed uncharacteristically impatient, "I didn't, and you know it. Why did she assume I was Peter?"

"I don't know. She just assumed it," Emily answered without looking up from the paper. Maybe he wouldn't notice her discomfort. She sneaked a quick shift of her eyes to see if he was buying it. Stern disapproval all over his face. Nope, no sale.

"Okay. She told me that I mentioned Peter in my sleep a few times. So I guess she made that leap herself." Emily didn't bother to explain that she hadn't corrected her. "Why didn't you correct her?" she reversed the blame. Smooth.

"I will," he defended.

"Good. You don't look like a Peter. You definitely look like a Jim, maybe a Jimbo. Can I call you Jimbo?"

She was really working to get a smile out of him. He had a fantastic smile. The nurses all loved him. She always got a little extra pillow fluffing and water-pitcher filling when he came around. She and Jim joked about it often. "Hey, Emily, if you want an extra dessert I could always come in wearing a tight t-shirt and chaps," he had joked once. She had laughed so hard at the mental image of the serious and austere Dr. James Serafino in chaps that she peed a little. Then she laughed even harder.

"No, you can't call me Jimbo or Bob or Mike—or Peter," he said a little too seriously.

"I've never called you any of those names, *Jim*," she emphasized Jim.

He realized that he was being extra testy about this. And he knew why. And he knew that it wasn't her fault directly. And it wasn't her fault that she called out to Peter in her unconscious mind. He knew that better than anyone. But the fact that she was calling out to him indicated an unhealthy circumstance. She never mentioned him, not even when she was reminiscing. She would carefully use a pronoun in place of his name whenever she could. Classic repression. And it always ended badly. He had to persuade her to contact Peter and clear this all up. That's the only reason he was concerned, he told himself.

"Emily, I just want what's best for you. Everyone deserves the right to the truth, and Peter is no exception. I can't help feeling that he should be standing where I am, bringing you newspapers and making you laugh. The truth is always better for everyone involved, including you. Will you think seriously about it?" he pleaded.

"Oh. Think *seriously*? Oh, I see. Because I've just been playing games here. You think I should think seriously about it? Well,

I guess if you say so. Let's see. Seriously? The truth is what you think Peter needs?"

Uh-oh, Jim was pretty sure he had just unleashed a monster.

"Here's the truth. Peter would have wasted years at my side, seeing me through this. And when I eventually die, he would be alone and older and bitter. It would have stayed with him the rest of his life and changed him. I don't want Peter to change. I want him to live in a world where he can concentrate on his medical career, have kids and a wife. A world where I'm a coldhearted bitch, but at least I'm not losing the battle to cancer. Can you understand that?" she asked this sincerely, not sarcastically.

"Yes. I can completely understand." *I'll be the one who ends up bitter and alone.* Out loud, he said, "But if you're calling names in your sleep, your conscience is plagued, and that's not good for your mental health. I know a little something about this, Emily." He was reminding her that this was, in fact, his area of expertise.

She wanted to change the mood in the room. She always looked forward to his visits because he made her laugh, not deal with reality.

"So is *Jim* short for *James* or *Jiminy Cricket*? Because you're acting an awful lot like my conscience right now. The problem is that you want me to become a 'real girl,' and I want to remain a wooden one."

"Touché, Pinocchio." He chuckled as he tapped her nose with his fingertip. "Just be careful this doesn't grow from all the lies. It's pretty cute the way it is."

He stood up to leave because he had to be at the office soon. He kissed her on the forehead, breathed in her scent without her knowing, closed his eyes to fully appreciate it, and pulled away with a perfected casual face.

"See ya later, gator," he said as casually as he could. *Classic repression,* he thought sardonically.

She smiled as he walked out the door and yelled hopefully, "Will you be back this week?"

"Being swallowed by a giant whale named Monstro couldn't keep me away, kiddo," he replied as he winked and smiled.

Her heart always lifted a little when he smiled at her like that.

After he left, a nurse came in and stated as a compliment, "Peter is such a great guy; you're a lucky girl," as she placed clean towels on the sink.

Without correcting the nurse's use of Peter's name again, she mumbled to herself, "Yeah, I was a lucky girl once. Now I'm a wooden one."

⌣

The heart cannot be fooled; the foolish cannot take heart.

⌣

She had to remain in the hospital for several months due to complications with her liver and spleen. Her hair was pretty much gone now, and her cheekbones were morbidly defined. Jim, true to his word, never missed a visit. He asked her about her articles and how they were coming along. She always brightened up a little when she discussed her writing. He loved to see the twinkle in her eye when she rambled on and on.

She told him that the angle of the story would be a comparison of living with leukemia and being a soldier in a war. He really thought that was fantastic and complimented her wholeheartedly. He talked less and less of her contacting Peter, which was ironic because she thought more and more of Peter. The chemo had been really rough, and she missed him and his quiet strength so much that it scared her sometimes. Not having anyone to kiss good night and say "I love you" to was very lonely, made lonelier by illness.

———

Illness ravages the body, loneliness ravages the soul.

———

CHAPTER 27

It was late one night, and Emily was feeling the effects of the chemicals flowing through her weakened system. She was trying to push back the bile rising threateningly in her throat, ignore the general discomfort, and concentrate on writing her third article in her series, "Leukemia: My Tour of Duty." From the light of her desk lamp, she squinted involuntarily toward the door at the sound of someone being wheeled in.

"We have a playmate for you, Emily," the nurses joked as they positioned the bed across the room from her. It was dark in the room, and Emily couldn't clearly make out the figure in the bed. As soon as they parked the bed they closed the curtains to perform some necessary adjustments to the IV. etc.

After about twenty minutes, the curtains opened unceremoniously. Emily was caught off guard by what her eyes beheld. Silent and pale, lay the tiny figure of a boy, hauntingly still, in the bed across from her. He was so heartbreakingly small and defenseless. The word *leukemia* seemed bigger than him. The single overhead light shining directly on his small, limp frame was a spotlight, causing his sallow skin to glow eerily, emphasizing his vulnerability and frailty.

Emily could not remove her eyes from the heart-wrenching image. He was so pitiable. His skin was so ashen with disease and chemicals that it appeared to have a greenish hue. And his eyes remained dissonantly vacant, open slightly from the pain reducing medication. Emily was frozen. She stared at him for hours, unable to remove her eyes from his image. The small child never moved a muscle.

Her mind continually recalled all the little boys who ran around with seemingly endless energy at the center where she and Peter had volunteered. They tested her patience sometimes. If she gets the chance, they won't test her patience anymore. Relativity. This little boy was far too young and innocent to be a soldier in this battle. It would kill Peter to see this.

———

The following week, Jim had come to visit with a dozen red roses and a birthday balloon for her. He said that he didn't know when her birthday was, so he brought them just in case it was that day. She was touched by that display of thoughtfulness. When he arrived, she and her new roommate, four-year-old Christopher, were playing checkers. Jim had brought him a balloon as well, and he was thrilled.

"Sanks, Jim. I wuv it!" he said with a giant smile.

It was so easy to make Christopher happy. His parents had stepped out for a short time to take showers, eat, etc. and Emily was keeping him company. She felt sick more than not but wanted to help with Christopher as much as possible. The pediatric ward had been overfull, and they had to put him in with her, so he missed out on some of the special things the center did for pediatric patients. In lieu of that, she sometimes played checkers with him or she read books to him. He was the sweetest little boy she ever met. The illness had made him appreciate everything even more, rather than causing bitterness.

Christopher really liked Jim too. Jim had brought him a baseball glove and a ball, in addition to some other small toys, but he never slept without that glove on his hand. Emily asked Jim if he thought it was wise to bring him something that a boy would usually play with outside, but Jim told her that he would play catch with him right there in that hospital room. He explained to Emily that Christopher loved baseball, and when a person loves something that much out of sight, out of mind doesn't work.

"When you love something, you have to face it and embrace it," Jim made his own little saying.

Emily felt that he was trying to sneak in a double meaning to teach her a lesson, but she didn't take the bait, just nodded in understanding.

"When I gwow up, I'm gonna play for the Wed Sox," Christopher said with complete confidence that he really would.

All their hearts broke in unison. They weren't confident that he would get the chance to even go to a Red Sox game. Emily adored the way Jim was with Christopher. It showed her a side of him that was warm and tender and selfless. It reminded her of Peter. When the three of them were alone in the room, they seemed like a small family, and Emily liked to imagine it. She would never let on, but she would fantasize in her mind. Loneliness was a wicked, wicked thing, and it could make someone behave strangely.

Maybe that was why—that afternoon when Christopher had been taken downstairs for tests and they were alone and she lay weak and exhausted in her hospital bed, she did a crazy thing. Jim was preparing to leave for his office, and he bent down as he always did to kiss her on the forehead. At the last second, she lifted her chin so that his lips landed smack on hers.

They held the kiss just past the platonic mark and opened their mouths slightly to let an ounce of sexuality in. After a few moments, he separated reluctantly from her and looked intently into her eyes. He saw only loneliness and shame hiding behind an apologetic smile. He stroked her cheek with the back of his finger lovingly, like he was admiring the feel of a fine silk suit that he had just tried on. But it didn't truly belong to him and probably never would. It was a tender touch full of what could have been.

"Emily, you didn't intend that kiss for me." He was head shrinking.

"I wish I did, Jim," she said in earnest.

"I know," he smiled sadly. He sat on the edge of her bed and held her hand affectionately. "You're sick and you're scared and you need confirmation of being alive. Love and sex are the ultimate in life-affirming activities. You miss Peter and the strength he gave you. But I'm not Peter. I'm very happy to be here for you. I want to be here when you need someone, but you can't replace Peter with me. We'll both end up resenting each other. When and if you ever kiss me again, I want it to be me you're kissing.

"When you get the results of your progress next week, I really think you should call Peter. The doctors have all told us that you've turned the corner, thank G-d. You left him because you thought you were dying, Emily. That was almost a year ago. Now he may or may not have moved on, but you haven't, and you have to face this before you can." His face changed slightly then. He went from professional looking with direct eye contact and certainty in his voice to lowering his eyes to their hands and speaking softer, almost shyly. "I'm not as strong and noble as you seem to think I am." He paused, kept his head down, and spoke even more softly with a catch in his voice. "If you kiss me like that again, Emily, I…well, I don't know…" he warned, shaking his head, then met her eyes with a hungry gaze.

A lonely tear fell down her cheek to match the loneliness she felt for Peter. Jim did not reach up to wipe it away; that would be up to her. It remained there, dried onto her skin, leaving a salty trail, long after he had left the room with his head hung down.

The following week was Christopher's bone-marrow transplant. He passed Emily as he was wheeled out the door and attempted to wave to her. It looked more like a salute because he couldn't lift his arm up very high with the IV attached to it, so she gave the snap of a salute back. Off to another battlefront.

"See you soon, Christopher! I'll be right here, waiting with your favorite book!"

He loved when she read to him from Dr. Seuss's *Sleep Book*. All the funny words made him laugh. The trick was to read it out loud as fast as she could to him without making a mistake, practically impossible with all the tongue-twisting words. *Foona-Lagoona Baboona*, *Hinkle-Horn Honkers*, and *Biffer-Baum Birds*. Christopher laughed so hard she never tired of reading it to him. "Pwease wead it again, Emiwee, pweeeeease," he would beg. How could she resist? They had become very close.

Somehow, he reminded her of Peter as a small boy. It might have been his sweet and kind disposition or his affection for her. Or maybe it was just that everything reminded her of Peter. So much for not thinking of him.

She prayed all night long for Christopher to do well today. The world seemed completely upside down to her when such a small, innocent child could be put through such a living hell. It tested her faith to its very core, but she prayed all night, anyway.

She had been up most of the night thinking and praying when around 2:00 a.m., she heard whispering. She listened closer and realized it was Joanne, Christopher's mother. Joanne was kneeling by his bed, bargaining with G-d. She pleaded with him, through a tear-choked voice, that if he needed to take a soul, to please let it be her own instead of Christopher's.

As Emily heard Joanne say the words "Let it be me," she thought of the Beatles' song "Let it Be." As she recalled the lyrics, she mused at how it seemed like Paul McCartney wrote those lyrics for this very moment. The image of that anguish, despair, and selflessness became a part of Emily that would never leave her. This was trench warfare. We were all just sitting ducks, and fate was locked and loaded.

Jim came in during the morning because he knew it was the big day for Christopher. They hadn't seen or talked to each other since the kiss. Although, it was the last thing on their minds right now.

"Hi, Emily," he said tenderly.

He knew she'd be upset today. He found her working feverishly on her article. She was looking so much better. She was really hoping that her article would stir more attention and bring even more awareness to the public about the disease and the medical community's efforts to find cures. She had originally offered to do the article simply to keep her hand in journalism throughout her treatment, but when she discovered the disproportionate number of children, that more than a quarter of kids with cancer were affected by different types of leukemia compared to other cancers, her own efforts became more altruistic. It felt really good to be doing something more important than writing just to write, more important than dealing with her own illness, and even more important to her than losing Peter. Peter would be so proud of her right now.

Jim was saying something as he watched her writing, but she didn't hear him. "I'm so proud of you, Emily," he repeated, unheard, to the top of her head as she wrote.

"Oh, hi, Jim," she said belatedly without lifting her head. "Give me one minute, okay?"

True to her word she lifted her head after about sixty seconds and bestowed him with a brilliant smile that said everything was fine between them.

"I'm so glad you're here, Jim," she said genuinely with a spark in her eyes that disease and poison couldn't erase.

When she was writing a story that she believed in, she became so passionate. It was the only kind of passion Jim would probably ever get to witness in her, so he relished it while he could. All he could think of when he looked at her like that was what a poor schmuck Peter was. The guy didn't stand a chance of a normal life after Emily.

"Guess what?" she dangled.

Jim thought he felt a spark jump out of her eyes and land on his shirt—she was so excited. "What?" he said as if playing a child's game.

"I just got word from a nurse that Christopher did extremely well and should be back home—I mean, in our room, soon!" She looked like a little girl on Christmas morning.

Jim's relief was clearly evident. He inhaled as he looked upward, closed his eyes, and exhaled, "Thank G-d." He was truly afraid for the little guy. He had talked with Christopher's parents on several occasions and offered friendly counseling for the family if they wanted it.

Emily was improving considerably. The test results indicated that the cancer cells were reduced significantly but not eradicated. As soon as the cancer was completely gone, and she was in remission, she would need a bone-marrow transplant in order to implant healthy blood cells to hopefully take root and grow in her bones.

Her parents were encouraged with the news and anxious to get her home and ready for the last round of treatment. Her father came to the hospital several times a week, and her mother still visited every day after leaving her office. They saw Jim visiting a lot more and more every week. They were growing concerned that Emily was misleading him, even if unintentionally. When they spoke to Emily about it, she waved it off as crazy. *He's just a friend*, she kept assuring them. They weren't convinced.

It had been a long row to hoe for Emily. She had landed in San Francisco ten months ago. They started the process of finding a bone-marrow donor right away, but it would take months, maybe longer. If she had had siblings, especially a twin, this process might have been shorter. She could donate her own marrow once she was in remission, but that would weaken her further and take longer. She spent two months preparing for treatment, four months on Gleevec, another two months preparing for chemotherapy, and still another two months receiving chemotherapy. She would get two months off now. Then she would be back for more chemo and radiation for a few weeks before they were ready to perform the bone marrow transplant.

The longer the treatment took, and the more she suffered, the better she felt about her decision not to tell Peter. This was actually a no-lose situation for her, she told herself. Either she went into remission right away and everything progressed as the doctors had wanted—win, or she was sick a long, agonizing time and suffered a grievous end, and that only reinforced her reason for leaving Peter in the first place—another win, sort of. Emily just seemed to be winning left and right. Therefore, those tears she shed when she lay in bed every night thinking of Peter must have been tears of happiness, not regret, she resolved.

The day came for Emily to leave the hospital. Her cancer cells were finally at an acceptable number, and she just had to wait for a donor now. On her last day with Christopher, as she was teaching him a new card game called war, he looked at her as if he had a question that he wanted to ask but was afraid to.

Emily made it easy for him. "What's on your mind, soldier?"

"I'm gonna miss you," he said honestly.

"I'm gonna miss you too, buddy. But I'll visit you all the time. Okay?" she promised.

"Weally?" he asked skeptically.

"Sure! I would miss you way too much if I didn't," she assured him.

Then he looked at her with disappointment, confusion, and sorrow. The look on his face was uncannily scary. It was the same exact face that Peter made when she told him she was leaving. It gripped her heart and squeezed until she had to inhale suddenly so she could breathe again.

As chills ran up and down her spine, she couldn't believe her own ears as he asked, "Do you love me, Emily?"

It took her a minute for the shock to wear off, then she answered, "Of course I do, Christopher. I love you, and I will visit you."

A flood of relief washed over his little face, and he said, "Okay, good. I believe you because my mommy said that you can't lie to people you love."

Tears filled her eyes as she found herself having to agree in spite of the contrast in her mind. She loved Peter so much, yet she had had to lie to him, hadn't she? His naïve words rang in her mind all afternoon. It was as if he had seen inside her past, her soul, and was testing her. Out of the mouths of babes…

As Emily left the hospital, she took in the scene around her seemingly in slow motion. There were doctors and nurses hurrying in every direction. There were patients who looked like death warmed over. There were brokenhearted families holding each other up in their grief. All that was missing was the smoke from the bombs. It was a war-torn scene, and she had her leave papers, with orders to report back for duty in just a few months. She reminded herself that she was glad Peter didn't have to be a witness to this tragic conflict.

CHAPTER 28

Emily was back at her parent's house, and in a couple of weeks, she was feeling a lot better. She spent a few days a week at the hospital, volunteering and especially visiting Christopher. He was having good days and bad. His body wasn't accepting the transplant as well as they had hoped, so he had to take a lot of autoimmune medicine. He felt too sick most of the time to play or read, so Emily would just sit in his room with his mother. The bond between a mother and child was incredible to say the least.

Emily had wanted to have children more than anything in this world. Peter's children. She knew now that that would never happen. The prospect of her body being able to recover well enough, without the need for ongoing autoimmune medication would be highly unlikely. Frequently, radiation in such high doses causes sterility. She wondered often, lately, what Peter had done after she left. She hoped he was happy by now. She hoped her heart wasn't broken in vain. She had not expected to be doing so well so soon, but she still had the bone-marrow transplant ahead of her. And quite often, Christopher's words about lying to people you love haunted her.

The months inched along, and Emily was getting used to having hair and not feeling nauseated all the time. She spent a lot of time with her parents. She hadn't been home all that much since she left for school years ago, so they had a lot of catching up to do. She saw Jim a lot as well. They had a very easy friendship. They never brought up the uncomfortable subject of the unintended kiss. They shared a lot in common, they made each other laugh, and Jim was very kind. She also spent a lot of time working on her series for the paper. It had done really well, and she was very proud of it. She was originally only supposed to write three articles in the series, but the paper signed her up for three more because of its success.

Her life was almost back to a new normal, an "after Peter" normal, though she was very tired most of the time. She had had to make several lengthy trips to visit Christopher because he had been moved to a different facility for trial medications. She spoke to Joanne often and stayed informed of his progress, which was slow but steady. His battle was uphill, and the troops were weary.

In the middle of her second year apart from Peter (her own personal AD), they found a bone-marrow-donor match. The reinforcements had arrived! She had to go back to the hospital for another round of radiation to prepare for her transplant.

She visited Christopher before she went in and explained to him that she would be in the hospital for a little while and wouldn't be able to visit him, but that she would think of him every day and come to see him the minute she was able to. And she reminded him that she loved him. He gave her a precious smile that told her that was okay and he believed her because you can't lie to people you love. She had a lot to learn about love and trust from this brave little guy.

Emily was very weak due to the higher dose of chemotherapy that was necessary prior to the transplant. It actually was intended to kill all of her own bone marrow in preparation for the grafting of new marrow from the transplant. And when the transplant was finally performed, it would take up to eight weeks of blood transfusions and high doses of antibiotics before they would know if the transplant was successfully grafting. Her hair was thin again, her skin pallid, and her stomach constantly retching. Transplant recipients are at high risk for infection, so extra care had to be taken from visitors.

Jim still came faithfully, scrubbing up and wearing a mask.

"You don't have to visit me this much, you know. You should be out dancing with what's-her-name," she told him.

To which, Jim replied, "I know I don't have to—I want to. And I haven't seen what's-her-name in months."

There was no way she was going to convince him, and she didn't have the energy to try harder. She heard a subconscious warning bell at the news of him not dating anyone, but she ignored it, actually hid from it, because she really liked him being there. She smiled to let him know that, because she was too weak to keep talking.

Little by little, with a few touch-and-go days, Emily felt better and better, though she would remain in the hospital for two months. The final tests were going to be performed in a few days. If the transplant was a success in replacing her cancer-ridden white-blood cells with cancer-free cells *and* she didn't reject the donor marrow, she would be considered to be in remission. All she could think of at this prospect was Peter.

The two months passed slowly, but the tests results were finally back, and the doctor came in to explain them when her mother and Jim happened to be in the room visiting. They were piercing the doctor with their eyes in intense concentration on what he was about to tell them. It was as if he were holding a grenade, and they didn't know if he was going to pull the pin and toss it at them or simply place it back in his pocket and leave the room. He let them off the hook quickly and was happy to inform them that the grafting seemed to be a success so far!

Emily wasn't even sure she heard correctly. She looked to Jim, but his face was turned and shielded from her view, intentionally—too much emotion. She looked to her mother and found her smiling through her tears, so she assumed she heard correctly. The relief was like a tidal wave washing over her, but she felt so differently than she expected at the good news. She thought she'd be overjoyed and elated, but she had mixed feelings of joy and guilt.

She had met many cancer patients since she'd been here. Many of them survived, while a good number didn't. What had she done differently than the ones who didn't make it? Nothing. She'd heard people say G-d spared him or she beat the cancer when referring to other patients who survived. She couldn't help but see the absurdity in these comments. They didn't mean harm, but what did this say to the families of those patients who passed away? That they didn't fight hard enough or G-d didn't choose to spare them.

Cancer is nondiscriminatory. Cancer is unpredictable. Cancer is difficult to treat. Cancer knows not who its victim is. Cancer could happen to anyone, anytime, and they may live or they may die. But it is not a punishment or a lesson learned; surviving it is not a reward for a job well done—it's simply good fortune. It is researched by science, it is treated by science, and it is explained by science. To read anything else into it is to take away the dignity and the honor of all who fall prey to it. As one soldier crouches in a foxhole next to his fellow soldiers and gets shot to death while his comrades escape to safety, is he any more or less worthy or is it just a matter of luck? She didn't want to be revered as having done anything to deserve remission. She was relieved beyond belief, but she was no more deserving than every one of the other patients here. She was not a hero any more than every other cancer victim across the globe who lives or dies.

And she was not out of the woods yet anyway. It would take a few more months to be sure that her body didn't reject the transplant. Now the only thing left was to stay on autoimmune meds, like interferon injections for an indefinite period of time to keep the new blood cells from forming cancerous cells.

As soon as she was able, she visited Christopher to give him the good news. She took one look at his emaciated body, and her blood ran cold. The trial medications were not working as well as they hoped. There was one more new medication they could try and he was to start it the next day. She told him she'd be there more now, and he smiled. His smile looked very different. It looked knowing, somehow. It looked serene and fulfilled. Maybe she was thinking of him too much lately, but Christopher's smile looked like Peter's.

Now all she could think about at this point was Peter. With the new life that was just seemingly breathed into her, she had a new thirst for life. It increased with each passing day, and she was 100 percent sure that she wanted to contact Peter and try to mend their broken lives back together. She started thinking about what she would say to him. She could hardly believe she was going to do this. It had seemed like a fantasy for so long. In her mind, she'd become the tragic princess locked in a tower and placed under an evil spell, and Peter was the brave prince who loved her truly and would rescue her, except she herself had cut his legs out from under him. She would wait one or two more months until all her tests showed her accepting the graft, then she would call Peter and hand him his new legs.

It was about two years after she had arrived in San Francisco, and she was doing remarkably well. The last big hump had been the possibility of her body rejecting the transplant, but she just had blood work done, and the doctor at last waylaid those fears. She was on cloud nine. She had just left the doctor's office with her fantastic news and rushed home to share it with her parents.

All the way home, she thought only of what she would say to Peter when she called him. First, she would have to find out what he was doing, if he was in a relationship with someone else. The possibility of that more than worried her, but she had to find out. Then if he was unattached, she would have to figure out a way to explain the last two years and hope that he could forgive her. There were a lot of hoops to jump through, but she was still in love with him and very anxious to try to rebuild their life.

As soon as she walked in the door, her good mood was stolen away. Her mother's eyes were red and swollen. She had answered a phone call for Emily. It was about little Christopher. He was gone.

It was a beautiful, sunny day in San Francisco. The weather seemed to be a reflection of Christopher's sunny disposition, even in the face of all that suffering. Not a drop of rain interfered with the procession. Jim and her parents joined Emily to pay their respects.

The funeral for Christopher was the saddest thing she had ever seen in her life, from the tiny-sized casket to the handful of photos from his short life, all ending at four-years-old. No pictures of his first day of school, no graduation, no wedding, no fishing trips with his children, no retirement vacations. There weren't many pictures at all, but in every single one, Christopher had a big smile on that precious little face. They all learned a valuable lesson about the human spirit that day, and they learned it from a four-year-old boy. Faith is a thin sheet of ice upon which one must tread lightly. The death of a young boy like Christopher is a fracture in that ice, a fracture that reminds everyone of the fragility of life.

Though it was painfully difficult, Emily decided to say a few words at her young friend's service. She told the sorrowful crowd that one of his favorite things to do was to have her read his favorite book to him. She continued to explain to them that his favorite book was Dr. Seuss's *Sleep Book*. He had told her that he loved it best because he loved to sleep. In his sleep, he could dream about doing all the things that he couldn't really do like swim, and run, and especially play baseball. Without explaining further, she took out the book and read from his favorite page.

> Speaking of dreaming, I think you should note, that the Bumble-Tub Club is now dreaming afloat. Every night they go dreaming down Bumble-Tub Creek, except for one night, every third or fourth week, when they stop for repairs 'cause their bumble-tubs leak. But tonight they're afloat, full of dreams, full of bliss. And that's why I'm bothering telling you this.

She stood silent for a moment while she collected herself. Then she simply closed the book and quietly wished Christopher sweet dreams, full of bliss. As she walked over to the small casket, she couldn't help but think that there should have been an American flag draped across it to mark this short life as the life of a brave soldier in the war against leukemia. She knew because she'd been his comrade, at his side in the trenches. She saluted him as she left.

As soon as she got home, with her soaked handkerchief in one hand, she picked up the phone with the other and called the hospital in Virginia where Peter had worked. She could think of nothing else. She needed Peter more than anything right now. Christopher's death occurring simultaneously with her remission wreaked havoc with her mind. She had just been about to celebrate when she got the news about Christopher and she couldn't shake the survivor's guilt she felt.

When the anonymous hospital operator answered, she didn't ask to talk to Peter. She simply asked if he was still the chief resident. The answer was no. The operator was proud to tell the unknown caller that he had left a few months ago to join a team of Doctors Without Borders. The hospital had no idea where he was sent.

As she thanked the operator and hung up, she was stunned into silence. All this time. She went through so much—a living hell. She came so far. And he's gone? Unreachable? She called the organization headquarters in New York, but they wouldn't give her any information—"Confidential and immediate family members only," was what they told her. It hit her like a slap on the face; she used to be his immediate family. They said she would have to call his family.

Fate really was unkind. She couldn't call his mother, not without talking to him first. She didn't want to face that music just yet, without knowing if Peter would receive her or not. She would simply have to wait until he returned. She occasionally called the hospital to find out about his return. But for months, she received the same answer over and over: "We haven't heard anything yet."

CHAPTER 29

In March of the next year, as she waited anxiously for word of Peter's whereabouts, Emily had finally finished her series on leukemia for the paper and was honored with a literary award and a handsome bonus. She donated the entire bonus to leukemia research in Christopher's name. Jim attended the award ceremony with her. She had been very depressed since Christopher's funeral, and she hadn't wanted to attend the ceremony at all. She didn't feel like she earned an award. She had simply written the truth. Cancer is hell—just like war.

Jim convinced her to go to the ceremony by saying that it would bring even more awareness to the need for additional research funds. She couldn't argue with that. He had learned how to appeal to her: through her sense of duty. He had learned a lot of things about her over the last two plus years. Loyalty, duty, and righteousness were her strongest qualities. He had stopped dating because he found himself constantly measuring up other women to Emily, and none of them even came close.

Emily noticed that their conversations never included recent dates or romantic escapades but never said anything. She had grown dependent on his friendship. She knew it wasn't fair to him, but she couldn't stop herself. Maybe she didn't want to. She blamed it on loneliness.

It had been several months since Emily had first tried to contact Peter. Jim never knew she had tried to contact him, and he never suggested it anymore. They were at the award ceremony when Jim asked her to dance. She accepted, and he led her to the floor. They fit surprisingly nicely together, and he was a smooth dancer. They talked and laughed and danced all night. It was the first time she laughed in a long while, and it felt like heaven. Jim was so happy. He wanted to be happy like this the rest of his life. He wanted her for the rest of his life.

They were walking home from the restaurant where the ceremony was held. The night air was chilly, and Emily rubbed her arms to warm herself up. Jim noticed and put his arm over her shoulders to draw her close to him for warmth. She felt slightly uncomfortable, but at the same time, she felt cared about, and that felt good. She looked up at him without words and smiled a thank you. They were only six blocks from her parents' place when Jim stopped under a streetlamp, turned toward her, held her hands in his, and asked her what her long-term plans were.

"I don't know. Long term is something new for me to think about," she answered honestly.

"Do you think you'll stay in California?" *As opposed to Virginia*, was what he was leaving out.

She paused as she studied his face. She knew where this was going. He had been such a great friend, a gentleman, and so patient and so loyal and so caring. He's the one who deserved the award, not her. He was looking at her now with sincere earnest and—love? She guessed she already knew that he was in love with her. She pretended, even to herself, that she didn't know, but she did. She didn't know if she would ever find Peter again. And if she did, if he would already have someone else or even want her back. She had to know all this before she could have a fair relationship with Jim. She wouldn't cheat him like that. Jim deserved to be number one in someone's life.

"I honestly don't know, Jim," was her carefully constructed answer. She gave him direct eye contact as she said it.

"Do you *want* to stay in California—with me, Emily?" He dared with an equally direct gaze.

"Jim, I don't know what to say to that."

"That says it all, Emily." He sounded very disappointed as he let go of her hands and took a step back with his head down.

"You don't understand what I mean, Jim. I haven't told anyone this, but I've actually been trying to contact Peter for some months now," she admitted, a little ashamed, though she knew she had no reason to be.

"Oh, I had no idea. Trying?" he asked, wounded but hiding it.

"Yeah. All I could find out is that he has joined Doctors Without Borders. They won't tell me where he was sent, strictly confidential, I guess. He should be back before too long, because their missions are typically only one year. I could call his mom in the meantime, but I probably wouldn't be able to reach him until he gets back anyway, so I figured, why involve her prematurely until I know what his status is? Same goes for his brother, sister, and friends. If I reach him and he's involved with someone, then I can just exit his life again cleanly. He doesn't—no one has to know about my leukemia or any of this. I just feel better about it this way. You know what I mean?"

They had started walking again, and as she asked the last question, she stopped and turned toward him for his response, his usual go-with-the-flow, don't-demand-anything response. He was just staring at her as if she weren't real. That's how he felt. He'd been so close, yet so far away all this time. He couldn't stand the not-knowing anymore. He wasn't angry, just in love.

They had stopped near her door. He pulled her to him uncharacteristically firmly and turned her so that her back was to the wall, literally and figuratively. He slid his fingers threw the short hair on either side of her head. He felt as though he owned that hair; it was his—it belonged to him because he saw it grow in from nothing—baldness,—not Peter. He knew it wasn't Peter's fault, but it wasn't his fault, either, and he was sick of having to be the good guy, the understanding one.

In a way, he did blame Peter. If Emily had been his, he would have moved heaven and earth to find her. What's wrong with this Peter guy anyway? *He's not worthy*, Jim told himself. He knew he wasn't making sense, that Peter was not to blame, and he was probably a great guy if Emily was so devoted to him, but he wanted to hate him so he could confess his feelings for Emily without guilt. He held her there proprietarily for a full minute, just searching her eyes for any glimmer of longing or even just a response to his longing. She didn't try to get free. She didn't take her eyes off his.

"Jim," she whispered.

Was it a question? Was it a plea? Was it an invitation? He didn't know. He never knew with her. Her signals were so mixed it made him crazy. He knew instinctively that he was at a fork in the road. He had to act now or never. For once, he decided to do whatever came naturally to him. He closed the space between them and opened his mouth over hers, moving his lips and tongue with all the desire he had pent up in almost three long years.

G-d, it felt good. She felt good and tasted good. This was right. She didn't pull away. She kissed him back. She definitely kissed him back. She hadn't been kissed like that in a very long time. The carnal urge to be alive, fully alive, was innate. She'd been so close to death. It had been all around her for almost three years, hovering over her like a vulture circling its prey. The rush of desire in her whole body was a drug. She could feel it racing through her veins and breathing life into her, awakening a dormant beast.

He drew away and looked at her closely to assess the damage. Seemingly none. He was anxious. He was in uncharted territory, and he didn't know what to do next. So he kissed her again, not as greedily this time, more slowly and more tenderly. When he pulled away and searched her eyes this time, what he found brought a smile to his own lips. Her lips were swollen, and her eyes were half mast with the grogginess of yearning. There was a slight blush on her soft, sunken cheeks that made her look more alive. She wasn't angry or even put off. She just looked relieved.

"Wow," she said.

"Wow," he repeated.

"Do it again," she whispered.

"Gladly." He smiled.

They stood there on the doorstep for a long while, kissing and holding each other in the damp San Francisco night air. They entered the vestibule to allow for more privacy and intimacy. With each kiss, they grew more and more familiar with each other. His gentle hands roamed over her small, weary frame as if she was on fire and he had to rub out the embers. Her body responded willingly and unconsciously. Her leg lifted to his hip in an effort to get even closer than their melded bodies already were.

As she pressed against him, she found no doubt of his desire for her. He kissed her whole face, her neck, and then moved south hesitantly as he undid the top two buttons of her silk blouse. He looked questioningly into her eyes; she closed them, dropped her head backwards, and pulled his head and his lips to her pounding heart. She moaned in pleasure, and he returned to her lips to answer the moan. They separated for air only for a moment and looked fervently into each other's eyes. They were both out of breath, lips full from the activity, and faces radiating with passion.

"Jim," was all she could manage, again.

He was feeling very brave and very confident, so he decided to go full throttle and tell Emily how he really felt. He held her small, frail hands in his and looked down at the image their hands made together.

With his head still down, he said, "Emily, I have something I want to tell you. I just think you should know the truth before we go any further."

"What?" she asked out of formality. She didn't really want to talk just now.

He looked up at her then with a hopeful smile and whispered, "I love you. I have since the day we met on the airplane a million years ago. I love you, and I want you to be mine. I know I shouldn't. I know you have unresolved issues. As a psychologist, I know you're not ready for a new relationship, but as a man, I want you so badly right now I think I may come apart at the seams." He paused, lowered his head, and added with pain in his voice, "Please, Emily."

She felt slapped, backhanded, right across the cheek. It was reality coming to call. As soon as she heard Jim's words, she thought to herself, *I already belong to somebody else and he said those same two last words when he begged me not to leave him.* She kissed him one more time to store up for the lonely road ahead of them but never answered verbally.

He noticed the lack of "I love you too" but was not surprised. He was happy for whatever she was able to give him. He was so happy to at least be able to tell her that he loved her. He was delirious to be holding her close and kissing her. He was happier than he'd ever been, except for the day the results came back negative for her cancer-cell test.

It was late, and she didn't want to lead him so far down a path that they couldn't find their way back. The more she kissed Jim, the more she wished it was Peter she was kissing. As her mind took control of the situation, Emily pushed him gently away. He knew exactly what she meant with that push, and he knew, personally and professionally that she was absolutely right, but he still wanted her. He was a psychologist, but he was also a man.

He took a few deep breaths to restore some oxygen to his brain, then he smiled and backed up reluctantly. He told her he'd give her a little time and space to figure this all out, but he wasn't going back to their old modus operandi. He loved her, and he wanted a life with her—with the real girl, not the wooden one. She told him how much she cared about him and really loved being with him, but she had a lot of things to figure out. She hung her head in a way that let him know that she was speaking of Peter. He held her chin up with one finger to kiss her lips one more time with exaggerated tenderness. It was a "Well, at least I tried" sort of kiss. Then he simply said good night and left.

As she lay in bed that night, she thought about Jim and his words to her. She relived the events of the evening. He was fantastic. Her body responded to his with undeniable desire. He was strong and gentle. She must have missed the intimacy of sex more than she thought. There's no doubt that she could have been very, very happy in Jim's bed and in Jim's life, if she had met him first before Peter. She pictured a future with Jim as her partner. Then she thought of Peter—of all the years they had spent together, then as he had looked when she left him, so hurt and broken—and cried herself to sleep from loneliness.

CHAPTER 30

Emily found herself wandering through the empty streets of San Francisco. The city was eerily quiet—not a soul in sight. Every familiar corner seemed somehow unfamiliar. Things that were well known to her now appeared to be strange. She peeked in the window of her favorite bookstore, but there were no books, only empty shelves. She went down the street to her favorite coffee shop to see the girl who cheerily sold her coffee every day. The girl was gone, and so were all the other employees; in their places were spooky marionettes.

She started to panic, and she became desperate for something she didn't know what. But she felt she had to start searching. She ran up and down the streets, from block to block, always sure that what she was looking for would be right around the next dark corner. Suddenly she saw the back of a familiar-looking man and yelled out, but he turned the corner without looking. She tried to catch him, but just as she turned the corner, he had gone into a store. She ran up to the store and followed him in. She heard a voice. It was Peter's voice!

She followed it. In a back room, she found a man with his back turned. She heard him speaking, couldn't make out what he was saying, but she was sure it was Peter. She spoke to him. Then the room became a bedroom, and he turned very quickly, grabbed her, and threw her passionately onto the bed. Suddenly she was naked, but he wasn't. He was heavily clothed, and she couldn't see his face. She said his name as a plea, "Peter, Peter," but he didn't answer.

He caressed her naked flesh, kissed her lips to hush her, moved his tongue across her breasts lovingly, and she responded ardently. She could feel her groin unfold as a flower after the rain, when the warm sunshine falls upon it. Her whole body became a receptor for his body. She wanted him so badly. She lifted her hips toward him to let him know that she was his and would do anything for him. Just as he slid gratifyingly into her, they both reached their climax, and he rested his body on top of hers heavily and possessively.

Something felt wrong—unfamiliar. Then he spoke closely in her ear, "Now you're mine forever, Emily." With a sudden burst of panic, she realized at the sound of his voice that this was Jim and not Peter! Oh my G——d! Oh my G——d! What have I done? she thought to herself. She tried to run, she tried to yell, but her body and her voice wouldn't work. She was straining to shout, but nothing would come out. Jim's face became clouded with disappointment and pain because he thought she was ignoring him, but she couldn't make her voice work. She heard a bell in the distance, a doorbell, or a bicycle bell, or a phone. That was it! A phone!

She pushed Jim off of her and kept her hand out to keep him away as she searched the bed for the ringing phone, knowing instinctively that it was Peter trying to call her. If she didn't answer in time, he would never call again. He would somehow know that she had slept with Jim, and he wouldn't want her anymore. She had to find that phone before Peter hung up forever!

———

She sat bolt straight up in her bed, sweating and panting, and now wide awake. She heard a real phone ringing and grabbed her cell phone from the nightstand. It was Jim calling, and it was nine thirty in the morning.

"Hello?" she said breathlessly into the phone.

"Hi, kiddo. Just called to say good morning. Did I wake you?" he asked.

"Yeah, but I'm glad. I was having an awful dream," she answered, feeling a little guilty.

"About what?" Jim asked suspiciously.

Emily thought for a second, woke up fully, and remembered that Jim was a headshrinker. As the details of the dream filtered into her conscious she decided there was no way she was telling him about this dream. He'd have a field day with it.

"Oh, nothing. I dreamt that all the libraries had closed for renovations at once, and I couldn't go to one for a long time!" she manufactured.

"Figures. You and your libraries. You're a nerd, but you're a cute nerd," he said affectionately.

"I gotta go. Wanna have dinner with me tonight?" he added as nonchalantly as possible.

"Well, yes. But no secluded front porches this time, okay? I just need to get my head together," she said sweetly. "I'm not saying I didn't willingly participate last night, but you're like a superhero of a kisser, like Superman or something," she added to interject a little levity to the situation.

"Okay, Lois," he joked back. "I'll pick you up at six, and I won't even bring my cape."

She laughed with relief that he got her message and no one had to get hurt—yet. However, in the light of day, and after the way that dream made her feel, it was very clear to her what she had to do. She had to call Peter's mom. It was going to be very, very hard. Phyllis was a loving person. They had always got along extremely well, but it's been a long time since the sudden breakup, not only chronologically speaking, but in life years, even longer. She had left so much unsaid and unexplained, Phyllis must certainly harbor resentment on behalf of her son. She had to really think about what she would say. She called Jim and told him what her plans were, and he warily agreed to give her the space to do this, saying unconvincingly that he understood.

———

She dialed Phyllis later that day, when she had worked out exactly what she would say. It rang six times, and with each ring, Emily's heart stopped. Suddenly there was the tinny, cold voice of an answering machine. She had decided ahead there would no messages, too complicated for that.

Now what? She headed to the computer downstairs for her daily search for Peter. She kept hoping that there would be an article about him somewhere. She absentmindedly Googled Peter's full name, combined with *Charlottesville* and the hospital's name, as she did every day. The indicator on the search engine twirled in a circle as the database was searched. It always gave her a mental image of a microworld with tiny, little micro-robots busily running in all directions, pushing buttons and calculating numbers. Computers amazed her. Unexpectedly, the twirling stopped, like a spinning prize wheel at a carnival, and something actually came up this time!

She was afraid to look, in case it was just another dead end. She squinted at the screen to soften the blow—and bingo! A website for a small bar in Charlottesville was advertising. It said that Dr. Peter Daniels had taken a break from his position at the hospital and was enjoying performing with his band at local hot spots. It went on to give a brief and uninformative bio and that he would be performing his first solo at the Ends of the Earth on Saturday, April 7, next month! She found him! She screamed and jumped and cried. She found Peter!

She silently thanked G-d and the tiny micro-robots in computer world. She was trembling with excitement. This was the happiest she'd been since she got the negative results to her cancer-cell test.

At dinner that night, Jim, however, was not as enthusiastic about the news as Emily was, though he hid it well. Above everything else, he did want Emily to be happy. As a psychologist, he knew that she needed closure to her relationship with Peter before she could move forward in her life with him or anybody else, for that matter. The circumstances of their situation lent themselves to more compassion and understanding than a traditional love triangle.

Emily checked her delight when she told Jim about the website that mentioned Peter. She would be leaving soon, and it overshadowed everything. She tried to let Jim know how much she cared for him and how highly she regarded him, but all her attempts made him sound like a close second best, a poor girl's Peter, so she refrained from making those comments any further. They avoided any more romantic interludes, but they did see each other every day. He made her promise to call him as soon as she knew anything. She knew he thought there was a chance for happiness between them, but he didn't understand how determined she was to be with Peter. The only thing that would stop her was if she found him married to someone else. Since he went to Somalia for a year, she figured he wasn't married. And that was very encouraging to her. At this point, nothing else would keep her from pursuing him, she thought.

She had believed her tour of duty was over when she received the news of her remission, her own personal VE Day, but again, there was collateral damage to every war, and this war was no exception. Parents, siblings—anyone who loses a loved one to a terminal illness would all agree. The hostages had not all been freed in this war. Jim had been held hostage merely for being an ally—an incredible ally, and their budding relationship was the collateral damage. He deserved more than she could give him, but he deserved honesty more than anything. Emily would ship out in less than two weeks, headed back East, to claim what's left of her civilian life. The soldier's weary return from the battlefield.

———

Emily's parents were sad to see her leave but understood her wanting to go. This was going to be very hard for her, and they knew that it occupied all her thoughts. They had a nice going away dinner for her and said their good-byes the morning she left. They let Jim take her to the airport because they were aware of the tension between them.

The drive to the airport was painfully quiet. Jim looked somber, and Emily didn't want to address the obvious elephant in the room, but she didn't want to trivialize it either with small talk. So they remained quiet. He walked with her, hand in hand, as far as he could go before security would ask to see his boarding pass. They stood facing each other. There was nothing he could say that wasn't already said, no message he could convey that his eyes weren't already conveying. He hugged her and pressed his lips to the top of her head, and she felt him tremble a little. The embrace lasted longer than a mere good-bye, but shorter than a "Please don't leave me." He knew she had to go.

As he held her, he asked, "Did I ever tell you that my family are originally from Verona, Italy?"

"Uh, nope, don't think you ever mentioned it," Emily responded with a sideways tilt to her head, puzzled as to why he was bringing this up at that moment.

"Saddest love story of all time, "Romeo and Juliet." It took place in Verona. I believe I am cursed in the romance department because of my heritage," he added with a sad smile. "There is no world without Verona walls, but purgatory, torture, hell itself," he quoted Shakespeare with flawless diction.

Emily's face showed her soul's sorrow. Her voice wasn't trustworthy, so she let her actions speak for her. She paused, looked at him with tears shining in her eyes, and gave him a tender squeeze and a slow kiss on the cheek.

As they released each other into their respective separateness, all Jim said was, "Just do me one favor, Emily. Please don't meet any other men by vomiting on them—that was our thing." Emily laughed through her tears, and Jim added, "I love you, kiddo," then he turned slowly, shoved his hands in his pockets, dropped his head, and walked away without lifting it.

CHAPTER 31

APRIL 2007
CHARLOTTESVILLE, VIRGINIA

Emily had told Peter almost everything. He sympathized with her when she explained how she reacted to Dr. Crosby's original diagnosis and they had had to sedate her. He felt compassion for her when she expressed her intense grief over having to leave him. He cringed and shuddered with her when she explained her treatment and the following bone marrow transplant. He shared in her pride over her journalism award. He held her tightly as she sobbed over little Christopher. He felt her desperation as she detailed her search for him. He kissed her gently with relief over her remission. And he watched her face closely as she told him about how she finally found the website about his performance at the bar and flew out immediately to find him. But he did not respond at all about Jim. Of course, that was only because she hadn't told him about Jim. She would eventually, she told herself.

For now, she wanted to lie back on that comfy bed, with her head next to his on the pillow, his warm, familiar body protectively pressed up against hers and the sun rising in the window. She could feel his heartbeat against her, his stubbly shadow of a beard from the long night, and the warmth of the sun on her face as it crept up over the window sill, like a timid child making sure that they weren't still angry before it entered the room. *Come on in, sunshine,* she thought, *you never have to hide from us again.* Her fingers were laced through his, and her other hand was gently stroking his arm.

"My mother never thought badly of you, by the way. Both my parents adored you and told me over and over that you must have had a very good reason for what you did. Even after my dad died, my mother still believed in you." He wants her to know all this. She needs to know all this. "I wish I had been able to think past my own pain and suffering. Maybe I would have figured it out," he thinks out loud. They are both quiet for another few minutes as that soaks in.

"Peter?" the softly spoken name disrupts the silence like a tiny pebble tossed into a perfectly still pond, making gentle concentric waves until the sound reaches his ears.

"Yeah?" he answers slowly in case he is dreaming, afraid to wake up.

"Why don't you sing when you perform at the bar?" She suspects there is a deeper meaning for this and wants him to talk about it but feels she needs to take a back road to get there so he won't suspect her.

"Well, I guess I haven't sung in public in a while, about three years actually," he says with a hint of sorrow and teasing accusation in his voice.

"Oh. I see," she replies with quiet remorse. They don't say anything at all while they sort out the implications, then she adds earnestly, "Well, I hope you sing again soon."

Then with the sun a full two inches above the window sill now, illuminating their faces fully and making their eyes shine even more brilliantly, Peter looks at Emily, smiles, and sings the first few stanzas of "You've Got a Friend."

As the lyrics about being there for her when she's down and troubled sink in, he can't go on because his throat is too thick with emotion. "Hey, Em?" He doesn't wait for a verbal reply but continues, "Those words are perfect. I'm on the record now. Please don't ever shut me out, again. No matter what you think you're saving me from. I don't want to be safe and happy. I just want to be with you."

She gives him a mock curious, accusing look out of the corner of her eye at this,

He immediately corrects himself, "Wait, that didn't come out right. I meant I want to be safe and happy *with* you. Oh, you know what I meant."

They both laugh playfully, roll into each other and relish in their recently reclaimed intimacy.

They get quiet again, and Emily looks seriously into his eyes. "I promise, Peter. I promise," she whispers with complete sincerity.

The evening's revelations have definitely shed a new light on the infamous breakup. They are no longer the villain and the wounded, the leaver and the left, the heartbreaker and the heartbroken. They are both simply victims of fate, innocent bystanders of unfortunate circumstances. Peter doesn't blame Emily anymore. He considers the fact that he may have done the same exact thing if the diagnosis was his and he thought he could spare her the pain. Secretly, he even thinks she is pretty damn remarkable to go through all that for him.

They lay there for a while longer just enjoying the new oldness of being in the same room together. The sun is fully up now, and they are exhausted. They doze off in each other's arms and awake nearly two hours later. In the half-conscious stupor of waking, Emily is momentarily surprised at the fact that Peter is next to her.

She sits up quickly, is startled, and exclaims, "Oh! I forgot I was back home."

Peter answers with a tender smile, "Welcome home, Em."

Home is good, she muses.

They spend the next hour or so eating breakfast together in Emily's room. Peter tells her that he has to go and explains that he has a very important appointment at noon and will call her after that. He says that he has so much more to talk over with her, and he really wants to finish their catching up today. He knows that if he waits too long to tell her about Ayanna, his delay could be misinterpreted. He is anxious to get everything out in the open and get started on their future together—if she accepts Ayanna into her life.

Emily explains that she has one more thing she needed to take care of while she is in town anyway and would be busy until about three or four. They agree to meet in the hotel lobby at four o'clock and have dinner together then go back to Peter's house. He decides right there on the spot that he'll tell her about Ayanna tonight after dinner. He's actually looking forward to it, even though he's not sure how she'll respond. They kiss each other with longing, and it's hard to part, but they know they'll be back together soon, so they say good-bye for now.

As soon as Peter closes the door, Emily showers and changes. Cloud nine wasn't high enough, she decided. She must be on cloud one hundred by now. Peter had obviously felt as much for her over these long three years as she had for him, and he was eventually just as understanding as she knew he'd be. She just wanted to pick right back up where they left off before the diagnosis and move forward. She had sensed a change in him, but with time, she thinks she can make everything the way it was.

She silently thanks all who were responsible for her happiness right now and set about the unpleasant task at hand—calling Jim to tell him the news. *Journalists usually love reporting a good scoop*, she thought, *but not this time.*

Emily picks up her cell phone and sits down on the bed. She flips it open and stares at it, as if it could tell her what to say and how to say it to make this easier for both of them. She bites her lip and dials his number. Jim picks up on the second ring.

"Emily?" he says anxiously as he reads the caller ID.

"Hi, Romeo," she answers as evenly as she can, nervously tucking her hair behind her ear.

Silence. He could already tell from her greeting that she wasn't coming back to him. "You're not coming back, are you?" he says, completely deflated.

She pauses, taken off guard by his directness. "No, Jim. I'm not coming back." She doesn't apologize.

There was nothing to apologize for. They had met and become friends. She had been very honest with him. She was in love with Peter. She did have some feelings for Jim, but not the kind of love that she had for Peter. Jim always knew that her first priority was Peter. She never pretended anything different. They had shared one passionate evening on her front porch, and that only cemented her feelings for Peter even further. There was nothing more to say. As they say, the heart knows what the heart wants.

"Emily, we didn't even have a chance to start," he tries to reason with her.

"I know, Jim. But I hadn't really finished what I had already started with Peter. I hadn't wanted to leave him in the first place. I felt that I had no choice. You, of all people, know that," she says to remind him of his position.

Jim said nothing in response because he knew she was right. It was an unusual situation. A blameless crime.

"Jim?" she stabs at the silence.

Finally, "Yeah?" he tries to cover his heartbreak.

"If I were the kind of person who could have turned my back on Peter and started an affair with you while he was away and unaware of the truth behind my leaving, then I wouldn't be the kind of person you would waste your time with," she points out. "Right?"

He was thoughtfully quiet for a moment, then, "Catch-22," he agreed with a gravelly voice. "Catch-22 sucks," he added, trying to laugh instead of cry. She had him, though. It was true. Her devotion, loyalty, and selflessness were the things he loved so much about her, yet they were the things that prohibited a relationship between them.

Silence for a prolonged attempt to control the emotion in their voices, then, "Jim, you know how I feel about you, don't you?" she wants to be fair.

"Tell me anyway," he says quietly.

She starts to cry because she doesn't want to hurt him. He had been by her side for almost three years, through the worst of it, and never let her down. That meant something to her; it meant a lot. But she couldn't build a relationship out of indebtedness. Jim wouldn't want that anyway. She really wished she could love him the way she loved Peter, but you only love like that once in a lifetime. She got chills at that thought. Could Peter's grandma have foreseen this whole situation?

She wished there was an easier way to do this, but a choice had to be made, and that choice was made long before she even left Virginia three years ago. Peter was her true north, but she did love Jim in a different way. She owed him the truth, no matter if it was right or moral to say this now. She had always been honest with him, and she would remain honest.

"I love you, Jim," she says with obvious tears in her voice. She says it sincerely, sadly, concededly, and purely, and then she closes the phone in slow motion without waiting for a reply. The snap of the phone shutting was like the sound of a rifle in her ears. This time it was more like Old Yeller than the yearling that she had to shoot, because instead of being her playmate and confidante, Jim had been her protector and strength.

She wasn't just throwing Jim a bone when she said I love you; she really does love him. But she realizes that a person can love people in different ways. Her love for Jim was born out of need, loneliness, and companionship. She loved Peter from a place in her soul that was involuntary. He was part of her, and she was part of him. Their souls were connected somehow. She would do anything in the world to make him happy; she would travel to the ends of the earth. And she did.

CHAPTER 32

Peter arrives back at the house he shares with Miranda and Ayanna at about ten in the morning. His arms are full of donuts that he stopped to buy. Miranda is feeding Ayanna when he walks in, and he can't hide the smile he's trying to suppress. Miranda is doing a great job caring for Ayanna, but she's more of a career woman than a mommy. He really appreciates the effort that Miranda has gone to in order to help Peter get settled with the baby.

"And how's our big girl this morning?" he asks happily, more happily than anything he's uttered since she's known him. She doesn't answer, just watches as he practically skips over to the coffee machine and pours himself a big cup. "Want some, Miranda?" he offers with a ridiculously misplaced smile.

"Okay, who are you, and where's Peter?" Miranda asks sarcastically. "And where the hell were you all night?" she feigns exaggerated annoyance with her hand on her hip.

They've fallen into a very comfortable routine of caring for Ayanna. They take turns waking with her, feeding her, etc., and they give each other a break when they need it.

"Hey now, Dr. Thomas, watch your language in front of the baby. Is that any way for the new internist at Mount Sinai to behave?" Peter teases. Miranda has been working on securing a fellowship back at Mount Sinai in New York where she did her residency.

"Oh, Peter, shut up." She smiles at him. This new, upbeat Peter is like a whole different person. Whoever he hooked up with last night did him a world of good. "So seriously, where were you all night? I was kinda worried 'boutchya."

Peter leans back against the counter, crosses his legs at the ankle, stirs his steaming cup of coffee and stares into the mug, watching the cream as it swirls with the dark liquid, making intriguing patterns that were open for interpretation. He's relishing his memory of all the events from last night. As his mind meanders through the ups and downs of everything he shared with Emily in the past twelve hours, the slow dawn of a smile full of possibility and anticipation broadens across his face. His brain has calculated the weight of Emily's leaving, Emily's lie, Emily's illness, and Emily's return to him, and his heart has tipped the scales in favor of pure joy that she's back in his life. She's back, and that's all that matters right now.

Somehow the secret knowledge of Emily seems to make it even more euphoric. He wants to share it with Miranda, but he needs to savor it for just a few minutes more. He can tell that Miranda suspects something and is getting impatient the longer he waits.

"Peter! What's going on? What is it?" Miranda yells at him excitedly.

As soon as Peter feels that her excitement matches his own, he begins, "Well, you remember the woman I told you about who I was engaged to a few years ago?"

"Yeah, yeah," Miranda urges him, along with her hands waving in time with her nodding head. "Go on!"

"She's back." he declares all at once and a little loudly for effect.

"Back? Like back in Charlottesville or like back in your life?" Miranda seeks more details.

"She came back for me," he answers without showing the deep emotion he's feeling. At Miranda's quizzical eyebrow lift, Peter adds, "It's a really long story, but let's just say she's back and she's not going anywhere this time." He has to look down into his mug again to keep his composure.

There's a small silence between them as they give the moment its due, then Miranda speaks softly and genuinely, "Peter, I'm so happy for you. I wish you both all the joy in the world." Then she turns up the volume as she orders him to go get changed and swats his leg with the cloth she's using as a drool bib. Their appointment for Ayanna is in less than an hour. Peter grabs a donut as he turns to go change.

"And I want to hear the whole story on the car ride, Peter," she calls to him as he climbs the stairs.

He takes the stairs two at a time, bounding up to his bedroom like a young boy as images of Emily pop in and out of his mind's eye. The top stair squeaks under his weight. That usually grates on his nerves, but today, he doesn't even notice. There are still boxes around his room that have yet to be unpacked. They had moved in only a few weeks ago, and he was slow at getting back into the swing of American suburban life.

He had been overjoyed to be able to bring Ayanna back to the States to raise her, but the easy-going, laid-back lifestyle after Somalia and the excitement of their exodus has resulted in a syndrome not too much unlike posttraumatic stress. MSF had warned all of them about the emotions and stress they might feel upon their return. Peter usually wasn't affected by things like this, but he had to admit he was wound a little tightly since they got back. Of course, he did have a newborn to care for, and he had lost a very dear friend recently. He was only human after all.

Within a week of landing in Richmond, Peter bought this charming old house on a quaint tree-lined street with lots of picket fences, rope swings, and detached garages from days gone by. The house was a Victorian style, with a big, welcoming wraparound porch, soft yellow exterior with white shingles, and flowerboxes at the windows. It didn't take Peter long to find a home for him and Ayanna. Emily had always admired the houses on this street, and he never even looked anywhere else. There were several for sale, but this one had a nice view of the park, so his decision was easy. He didn't even negotiate the price. They went from drive by to dotted line in just a little over twenty-four hours.

Now as he looks around, the house seems changed somehow. It has promise. It has possibilities. It has a future. He showers and changes hurriedly and is back downstairs in a flash.

During the length of the entire twenty-minute drive downtown, Peter told Miranda all about what Emily had been through in the past three years. He explained why she thought she had to leave. And he talked about what he knew of her medical prognosis at this point. By the time they get to the Social Security office, Miranda feels as though she had met Emily herself. He is still rambling on and on as they enter the lobby and never notices who just stepped out of the elevator just several feet away.

————

After Emily's call to Jim, she makes mental plans to complete the one last thing on her checklist. The last time she had seen Dr. Crosby had been for her diagnosis. She swore she would never return to his office. She swore a lot of things, though. She feels like she owes it to him to apologize for the way she reacted and to let him know that she was in remission. He had always been so kind to her, and she didn't want to leave things the way she left them. Because Peter was in the medical community, she had developed more than a patient-doctor relationship with Dr. Crosby and his staff. They had been invited to many Christmas parties together and other social gatherings and were definitely considered friends.

She knew his office closed for lunch, so she planned to arrive just before. His office was a quick cab ride about ten miles from her hotel. She had checked the phone book to make sure he was still practicing in the same office and just reading the name of the street even gave her chills.

As the cab pulls up to the modern-looking brick building, Emily muses at how different it looks, even though it is exactly as she remembers it. Her hands go cold, and her heart rate quickens as she looks up toward the fourth floor where Dr. Crosby's office is. She had come this far so she wasn't stopping now. She suddenly becomes aware that she didn't call in advance and she hopes that he's able to see her.

The ride up in the elevator seems indefinite, and she prepares words in her head for her meeting with the kind old man. As she steps out of the elevator and approaches the door, she feels as if everyone in the hall is staring at her and knows why she's there. The door closes behind her, protecting her from their scrutiny. She crosses the waiting room and taps on the frosted glass then waits for it to slide open.

Her hand is trembling as she waits patiently. After a very brief moment, the glass slides, as if in slow motion, and the familiar face of the receptionist lights up with recognition. The woman is speechless. Then finally, "Emily Waters!" she begins to shout to everyone in the office. "Look, it's Emily."

They scurry her back and hug her and squeeze her. Everyone is so happy to see her looking considerably well. They hadn't heard a thing after she disappeared.

As they're all making a fuss over her, she hears a man's gruff voice from behind her. "Ms. Waters?" She turns around slowly to find Dr. Crosby, slightly older looking, standing, stethoscope around his neck, glasses low on his nose, and hands clasped neatly in front of him. He offers a warm smile and open arms, which she falls into happily.

They hug quietly for a few minutes, and Emily is instantly very glad that she decided to visit them. What a reception.

Dr. Crosby gently releases her to hold her at arms' length and take an inventorial look. "How have you been, dear?" he asks with deep concern.

"To death's door and back, honestly. But I feel fantastic right now, Dr. Crosby," she answers truthfully.

"Well, we're all just going to lunch. Can you join us?" he asks.

"That would be wonderful," Emily replies.

And they head off to the elevator as a pack; Emily is feeling very celebrity with an entourage. Yes. Home was good.

She gives a quick recap overview in the elevator, answering some of the basic questions, like where she received treatment and whether they did a marrow transplant. They were deeply engrossed in conversation as they all stepped off the elevator and into the lobby. Emily didn't hear the familiar voice until she was right behind it.

———

It's Peter. He is only a few feet away. Her head snaps in his direction. She is hidden by the crowd, but she can clearly see him holding an infant, walking with a pretty young woman into the Social Security office in the lobby. She supposes this was the appointment he had spoken of.

Tammy, the receptionist, noticed him just after her. "Hey, Emily, wasn't that Peter?"

"Yeah, I think it was," Emily answers distractedly as the door closes behind the pair with the baby.

Emily has stopped walking and is just staring at the closed door as people pass by all around her. She can't move or even blink. A shiver crawls up her spine as a warning. He could be helping out a friend. Peter would never be duplicitous. Peter wouldn't lie to her. Peter wouldn't tell her he loved her and sleep with her if he had a wife and child. Would he? Of course, Peter probably thought she'd never lie to him, either, but she had. Was he simply out for revenge? He had been awfully angry at first. Suddenly Emily awakes from her daydreaming and decides that she has to know.

"Do you want to go say hi and then meet us at the coffee shop on the corner after?" Tammy asks, noticing Emily's distraction.

"Okay. Yeah. Good idea. I'll see you there in about ten minutes. Thanks," Emily answers as she keeps her eyes on the door to her fate.

Her entourage walks away, and she feels smaller and smaller as they became further and further. She forces her feet to move, and she enters the overly crowded office very stealthily. She spots the couple immediately. They are standing at a desk, smiling and shaking hands with the clerk on the other side as if in greeting. They must have just begun their appointment. The room is lined on either side with desks. Down the center of the room is a line of people waiting to speak to the clerks behind a counter at the far end of the room. If Emily stands in that line, mixed in with all those people, she would not be seen. Peter is at the second desk on the left side of the room. Now the pretty woman is sitting in the chair next to him, and he is still holding the infant.

As they speak, seeming to explain their situation for being there, the clerk behind the desk is smiling at them, as if sharing some wonderful news. What is he telling her? Recent wedding? New baby? This is looking more and more damning. As Emily moves up in line, she can hear them speaking but can't yet make out their words. Emily moves slowly up the opposite side of the line of people, acting as if she was looking for someone further up the line. Within a few moments, she is close enough to hear them but still shielded by several people in the sloppy line. She hears Peter say something about a foreign-born US citizen, a birth certificate from the American consulate in Djibouti, and something about medical insurance.

Then the clerk answers loudly while nodding in understanding, "Okay, Dr. Daniels. No problem. I'll just need you and Miranda to fill out this form SS-5. Then I'll need your daughter's birth report, Miranda's ID as the mother, and your ID as the father. Once I file this, it should only take about two weeks for you to receive Ayanna's card in the mail. There's a phone number on the back of your copy of this form, in case you don't receive her card. Call any time."

She is smiling so sweetly at Peter and the woman that Emily wanted to smack her. He doesn't deserve that smile.

Emily is officially in shock.

By the time the clerk is done with her instructions, Peter had filled out the form and handed her all the necessary items. Before Emily knew it, they were standing up and shaking hands in salutation.

Emily is glued to the floor.

Peter and the pretty woman are collecting all the baby things they brought in and turning to leave.

Emily is frozen in time.

CHAPTER 33

Peter is looking around the floor to make sure nothing was dropped and left behind. The pretty woman heads toward the door first. Peter follows carrying the baby girl, his daughter, if she had heard correctly. They pass by her on their way out but don't notice her through the line of people she is standing on the other side of. As they go through the door, Emily still is stuck in the same spot, her eyes fastened on them. Peter turns to look back into the room, as if he sensed something. Emily had moved behind the group of people next to her. There is no way he could possibly see her.

Peter and Miranda head outside with Ayanna and are standing on the curb. Miranda tells Peter that she'd love to stop for a bite at the coffee shop, if that's okay with him. He looks at his watch and sees that he still has a few hours until he has to meet Emily at her hotel, so he agrees and they head down the block to the restaurant.

As he's opening the door, something up the block catches his eye. It's a woman getting into a cab. The woman looks an awful lot like Emily from a distance. He laughs at himself because he obviously can't get Emily out of his mind. He thinks about how he's going to see her this afternoon and tell her all about Aya and Ayanna and how he brought the baby back with him to raise her.

He doesn't really know what to expect as her reaction, and he's not sure what the future holds for them, but he feels that Emily will love Ayanna instantly and welcome her with open arms—if Emily is the Emily he remembers.

He and Miranda sit down for a quick bite and chat about her plans to head to New York late next week to start her fellowship. Peter is happy for Miranda, but of course, he'll miss her help. He'll be starting back at the hospital soon, so he'll have to arrange a sitter. Phyllis told him she'd come in for as long as he needs her. She can't wait to meet her new granddaughter. Peter and Miranda talk on and on, as Ayanna sleeps in her car seat. They lose track of the time because Ayanna is sleeping so peacefully. Miranda asks a lot of questions about Emily, and Peter tells her that he plans to pursue a future with her. He knows they have some issues to work out, but he's confident that they will.

Peter is enjoying being able to talk about Emily and the future without a bitter taste in his mouth for a change. He feels like a man who's just been set free from a life sentence of hard labor. He feels lighter somehow. It shows in his face, and Miranda is so happy for him. She thinks about what a great guy he is and how much he deserves to be happy.

"So what time are you supposed to meet Emily?" she asks.

"Around four," he answers. "She had some things to take care of this afternoon."

———

As they're talking, a group of people walk past their table on their way out the door. It's Dr. Crosby and his staff. Tammy approaches him and says hello. They haven't seen each other in a few years, and she asks how he is. They make small talk, then Tammy asks if he saw Emily about an hour ago at the Social Security office.

Peter's face went white as a sheet. Before he asks Tammy what she meant by that, he already knew. Tammy explained that they hadn't seen Emily in a few years but she stopped by just before lunch to say hello. They were all heading out to lunch together when they saw him in the lobby. Emily had told them she was going to stop and say hello to him then meet them in the coffee shop, but they haven't seen her since.

Peter's hands cover his face, and he rakes his fingers through his hair as he curses under his breath. All eyes were on him, but he didn't feel like explaining. He can only imagine how it must have looked to her. Maybe she even overheard them explaining that Ayanna was their daughter! He gives Miranda a look, and she is already sliding out of the booth. They head home as fast as possible so he can drop them off and get to the hotel. He curses himself over and over for not telling her right away and for not getting her cell-phone number before he left this morning. He had already called her hotel room, but she didn't answer. His mind is going crazy with worry. He tries to calm himself down but can't.

By the time he gets to the hotel, it's almost three, a whole hour before he was supposed to meet her. He had called her room about a dozen times already, so now he asks the front desk to ring her room. They look her up in the computer and very casually, unemotionally inform him that she checked out over two hours ago. He hears them say this, but his mind can't register it.

"Pardon?" he says, buying time for his mind to accept this horrible news. He feels as though his head just hit a brick wall.

They explain again that she checked out earlier, but he's not listening. He's thinking, thinking, thinking. What should he do? Where should he go? She could be anywhere! He searches through his phone to see if he still has her parents' phone number. Nope. He calls information. Not listed. He's not surprised because of the nature of her mother's work. He only has one alternative: call his mother.

It's ringing. By the fourth ring, his mother answers. He tries to ask for Emily's parents' number without arousing suspicion.

Ha! His mother is like the Spanish Inquisition all of a sudden. He simply sums up that he saw Emily yesterday they talked a long time and both still have feelings for one another. He wants very badly to have her back in his life but there's been a terrible misunderstanding today and he needs to reach her parents as soon as possible. The whole time he's talking, his mother is looking up the number and has it ready for him when he takes a breath.

"Thanks, Mom. You're a lifesaver!" he says with emotion.

"Good luck, honey. Please call soon and fill me in!" is all she says then hangs up so he can hurry.

Peter dials the number his mother gave him, but it goes to voicemail.

"*Ugggggggggggggggghhhhhhhhhhhhh!*" His voice echoes eerily in the middle of the quiet, polished five-star-hotel lobby. He sits on a sofa in the lobby for about an hour, constantly dialing and redialing her parents' number. He's hoping against hope that she'll walk through that front door by some strange miracle. Hasn't he been through enough already? Could fate be this sadistic? Just before he thinks he's going to have an all-out meltdown, he decides very calmly that there is no way in hell he's losing her again, especially over a misunderstanding! If she learns the truth about Ayanna and Miranda and still decides to leave him, then he'll accept that, but not this. No way.

At five o'clock, he finally gives up and goes home. He has no idea if she's even still in town. When he walks in, Miranda obviously sees that he was unsuccessful.

"Did you even find her?" she asks.

"No. She checked out. She's gone…again," he mumbles.

Miranda doesn't know what to say. So she doesn't say anything.

Peter picks up Ayanna, sits in the rocking chair by the window, and lays her against his heart. He rocks her like that for over an hour, just staring out the window. Miranda offers him some supper. She had made herself some chicken and rice. "No thanks," he mutters.

The day fades drearily into night, and the mood is beyond somber. After they put Ayanna to bed, he calls San Francisco again and again, but no answer. He leaves several voicemails, only stating that he has to speak with Emily urgently. He falls asleep on the couch in front of the TV, and when he wakes up in the morning, it hits him fresh and new all over again. At 8:00 a.m., he starts calling San Francisco again. He calls once every hour, in between caring for Ayanna. By about the millionth time he calls, he's so used to the incessant ringing of the phone that when a person actually answers the phone, he's dumbstruck.

"Emily?" he stutters.

"Peter?" she responds incredulously.

"Oh, thank G-d," he says. "Why'd you leave? I have to explain something very important," he begins.

"No explanation necessary," she says coldly. "I saw you and your family at the Social Security office yesterday, and I immediately took the red eye back home. I can understand why you'd want to hurt me, Peter, but I won't be a part of the pain you'll bring to your family, especially a tiny baby. You've changed, Peter. If I did that to you, I'm sorry. But we're through. Don't ever call me again." And the line went dead.

He heard the pain in her voice, and it was like a knife to his chest. Of course, he calls back over and over, but this time it doesn't even go to voicemail. He can't email or text her to explain. His mind is moving a thousand miles per hour, and he is desperate to explain everything to her. The urgency he feels is like a tornado in his soul. Within minutes, he realizes that there is only one way. He would take that same red eye tonight.

He lets Miranda know that he'll be back in a few days, plenty of time for her to get to New York. She tells him to go and not worry about Ayanna; they'll be fine. He thanks him profusely, throws a bunch of stuff he doesn't even know what in a bag, and heads out to the airport in Richmond. He is on the flight by eight o'clock that night. He hasn't showered or slept in over twenty-four hours, he has no idea what he packed in that bag, and he has no clue what he'll say to her when he sees her—if she'll see him. But he's not going back to Charlottesville without a fight. He's learned a lot about people, life, and himself in the last few years, and one thing he knows for sure—some things are worth fighting for. Emily was his thing.

By the time he lands in San Francisco, he's calmed down a little. He's pretty sure he remembers where Emily's parents live. He rents a car and heads north from the airport toward Union Square. They only live a few blocks from there. By the time he gets to the city, it's well after midnight.

He checks into a hotel that is only a few blocks away from where he remembers the house being. He falls into the bed and gets a few hours of restless sleep. He wakes late and looks in the mirror. He even scared himself. Some hygiene is in order. He does his best. An hour later, he's shaven, showered, and changed. He had managed to pack something decent to wear after all.

He heads out the door and into the uncertainty of his life. He walks the few blocks toward Emily. It is now one o'clock in the afternoon, and he has no idea if she'd be there or if she'd even answer the door to him. But he is forging ahead anyway. As soon as he sees the familiar building, he recognizes it right away. He walks confidently up to the custom-crafted, walnut-stained, intricately carved elegant front door and pushes the doorbell.

As the chimes sound somewhere inside the beautiful townhome where Emily is, hopefully hearing them, he seems to feel the electricity flow through his whole body. He waits for the ensuing sound of her light footsteps approaching the other side of this confounded obstacle in front of him. So many scenarios fleet through his mind as he waits. But he remains steadfast. His mind is distracted by the images it conjures, but he is snapped back to reality when he hears the doorknob turn.

CHAPTER 34

Emily has just returned home after doing some marketing in the morning. Her parents are away for ten more days, and there was nothing in the house to eat. She's trying very hard to fill her days with tasks in order to keep her mind off recent events. *Two down, an infinity to go. How much can one heart take?* she wonders.

As soon as she places the last apple in the fruit bowl on the counter, she hears the doorbell ring. She considers not answering it since it's probably just FedEx or something anyway, but after the second ring, she reluctantly decides to see who it is. She walks unceremoniously to the door and opens it. When she sees him, she is absolutely floored. What the hell was he doing here?

"Jim!" she almost screams in shock.

"Emily?" he seems just as surprised.

Then at the same exact moment, they both say, "What are you doing here?"

Emily emits a nervous laugh, and Jim looks down at his feet as they shuffle on the doorstep.

"I was just stopping by to return a book your mother lent me, actually," Jim says to Emily's feet.

"Oh. My parents went away. They won't be back for over a week, but I can take the book for you if you'd like," Emily offers.

"No, that's all right," he says a little shakily as he slowly moves his hands in back of him, obscuring the book he was holding. But Emily already recognized the book. He was busted. "I'll just hang on to it until she gets back, I guess. I wanted to talk it over with her anyway." Unconvincing.

"What are you doing back in San Fran so soon?" It's Jim's turn to ask the questions.

As Emily tries to answer him, she can't help noticing the way he is looking at her. He glances at her furtively then quickly away as one might reach with their hand for something that's too hot to hold. Emily was not at all prepared to answer that, and she feels a little ambushed. She doesn't want to lie, but she doesn't want to go into the whole mess either.

She gets that old familiar wicked glean in her eye then, and Jim isn't able to look away as she speaks, "I'll tell ya what. I won't ask why you have a photo album of me from when I was five, and in return, you won't ask me why I'm back unexpectedly, deal?"

His eyebrows rise in surprise that she knew he had the photo album, and he says shyly, "Oh you saw that, huh? Okay. Deal."

They stand silently in the threshold for a few moments. Emily has to admit to herself that it feels very good to be in his company. He lifted her spirits better than anyone she knew. She can't help but smile at him. He smiled back. *This is ridiculous,* she thinks.

"Jim? Would you like to come in?" she finally invites.

He pauses, looks up and down the street and behind him, as if looking for a reason not to go in, then drops his head in defeat. When he looks back up at her, he's squinting in indecision.

"Sure," he answers as if against his better judgment. He enters Emily's home cautiously as if he is the fly stepping onto the sticky, treacherous silk of a spider's web. He has to be careful lest he's caught again. He only barely escaped last time.

"So how are you?" he asks as he enters and removes his jacket.

"Okay," is all she says. At least she's not trying to pretend nothing's wrong.

They stare at each other for a few seconds, trying to think of something else to talk about besides the elephant in the room. Food or the weather. The weather's boring so, food it is.

"Would you like something to drink or eat?" she asks politely. Before he has a chance to answer, she starts listing his choices, "I have fruit, cheese, bagels…"

"You know? A cup of hot coffee would be great, thanks. It's so damn cold outside," he answers. And they're on to the weather.

"Yeah. Colder than usual," she agrees.

He follows her into the kitchen where she starts getting two cups of steaming hot coffee and some cookies together for them. They make small talk about general things. Of course, Jim asks how she's been feeling and if her medication is agreeing with her. She can't help but feel close to him as he talks about her parents, her illness, her medication, her recent article that won the award.

Her mind automatically compares the intimacy she feels with Jim regarding the last few years of her tumultuous life with what she's shared with Peter the last few days. She's known Peter longer and shared a deeper relationship with him, but right now, Jim seems more like family. She knew this wasn't fair because she was the one who shut Peter out. She left him. She told him that she hoped he would find someone else. And he obviously did. Did she expect him to be alone the rest of his life just because she left?

It wasn't really the wife and baby that were angering her. If he had told her up front about his new family she would have been heartbroken, desperately sad, and forlorn. But she wouldn't have been angry at him. She would have cursed fate, but she would have forgiven and understood Peter. But what he did was unforgiveable. After she told him that she only left him to protect him from heartbreak, and that she had a life threatening illness, and that the last three years were hell, he simply jumps into bed with her, lies to her about loving her, and leads her to believe that they still had a future together. He was really convincing too. Dammit.

She realizes then that those few hours were probably the happiest of her life. She really believed that all was forgiven and that he never stopped caring for her. The feeling of relief and joy was euphoric, but short-lived. He probably never even intended to meet her in the lobby that afternoon. He got his retribution and was on his way home to his wife and child. Double whammy. She could never offer him children now. With abrupt, deep, dark despair, she realizes in a panic that she'll never have what he has. She'll never have someone she loves as much as she loved Peter. And she'll never have children.

"Whoa. Your face went from dreamy to sheer terror in the span of about thirty seconds. What were you thinking about?" Jim is concerned.

Emily shakes her head to clear it as she becomes aware that Jim's idle conversation about his new sailboat had trailed off somewhere during her silent reverie and he was just watching her face as she got more and more lost in the nightmare she was having.

"Jim, I…" She doesn't even know where to begin. She's at rock bottom. The levee breaks, and the sobs rattle her body. She covers her face with her hands to hide her misery. Jim is on his feet and holding her close in one heartbeat. He has already given up any chance at not getting his heart crushed—again. Nothing could stop him right now from holding her and stroking her head and whispering soothingly in her ear to try to calm her. He realizes painfully then that nothing could stop him from loving her.

The moments turn into minutes, and they are still standing in the middle of the kitchen holding each other up. As they embrace, her cries quiet down. She leans back a little to smile weakly at him and let him know the breakdown has passed.

He doesn't release her but holds her even tighter. He's staring into her glossy eyes and wondering if there is anything in this world that he would rather be doing than holding her like this right now, even if it's only to comfort her heartbreak over another man—again. Nope. He could stay just like that in that kitchen, in her arms, staring into her soul for the rest of his life. He feels bad for enjoying this opportunity to hold her at the price of her happiness. She is extremely vulnerable right now. He can see it in her face.

She's looking back at him with need and desire, but not love. He knows that. He knows that to kiss her now would be the wrong thing to do. Even to respond to a kiss that she initiates would be the wrong thing to do. But he doesn't really give a crap. That's why, as she slowly reaches up on her toes to lightly touch her tender lips to his, and he feels her sweet breath on his cheek, and her warm body pressed up against his, he bends his head and covers her mouth with his slowly in a kiss that completely removes them from the rest of the world and all of the pain in it.

Their lips are melted together and fit perfectly. Their tongues dance together in a rhythm that is pure desire. His hands slide down her back proprietarily, and he cups each cheek of her buttocks just this side of too roughly. She can tell he's doing everything he can to be gentle, but the unacknowledged desire in him is threatening to unleash. She knows she's not being fair to him. She knows she's kissing him for all the wrong reasons. She knows she can never love him the way she loves Peter, but she needs to be loved and desired so badly right now that she finds herself kissing him with wild abandon. And it feels pretty damned good. At least it takes the loneliness away.

His hands are exploring her entire body now, and she only wants more. She wants him to caress, squeeze, and own every part of her being. She encourages him by kissing him with a ferociousness that's foreign to her. She has never kissed anyone like this before. She's practically climbing up his body now, and her legs are wrapped around him. He's holding her by her bottom, and their mouths are inseparable. They're breathing so hard that it's making them both a little dizzy.

They break away for a second to look into each other's face and see if they're thinking the same thing. Flushed cheeks, bruised lips, wide eyes, panting mouths. Yep. They are definitely thinking the same thing. Jim makes a very slight gesture of a nod in the direction of her bedroom. Without taking her eyes off his, she nods just as slightly in agreement.

He carries her upstairs just as she is, with her legs wrapped around him and her head on his shoulder, nibbling on his neck. By the time they get to the bedroom, they're kissing savagely again, and he lays her on the bed and undoes her jeans without removing his mouth from hers. She pulls his shirt over his head, letting out a whimper for the split second that their lips are torn apart. He slows the kiss down and pulls away as he starts to unbutton her blouse. His lips have a new occupation now. He sucks gently until each rosy tip is at full attention. She can hear and feel him moan. Her hips rise toward him involuntarily. He cups and caresses each breast before leaving them, then slides his hands slowly, slowly down her belly, stopping at the lacy waistband of her silk underpants.

He doesn't go any further until he looks into her eyes for her reaction. Not her permission, only her reaction. He's not Peter. Her mind betrays her as it forces out images of her first time with Peter. He so desperately needed her approval and permission before he took what he wanted. Man, she loved that. Jim was gentle. Jim was loving. Jim was skillful. But Jim was Jim, not Peter.

She closes her eyes, lays back her head, and lifts her hips. He slides the silk down painfully slowly and kisses the trail his finger makes as it goes. When she is fully exposed, he tests her readiness with his thumb, sliding it ever so gently across her most delicate body part. Her reaction is the one he hoped for – a whimpering moan accompanied by a thrusting pelvis. She is ready for him. He slides his own jeans and boxers off and lowers himself on top of her. He uses his knee to tenderly nudge her legs further apart.

He is quite obviously ready too. But he knew that the moment he walked in the front door, he is about to finally, finally, take what he deserves after loving her silently for so long. He can't believe that an hour ago he thought he'd never see Emily again and now he's in her bed, about to make love to her. He knows full well that he is doing everything he instructs his patients not to do. He doesn't even know yet what happened to make her come back to California. He no longer cares. He only wants her in any way she is willing to give herself. He tells himself that she'll learn to love him or he'd die trying to get her to.

He brushes back the hair from her face so he can see her clearly as he claims her. She looks ready. She looks brave. She looks slightly frightened. Perfect. He takes a deep breath, and as his most private flesh barely touches the slick outskirts of hers, there is a thunderous knocking at the front door accompanied by an insistent, rapid-fire ringing of the doorbell. Jim is frozen—frozen in hell. He gives her a look that says, "Can we just ignore that?" but he couldn't ignore that racket if his life depended on it. The noise puts a little panic in both of them. Emily draws the sheet up to cover her bare breasts, the breasts that she so willingly let him nibble a few moments ago. He knows that they can't continue until he gets rid of whoever is at the front door.

Afraid of losing whatever momentum got them this far, he tells her to stay just like that and he'll be right back. He motions with his hands as he says this for extra emphasis, so afraid she'll change her mind. As he slides his jeans on and pulls on his t-shirt, he gives her a wink and a shy smile that she returns. *Good. She's still in the game*, he thinks. "Be right back. Don't move a muscle," he says happily as he hurries down the stairs to the front door.

All the while, the banging and bell ringing has grown even more demanding. He finally opens the door with a *whoosh* and almost shouts an impatient, "What!" Instead, he forces a controlled "May I help you?" through somewhat clenched teeth.

After he asks, he completely takes in the sight in front of him, and his blood runs stone cold. It couldn't possibly be. But he's pretty sure it is.

CHAPTER 35

"Peter?" he says in total bewilderment.

The doorbell-ringing culprit is standing there, inappropriately dressed and freezing, roses in one hand, the other hand in a pocket to keep warm. Without noticing that the man who opened the door knew his name, he asks through shivering teeth if he could come in but steps in without an answer anyway. As he enters, he asks the door man if the Waters' family still live in this house.

Jim simply nods, completely speechless.

Peter shows great relief at that bit of news. *Right house.* "Is Emily Waters here then?" he asks overly anxious.

Jim can't speak. The raging war in his head is leaving one explosion after another on his brain cells. He could say no, turn Peter out and never tell Emily, and proceed to ravish her waiting hot body. He could say, "Yes, but she doesn't want to ever see you again, so get the hell out of our lives." He could say, "Emily who?" He could just kill him and claim temporary insanity—he is an expert on the subject—though his insanity feels less temporary and more permanent at the moment.

As he's thinking of possible answers to the very simple question he was asked, Peter grows impatient and asks louder, "Is Emily here, man?"

"Shhh." He looks over his shoulder and up the stairs, giving away her location. Peter's eyes follow his up the stairs, and just at that moment, they both see Emily, fully (re)dressed, coming slowly down the stairs as if there were two wild animals in the living room. Well, there were. She could almost see and hear both their minds working, calculating, concluding.

Jim's head drops as if in mourning for what almost was. So damn close.

Peter's hand that held the roses drops to his side at recognition of what he could only assume was his interrupting their tryst. He takes a step back and makes a face that looks like he's been slapped. He squints and looks away as if the knowledge is too much for him to bear.

Emily immediately feels sick to her stomach from the guilt at having caused him this much pain. She doesn't know why she feels guilty. Didn't he just do the same thing to her? But the agony on his face is more than she can stand.

"Peter, why did you come here?" she asks very quietly.

Peter lifts his head, takes a few steps toward the bottom of the staircase on which she has paused at the halfway mark, looks her directly in the eye, and says in the most pleading and sincere tone he can muster, "Because I love you, and I couldn't lose you all over again."

Emily can't believe what she's hearing. How can he stand there and tell her he loves her with a wife and child at home? She's still on the stairs looking down on them both.

Jim has his eyes diverted to the floor. He can't leave the room, but he doesn't want to get in the middle of what he secretly hopes is a breakup and final good-bye. He feels instinctively that if he stays in Emily's sight, she'll choose him. Peter is just staring at her, shoulders slumped, arms hanging loosely, as if the air has been knocked out of him.

"I don't understand you, Peter," she spoke slowly as if he were a madman. "You have a wife and child at home." At this information, Jim's head snaps up in shock, mixed with a little hope. "You shouldn't be here. You never should have said and done all those things to me two nights ago. You have to leave and let me find the happiness you obviously have found. You got me back. We're even now. I get it. You can go back to your life and feel secure that you've crushed me emotionally." As she says the last few words, her voice cracks and tears spill down her cheeks unchecked.

Jim, admittedly encouraged for their budding relationship by this news, can't help but take a few involuntary menacing steps toward Peter in Emily's defense. Peter returns Jim's glare and stands his ground. He knows that Jim is misinformed but offers no concession in his returning stare. The steel look on Peter's face stops Jim from advancing.

Peter slowly turns his attention back to Emily. "True. In all our confessing and sharing the other night, I left an important detail out. As it appears, you did as well." Peter's eyes shift fleetingly toward Jim. "But that's just it. I haven't done any of what you think. I'm not married. It's very complicated, but what you saw at the Social Security office was not what you think." He gives another irritated sideways glance to Jim. "Can we talk about this in private, Emily? Please? Give me five minutes to explain the truth, and then if you don't ever want to see me again, I'll leave."

Emily thinks for a minute and says, "You can say what you have to say in front of Jim. He knows everything anyway." She wasn't about to ask Jim to leave after the unfinished business they had upstairs.

Peter isn't happy; they can both tell. "I can't do that. We have to speak alone."

Jim and Emily exchange puzzled glances, and Jim makes an executive decision. It's too awkward in there for him, so he excuses himself to the kitchen. "I'll be right here if you need me, Emily," he says to Peter's face as he passes him.

Peter keeps eye contact with Jim but doesn't utter a word to him.

Emily keeps her perch on the stairs and commands, "Go ahead then, Peter. What's the big secret?"

Peter moves closer to the stair railing so he can lower his voice and pauses as he tries to put the words together to explain the whole situation. "When I was in Somalia," he starts out slowly, "I met a brave young Somali girl whom you would have loved. She was seventeen, married and newly pregnant. Her pregnancy developed complications, which led to her death in childbirth."

Peter had to stop for a full minute and look away as he collected his emotions. When he turned back to face Emily, she could see the genuine pain and affection in his face. "I loved that girl like a baby sister, Emily." He pauses another moment then continues. "She gave birth to a little girl, the little girl you saw me with the other day—Ayanna. I promised Aya, the baby's mother, on her deathbed, that I would raise Ayanna as my own. Miranda, the woman you saw me with, is a co-worker from MSF who was with us in Somalia. She had become very close with Aya also and agreed to help me bring Ayanna back to the US so I could keep my promise to Aya.

"Adoption is not allowed there. So there was no other way. We filled out forms stating that we were the natural father and mother of the baby. It's a felony. At the very least, we'd be charged twenty-five thousand dollars, or worse, we could be imprisoned for a long, long time. And worst of all, Ayanna could be deported—to a living hell. I had to get her a Social Security number for medical-insurance purposes, and that brings us to the day you saw us at the SS office." He finishes up very neatly and watches her face for her reaction. Nothing. "Em, I could get in some pretty big trouble, life-altering trouble, if this ever got out.

I'm putting my life in your hands by telling you all this. That's how important you are to me." Still nothing. "Em?"

Emily lowers herself slowly onto the step behind her to sit down, puts her face in her hands, and stares vacantly into the space in front of her. Peter becomes concerned and rushes around the railing to climb the stairs and hold her. Five or six minutes pass before Emily can speak. "Oh my G—d, Peter. Oh my G—d. Oh my G—d." That's all she says over and over. The tragedy in her voice is real.

They just sit together on the stairway, halfway up and halfway down, for several minutes while everything sinks in.

"So that's the truth behind the drama. I just wanted you to know that I would never, ever do anything to hurt you—ever. I have no desire for getting back at you. That's your own guilt talking, I guess. I love you. I will always love you. I intend to raise Ayanna as my own daughter. I had started to believe in the last forty-eight hours that you would raise her with me, but I can't make that decision for you." Peter turns her blank face toward him with one finger under her chin. "Do you understand that I want to marry you and be a family?"

She was hearing him and seeing him but still incapable of responding. She was clearly in shock. It is all too incredible to be true. Her mind is like a hamster on a wheel, running wildly and getting nowhere. Peter knows she needs a little time to process it all. He is reluctant to leave her but has said and done all he could and knows the rest is up to her.

"I'm staying at the hotel across from Union Square where we stayed the last time we came in town together. I'll be there until tomorrow. Miranda has a fellowship waiting for her in New York, and I promised her I'd be back soon. If you want me, you know where to find me." He kisses her mouth and stands up to leave. As he opens the door, he turns back to Emily, still sitting blank faced on the stair, and says, "Oh, and please say good-bye to…uh, Jim was it?" He drops the roses on the table as he goes out.

The roses are blood red, and she stares at them until they blur into one giant pool of blood. There isn't a sound in the room. The silence seems incongruent with the whirring in her head. She wants to stand up but can't.

She must have been sitting there for half an hour when Jim finally comes out of the kitchen and finds her unmoving on the staircase.

"Emily? Are you okay?" Jim asks with great concern.

"Yeah," she answers vaguely.

"Well? What happened? When did he leave?" Jim starts.

"He left about a half hour ago," she answers just as vaguely as the first time. She's staring straight ahead, seeming not to be aware of Jim at all.

"Emily," Jim says a little louder to snap her out of it.

It works. Emily snaps to. She turns her head slowly toward Jim.

Her eyes focus on him, and she asks strangely, "Jim, why did you have my photo album? Our deal's off now because you heard why I came back, so why did you have my photo album?"

Jim is a little concerned with her oddly serene behavior, and he only blames himself. He knows he'll burn in hell for taking advantage of her at a weak moment like that. He knows it, but shamefully, he would do it all over again. He'll forever taste her skin and feel her softness. The whole event is burned into him like a branding iron. And he's glad of it. But right now, he feels like the biggest heel in the world.

"I…uh. I was planning on using some old photos to make a gift for you. That was before your phone call the other day."

She makes a sad face of deep sympathy and pity.

"I really believed that you would come back to me. I even tried to make myself believe very recently that you could love me and care for me, but I'm not blind. I saw the way you looked at Peter the minute you came down the stairs. I'm not blaming you or condemning you. I'm just facing facts. And I'm so sorry for my actions—" He was speaking to the floor.

"Jim—" she interrupts as she starts to deny or explain or something.

But he doesn't let her. It doesn't matter. He puts his hand up to halt her. "Emily, I'm trying to apologize, not accuse. You've always been very honest with me. Now let me be honest with you. I love you. I fear I always will. There will forever be an Emily barometer on my heart. But that's my fate, not yours. I really, really want to be your friend. I'm actually glad we were interrupted like we were. Or I'm sure I will be in a few days anyway." He tries to make it light.

"As a professional, it would have been a train wreck to have finished what we started upstairs. It's bad enough, the damage we've already done. Above everything else, I want you to be happy. If that means letting you go, then I have to let you go." His voice is a little shaky as he says the last six words.

Emily doesn't say anything in return, just lets one sad tear roll down her cheek. He smiles at her to let her know he's okay, and she gives him a teary smile back and mouths the words "I love you."

He knows what she means, and he mouths it back. As he grabs his jacket to leave he asks, "What did he say about the wife and baby anyway to make you change your mind?"

"He's not married after all. I was mistaken," she answered vaguely, looking right through him. Then she focused clearly on Jim's face and added softly but genuinely, "And he said to tell you good-bye."

Jim nods. "Guess I would have told you to do the same thing." He snorts lightly through his nose, winks, and leaves her without another word.

Jim had to ask her what Peter said so that she wouldn't suspect the fact that he had heard every word. And he had to admit to himself that Peter was just about the most admirable guy he knew. Well, at least it took the sting out of losing Emily to him—a little.

CHAPTER 36

Within five minutes, Emily has grabbed her purse, coat, and cell phone and is running out the door, down the steps, and up all four blocks to Peter's hotel. She makes it there in record time. He never tells her the room number so she has to stop, out of breath and crazed, at the front desk to ask. She bolts to the elevator and presses the button a dozen times before it finally arrives. She practically jumps into it and rides, anxious as a caged tigress, four floors up to Peter's floor. She runs down the hallway and stops in front of his door. Her heart is pounding in her ears, and she has to take a few deep breaths to collect herself. She's trying to recover from the aerobic workout and from the adrenaline rush.

She only knocks twice before Peter appears in the open doorway. He doesn't say anything, just stares at her. He can't get the image of that guy, Jim, out of his head. She knows this. She can see it in his face. She has to work hard, but she's going to make him get passed all this, whether he likes it or not.

"Aren't you going to ask me in?" she asks.

Peter just steps aside and gestures her in.

She starts talking. "Peter, I'm not going to apologize for jumping to the wrong conclusion. It was a ridiculous situation. I stood in that office and heard you say, point blank, that you and that woman were the baby's parents! I was left with nothing else to interpret except you were married with a child. No one on this planet would have suspected the truth! I will say now that I am horribly, horribly sorry that I didn't give you a chance to explain before I left so abruptly. That was wrong."

Peter showed nothing. He may as well have been playing Texas Hold 'Em.

Her tone turns beseeching and her eyes grow worried. "Peter, I love you. You have to know that by now. I'd do anything in the world for you." She tries moving toward him, though his body language is not inviting. She reaches up to put a hand on his shoulder, as if testing the waters of a dark, mysterious pond. She's never seen him like this. He's very intimidating.

He finally draws his breath to speak. "Who's Jim?"

"A friend," she answers honestly.

"How close of a friend, *Emily*?" He keeps his voice oddly calm and raises one eyebrow slightly with suspicion. He knows that he hasn't been celibate this whole time. But he wasn't the one who left. He wasn't the one who claims that it was only for her "own good." He wasn't the one who claims to have loved her too much to let her suffer the illness with him. And he wasn't the one who insists that he was in love with her the whole time and thought of her every day. Though, that last part could apply to him, anyway. For all he knew, she could have been in a new relationship with no intention of ever returning to him.

Emily's head drops in shame. "Truthfully, very close, but not like you think—" she starts to explain, but he cuts her off.

He grabs her and pulls her to him. He can feel her boney shoulders and is reminded of what she's been through the past few years. His heart softens, but only slightly. He lifts her chin so that she has to face him. He searches her eyes intensely for deceit. His face shows no emotion whatsoever, and it unnerves Emily. Her eyes shift to the side in her discomfort from the scrutiny. He demands her full attention and overreacts when she looks away.

With a grunt of withheld anger, he kisses her hard. Too hard. She thinks she tastes a little blood. But she doesn't complain. He pulls back and searches her face for her reaction. There are unshed tears in her eyes, there is agony in her eyes, and there is deep regret, but there is absolutely no guile. Not enough. He needs more reassurance.

He throws her down on the bed and covers her body with his. He kisses her hard again. She makes no move to push him away or return the kiss. At her lack of response, he loses his ferocity slightly. When he pulls back and looks at her this time, his face is a little softer. No words pass between them. There are no words for a moment like this. Actions speak louder. He kisses her again, and this time she kisses him back gently, lovingly, sincerely. Now she tastes salt in his kiss. She looks at his face, and his eyes are closed. When he opens them, she finds that they're misty.

In a soft, calm whisper laced with sincerity, she breaks the code of silence. "Peter, I love you. I love you more than anything or anyone in this world. Please, please believe me," she begs.

He pauses briefly to control the emotion in his throat, but his voice cracks a little anyway. "I do. I do believe you. And I love you too, Emily."

He pulls her close to him, and lets his body do the talking. She can feel his heart beating against hers, and she can hear his ragged breathing. Their bodies can't seem to get close enough to one another, and she just wants this moment to last forever. She can feel him relax and let her in. She knows the worst is behind them. She strokes his neck as she feels him get more and more relaxed. They just lie on the bed together in silence.

She can feel the forgiveness now. He nuzzles her temples tenderly in apology and kisses her bruised lip. Their senses are flooded with each other's touch, smell, and image. Whatever invisible, chemical, subconscious thing that was responsible for their original attraction to one another has returned and multiplied. They are inseparable—one. It's not even a choice anymore. Peter is Emily's, and Emily is Peter's. The rest of the world has fallen away. The past three years are losing significance. They were both lonely and hurting and only human. They can't change what has happened; they can only look forward to the future and begin again.

The better part of an hour passes before either of them speaks.

"Emily?" Peter invokes.

"Yeah?" she answers groggily.

"Back at the house, I told you about Ayanna, but I think you were too shocked to react," he probes.

Emily looks up into his eyes and with total humility says, "Yeah, my mouth was full of foot at the moment."

Peter chuckles. "Well, I should have told you the night before, but there didn't seem to be an appropriate moment. So much drama that night, you know? I had it all planned out for telling you the next day. She's so precious to me, Emily. I know that sounds weird, but do you know what I mean."

"Yeah, Peter, I know exactly what you mean. You mean that you are the most fantastic friend anyone could have. You are the best specimen of humanity that I know. And you will be the most incredible dad to Ayanna." She isn't looking at him as she says this. In fact, her face is hidden.

Peter can detect a distinct note of sadness in her voice. He gently turns her head toward him to see her face. Her eyes are shiny. "What's behind that look, Emily?" he asks tenderly.

She decides to just be honest and straightforward for once, takes a deep breath, and tells him gently, "Peter, I can't have any children now. I survived, but it had a price." She had known this for a long time and had dealt with it already, but somehow, telling Peter made it a fresh wound all over again.

Her tears are falling fast now, and Peter can only hold her. He is immensely sad for her because he knows how much having children had meant to her. He could say comforting things about adoption or fostering, but now is not the time. He just shares in her feeling of loss and lets her know that he understands. Adoption isn't really the issue, anyway. The issue is that she no longer has a choice. Cancer has taken a hostage, a prisoner of war, who would never be rescued—her unborn children. Peter's heart aches for her, and he holds her tighter in his effort to comfort her.

"Emily, while I was in Somalia, I learned so many things. But one of the most valuable things I learned was from Ayanna's mother. Aya faced so much adversity and so much grief in her short life on earth, but no matter what came her way, she always told me the Lord will not give you more than you can bear. I faced some difficult decisions while I was there. And each time I did, I was always stunned to realize that I could handle it. I believe she was right. The Lord or fate or life—or whatever you might call it—doesn't give us more than we can bear. It may not always be what you would choose, but you have the strength to get through it. I wish you had a chance to know Aya. Sometimes it felt like she knew you. Once in a while, I would mention you when I was talking about life back in the US, and I think she became very fond of you."

Emily is smiling slightly now. The sound of Peter's comforting tone, the warmth of his body, and the knowledge that he had spoken of her to Aya is life giving.

Emily's tone becomes less somber and more positive. "We've lost so much time, Peter. But you know, maybe it all served a bigger purpose," she suggests pensively.

"In what way?" he prods.

"Well, if I hadn't left you when I did, and you hadn't traveled to Somalia when you did, we wouldn't have Ayanna. Maybe it was all for a greater good, Peter," she says with renewed hope as she looks up at him for confirmation.

By the look on her face, he realizes that she has said something that requires a response from him, but all he can hear is, "*We* wouldn't have Ayanna." *We.* His heart is lifted, and he recognizes the old Emily, his Emily, instantly. He feels the warmth flood his body and spread across his face.

"Would you come back to Charlottesville with me, Emily? I really want you to meet Ayanna." Peter knows that Emily will love and care for Ayanna as her own, just as he does, not only because Ayanna looks so much like Emily, with her dark skin, curly hair, big black eyes, and shared African heritage, but also because he knows Emily's soul and will never doubt it again. Peter wastes no more time and gets straight to the heart of the moment. Down on bended knee, looking into the most beautiful face he'd ever seen, he states instead of asks, "Let's get married right away." More tears of course, but he knows that they're tears of joy this time, accompanied by a big, bright smile and a rapidly nodding head.

They celebrate their reconciliation all night long in each other's arms—again and spend the next day packing Emily's few things up from her parents' home and shipping them to his home, their home, in Virginia. She would have to give her parents the good news when they got back from their trip to India. They had left town on some child-advocacy business the day after she left to find Peter. She knew they would be very happy for them both because they had scolded her often for leaving him in the first place.

Peter and Emily were on a plane two days after he had landed in California. It feels good to him to be going home, their home together with their child. They hadn't been home in such a long, long time.

The crib is set up near the window and the sun is filtering through the sheer curtains, casting a warm light on the baby as she sleeps peacefully, in complete bliss to everything around her. The room is warm, in temperature and in color. It has been painted a tender, muted yellow. It smells of baby things–powder, lotion, baby soap. The window is open a tiny bit for fresh air and the birdsongs mixed with the neighborhood sounds of children, lawn mowers and barking dogs are drifting in on the breeze and lulling the room to sleep with the baby. Emily analyzes the nursery. There are simple decorations about. In addition to the crib there is a rocking chair, a dresser, a few pink teddy bears, and a big white shaggy rug over a golden wood floor. On the dresser is a photo of Aya, smiling caringly as she sits among a group of children in her country. And in the corner, resting against the wall subtly, looking over the entire room like a shepherd over its flock, is Peter's guitar – the guitar that Aya had made Peter promise to play, the guitar that enabled Emily to finally find him, the guitar that had brought them back together, just as Aya had prophesied. It seems to smile at them approvingly as they hold each other in that warm room.

—

The wedding was two weeks later. The University of Virginia has the most enchanting and charming old stone chapel with authentic stained-glass windows, a real working belfry, and unbeatable Old World appeal. Many couples throughout the years have held their wedding ceremony there. Peter and Emily, however, are not like many other couples. They held their ceremony in the east wing of the Alderman Library, Emily's church, overlooking the lawn where they had shared so many wonderful memories from simpler times.

With sage reference books, classic novels, sweeping epics, and heart-wrenching love stories as the faces in the pews, they exchanged vows to love, honor, and be truthful until death do they part. Emily's parents flew in and joined the bridal party of Phyllis, Michael, Jennifer and their spouses. Avery and Hugh were completely bewitched by Ayanna and held her as much as they could. They had a warm, intimate reception dinner afterward at their home. Peter played his guitar and sang for his new bride. It was perfect.

That night Peter and Emily finally realized their dream of becoming husband and wife; but they had been soul mates since the day they met. Peter made a silent prayer of thanks to Aya before he had walked down the aisle. He knew intuitively that she, from up above, had something to do with this. He was a man of science, but he never underestimated the power of a woman's heart. He had seen it in action firsthand. Peter and Emily had each spent three years in their own living hell and had made it through whether by sheer will or pure luck. It would take more than wars, floods, droughts, disease, time, and distance to keep them apart.

As they embark upon their new life together as a family, they innocently believe that all their troubles are behind them. That is, until they hear the chilling details about Avery and Hugh's trip to India. Later that night, in the shadows of their darkened room, Peter turns to Emily and asks if her passport is current.

Lightning Source UK Ltd.
Milton Keynes UK
UKOW07f2120141214

243121UK00014B/173/P